LETHAL - A DARK COLLEGE BRATVA ROMANCE

The Ares Academy Book One

Arianna Fraser

STA, LLC

Copyright © 2023 STA, LLC

All rights reserved

The characters and events portrayed in this book are fictitious. Any similarity to real persons, living or dead, is coincidental and not intended by the author.

No part of this book may be reproduced, or stored in a retrieval system, or transmitted in any form or by any means, electronic, mechanical, photocopying, recording, or otherwise, without express written permission of the publisher.

ISBN-13: 9798865760788
ISBN-10: 1477123456

Cover design by: Art Painter
Library of Congress Control Number: 2018675309
Printed in the United States of America

To my clever, handsome and deeply troubled husband, who comes up with the very best plot twists.

To my dear Christy, who might find herself in a certain Dean, particularly her love of power tools.

And to you...
A sincere and whole-hearted thank you for reading Lethal. Proceeds from this book benefit the two crisis nurseries in my city. The crisis nurseries here are non-profits that are here for families who are overwhelmed and in desperate need of help. Their little people can be lovingly and safely cared for while their parents are hooked up with services for anything from housing, employment, mental health, and more. Thanks to your kindness, I've had the chance to purchase much-needed items, like cases of diapers, industrial-sized boxes of goldfish crackers, books, formula, toys, and more.

And socks. Those kiddos can never hold on to a pair of socks.

FREE BOOKS!

Join my email list and I'll shamelessly bribe you with a free book. You can download your free copy of The Reluctant Spy - A Dark Mafia Arranged Marriage Romance here. dl.bookfunnel.com/6xud62rmg0

I'm too lazy to spam you, so you'll only see an email monthly when there's giveaways or a new release - like Book Two in The Ares Academy series - which will be released in December 2023.

SPOTIFY PLAYLIST FOR LETHAL

Do you get into a story more when there's a music playlist to inspire you? Find the Spotify playlist for Lethal - A Dark College Bratva Romance here.

PREFACE

Lethal - A Dark College Bratva Romance is set in the brutal world of organized crime. These twenty-somethings are not messing around.

As such, there is violence, explicit sex between consenting partners, arranged marriages, kidnapping and oh, so much profanity. Additionally, there is a scene of attempted sexual assault and one of torture. Neither scene is explicit, particularly detailed, and they are brief. But it is extremely important to me that you are aware of and comfortable with the subject matter.

If these things are not to your taste, please find something that you might enjoy more, but I thank you for stopping by. Reading is meant to be a pleasure!

Still here? Excellent! Grab a glass of wine or a bag of Cheetos and let's get started. As always, thank you for reading and supporting my stories.

~Arianna

PROLOGUE

In which Lucca struggles with his invisible family status.

U2 - Invisible

Lucca...

"What are you doing?"

Konstantin, my roommate, kicked open our door, the way he always does, already pulling his sweaty shirt over his head.

I put my phone down. "Nothing."

He throws his shirt at the hamper that housekeeping begs us to use for dirty clothes. He misses. How can such a lazy bastard be so gifted in ice hockey and soccer yet never hit the laundry basket? "Aleksandr and I are heading over to the lighthouse later, are you coming?"

The lighthouse.

The moldering stone edifice where our classmates go to get high and if they're lucky, get laid. It's always amused me because we can drink on campus, hell - they have a full bar in the dining room - and our suites are vastly more comfortable for fucking. Somehow, the allure of slabs of stone that can land on your head at any moment is too much to resist.

Still. "Maybe."

"Yeah, hedge your bets," he says dryly, pulling off his sweats and heading into the bathroom.

Picking up my highly illegal phone again, I read the bullshit in the society column from the *Boston Globe*.

Dario and Cora Toscano celebrated their marriage with a huge gathering at the home of her parents, Senator Carlton, and Claire Thorne. The lavish party's guest list included Massachusetts Governor James Conrad, Boston Mayor Meghan Flannery, and several celebrities, including...

There's column after column of this ass-kissing. Enlarging a picture of my brother and his new bride, I study them together. She's beautiful, too gorgeous for an asshole like Dario, but they look happy together. Throwing my phone on the bed, I pace, wondering if Cora and Dario got my gift. How did my dear brother explain his "invisible brother?"

Or did he just pretend I don't exist, the way the rest of my family does?

Fuck them all.

CHAPTER ONE

In which Tatiana discovers that nothing good happens at 3:36am.

Oingo Boingo - Dead Man's Party

Tatiana...

"Get up!"

The hand shaking my shoulder nearly knocks me off the bed.

"Miss Tatiana, we must leave now! Get up."

Opening my eyes and slapping at the arms hauling me from my covers, I wheeze, "What the hell? Stop it!" It's Lev, his mouth tight and he's pale. Glancing at my phone, I see that it's 3:36 a.m.

I've seen my bodyguard angry, amused, infuriated, and more over the last ten years, but never afraid. Now, he's afraid.

"Lev, what is happening? What are you-"

"Listen to me," he says sharply, precisely. "You are in danger. We need to leave *now*."

Rolling gracelessly out of bed, I shove my hair out of my face. "Let me get dressed. What kind of danger?"

Lev shakes his head. "No time." Grabbing my arm and yanking me from my room ends that line of questioning and I stumble down the stairs after him. The usually present household staff and my father's soldiers are noticeably absent. It's only Lev and me.

"Where is everyone? Where are my parents? They should have

been home by now- Lev!" Digging in my heels, I force him to spin and look at me. He's gritting his teeth, eyes narrowed. "Where are they!"

"Your father trusted me to keep you safe," he hissed, "now walk out this door or I will carry you out."

Nodding, I follow him out the door, so scared that my teeth are chattering.

"Please Lev, I am begging you, what is happening? Where are we going?" We're blazing down Highway 1 toward the airport and he is not following safe driving guidelines, speaking rapidly into his headset, ignoring me. The SUV is armored and not the usual one I ride in. This bullet-proof monstrosity is for my *otets*, or my brothers. Not for me. I'm not a security risk.

I'm just… the daughter. My parents were never cruel, though they made it clear my value was as a bargaining chip. Though other Bratva daughters often had arranged marriages set as early as fourteen - like my friend Mariya Morozova - I'm twenty and unattached.

As far as I know.

I wouldn't be the first Bratva princess who ended up at the altar without knowing what was happening to me until they were lacing me into my wedding dress.

Disconnecting from his call, Lev finally looks at me in the rearview mirror. "Let me get us to our destination and we'll talk, all right? I promise you an explanation."

He looks like he's dreading that explanation, and the knot in my stomach ties that much tighter. Looking out the window as we turn, I see we're heading for a darkened airfield. It must be one of the private airstrips that circle the Vancouver International Airport.

"We're flying out of here?" I ask anxiously. "Without my

parents?"

Lev ignores me, racing down the road toward the small grouping of darkened airplane hangars. There's a jet parked outside of one. Its running lights are off, but I can hear the engine. He pulls up in front of the stairs and opens my door before I have time to get my seatbelt off.

"Wait, hold up!" I dig my heels in, trying to make him slow down as he hauls me toward the jet. "You promised me an explanation!"

Two of my father's men hurry down the stairs, guns out. "Any sign of them yet?" Lev asks them, keeping me moving.

"Not yet," Nikolay says grimly, his weapon held up as he makes a visual sweep of the airfield.

This is bad. This is very bad. Nikolay is one of my father's top soldiers. He rarely travels without him.

"Where are my mother and father?" I nearly scream.

Without breaking stride, Lev throws me over his shoulder and takes the boarding stairs two at a time. I don't recognize this plane; this isn't one from the Aslanov fleet. It's still luxurious, with gray and cream leather seats and elegant wood detailing. I'm carried past a flight attendant, a smile frozen on her lips as I writhe and kick against my bodyguard's grasp.

He's barely put me into a seat and strapped me in when I feel the jet move, the high whine of the engine ready to take off. "Are you insane?" I shout at him, clinging to his jacket. "What the hell is happening!"

Lev continues to ignore me as he looks out my window, his brows drawing together. "Tell that pilot to take off before I shoot him and fly us out myself," he orders the now-terrified flight attendant.

Following his gaze, I see headlights - three cars, I think - closing in on us. The jet's cabin shakes as the engines scream, pushed to their limit as the wheels lift off the tarmac. There's a thud to my left and I turn to see an odd starburst pattern in the window just in front of me; cracks snaking out from a small hole in the center.

"Did- they just shot at us, didn't they?" I gasp. There are two more solid thuds along the body of the jet as we finally lift off. More headlights join the others, but we're out of their reach now.

Lev leans over to examine the bullet hole. "It cracked the outside window, but the interior one is secure," he said, back to his cold and calm bodyguard demeanor.

Grabbing onto his jacket, I fist the material. "Now. You're going to tell me what the hell is going on. *Now.*"

"*Privet sestra,* hello sister," my brother Roman says, trying to force a smile for me. My oldest brother was always the one to shield me from our father's anger and impatience, the brother who pushed to allow me some normalcy in my life. Thanks to him, I was able to attend Simon Fraser University for the last two years, though I was the only one taking notes during the lectures with a bodyguard sitting next to me.

After we were at cruising altitude, Lev had placed an open laptop in front of me and connected to the incoming video call from Moscow, and my brother appeared. His usually immaculate bespoke suit is ripped and there's a rust-colored stain that looks suspiciously like blood on his dress shirt.

"*Ya skuchal po tebe,* Roman, I've missed you," I try to smile back. "What's happened? It's bad, isn't it?"

"*Da,*" he says flatly. Roman is also the brother who will never lie to me, even when I almost wish he would.

Firming my lips, I nod. "Tell me."

"Our parents were returning home from the meeting in Seattle when their jet exploded."

There are words trying to make their way out of my mouth but none of them make sense. I make a noise instead, moaning like a wounded animal. "No," I shook my head firmly. "I spoke to *Mat'*, to Mother, two hours ago! They were fine! Your intel is *govno*, it's shit!"

Roman doesn't correct my cursing, he just looks at me sadly. "It's true, *malen'kaya iskra*, little spark. I'm sorry."

"This is... No." I shake my head. "No. That's wrong." The stupid laptop screen is blurring this is a crap connection and... Oh. I'm crying. Putting my fingers against my wet cheek, I watch his image waver and dim.

"I'm sorry to push you into this next step before you're ready," he says gently, "but we don't have much time. There have been hits on both Ilia and me-"

"Oh, my god are you okay? What about Ilia? Your suit looks all torn up, did they try to bomb your car? Your jet?" I'm babbling. Everything is slightly off-center. The lights, the underwater sound of my brother's voice, trying to tell me that he and Ilia are safe.

"...The hits came from four different groups, and none of them are recognizable. But we took captives," Roman said coldly. Captives. That means torture and for the first time, I'm all right with it. I want to watch. I would even help.

"How did they..." my voice broke and it took me a moment. "How did they get a bomb on *Otet's*, on Papa's plane? His security is state of the art, how could..."

I can hear people trying to whisper information to Roman and there are pieces of paper put in front of him. He keeps his gaze on me. "*Malen'kaya iskra*, we do not know who's behind this. None of our spies or our intelligence network had picked up the slightest hint of an attack. And they coordinated three; Father's jet, my motorcade in Moscow, and a firebomb in Ilia's New York apartment. It took out half the building but he's fine."

"You said there were four attacks," I said numbly.

His gaze moves to the left, where Lev is sitting next to me. "A group of soldiers breached security at the estate in Vancouver. We believe it's the same group who tried to shoot you out of the sky as you were taking off. Lev's quick actions are the only thing that kept you alive."

"I know we have enemies," I said, trying to enunciate through numb lips. "But you weren't expecting this? At all?"

Roman shook his head, eyeing me with concern.

"Who could be powerful enough to pull that many soldiers together?"

"None of the Six Families would be suicidal enough to try this openly," he agreed. "But working with another organization…"

"One of the cartels?" I ask, "Mafia? The Irish?"

His jaw tightens. "That's what I'll find out. Whoever they are, they'll pay dearly for killing our parents. I will burn every one of them to ash."

Finally realizing our parents are gone breaks me, and I wrap my arms around my stomach, rocking back and forth as I weep. I think my brother is trying to comfort me, but his voice is just static.

"Miss Tatiana?"

Lev is leaning over me, his hand braced on my headrest.

"You know, my father was always the one who insisted you call me Miss Tatiana," I said. I've been crying and staring out the window and crying some more for the last six hours. "Maybe you could drop the 'miss' and just call me by my name?"

He looks a little alarmed by my suggestion, finally nodding and smiling. "Tatiana."

"Thank you." I don't recognize my voice. I sound like a stranger. Flat, and blank. "I think... that's nice to hear." Lev has protected me for half my life, I've spent more time with him than anyone and he's my family in every way that counts. Right now, though, he looks torn between grief and guilt.

"We're landing in New Jersey to refuel," he said. "The *Sovietnik* will be there to speak with you."

Sovietnik. Titles from the Aslanov Bratva that always make me feel distanced from my brothers. As if there are far more important things they are called to than merely being my family. I understand, most of the time. They have their roles, just as I do. Though theirs have meaning, mine feels primarily decorative.

"Are you sure Ilia's all right?" I ask, "The explosion... did anyone get hurt in his building?"

Lev smiled reassuringly. "This is one of the new Aslanov properties. There are only three residents aside from your brother and they were all out of the building. He was uptown at the time; they must have had faulty intel."

"*Slava Bogu,* thank God." I rubbed my forehead. "Is this meeting safe? I don't want to put him in danger."

"He's flying in via helicopter, and this jet is listed under another flight path," Lev reassured me.

"About that... Whose jet is this?" I ask, "I know it's not one of ours."

"We needed a jet your family's enemies couldn't track; this one belongs to the Morozov Bratva." He looks up as the pilot announces our approach. "Time to fasten your seatbelt and put your tray in the upright position."

"Still not funny Lev," I sigh, "you've said that every time we fly."

"And you still giggle a little every time I do," he assures me, ruffling my hair. For just a moment, I'm ten again and he's my new bodyguard, trying to make me laugh.

"*Malen'kaya iskra!*" Ilia lopes up the boarding stairs and halfway through the cabin before I could unbuckle my seatbelt. "Are you all right?" Hugging me fiercely, he whispered, "I am sorry about *mat' i otets,* so sorry."

Having my brother's arms around me ends my fragile self-control and I sob, holding on to him as tightly as I can. "How could they be gone?" I wept, "I spoke with Mother last night, I don't understand any of this."

Pulling away, my tall, strong brother's face is pale. "We don't either," he said, leading me to a bank of seats at the back of the jet and sitting next to me. "This came out of the blue. Of all the chatter we monitor, the intel our spies gather… there was nothing to indicate this."

Running my hands through my hair, I try to gather my thoughts. "What's the next step? A funeral, and-"

Taking my hands in his, Ilia squeezed them gently. "We are not having a funeral for them."

"*What?*" That came out much louder than I planned and everyone in the cabin turned to look at us. "Of course, we're having a funeral, what are you even-"

"Listen to me," he said urgently. "We do not know who is friend or foe right now. There aren't enough guards in the entire Aslanov Bratva to secure the church and cemetery if we don't know who we're guarding against. Roman and I are going to war against an unseen enemy. In the meantime, you are in danger."

My brow furrows. "What? I'm just… the daughter. I don't have any power, there's nothing to gain from killing me." I don't feel the tears until Ilia pulls out his pocket square and dabs at my wet cheeks.

"We are at the very beginning stages of this investigation, but one of the few things we have learned is that you are a specific and valued target. The soldiers who breached the security at the estate didn't use explosives, like the other three groups. If whoever this is wants to gain a foothold with our Bratva behind them, taking and marrying you is a smart move."

"Does this mean I can't go back to school?" I wince, "That sounds so selfish, I'm sorry."

Ilia tilts his head, looking at me closely. "To Simon Fraser University? No. But… Roman and I have found what is possibly the most secure spot on the planet for you."

My gaze moves to Lev, who is nodding, even though it looks acutely painful to do so. "Where?"

My brother smiles triumphantly. "The Ares Academy."

CHAPTER TWO

In which Tatiana reluctantly agrees to The Worst Idea Ever.

Tatiana...

"You're kidding me."

Ilia shakes his head. "I know the stories Roman and I have shared can make the Academy sound a little scary-"

"Scary? You almost died there. *Twice*, remember?" I snap. "Students learning how to poison and torture and murder people more effectively? It's been ten hours since Lev dragged me out of bed, that I learned my parents have been murdered, that my brothers don't want me with them and, oh, yes. I'm some sort of juicy target for these murderous pigs. Have I hit all the highlights here?"

He sighs, rubbing the back of his neck.

"Why would you even joke about sending me there? Not to mention that they would never accept me. I'm twenty. It's what, a month into the school year and once the students get dumped on that island, they can't get off until June!"

Patiently waiting until the anxious flow of word vomit is over, he leans over to the bar to get me a bottle of water. "Drink this. Take a moment."

Glaring at him over the bottle as I drink, I try to regain some self-control. I know Ilia is being patient. While everything in my life just crumbled around me, tears and hysteria have never been welcome in the Aslanov Bratva. Taking a deep breath, I try to focus. "Okay. I'm sorry. I can listen."

"You're correct," he allows, "about most of this. You should be with us. You should be protected by us." His lips pressed tightly together and I can feel his grief and guilt. "We have threats coming in from every direction. Whoever it is has a literal army. And now we know you are a target. Roman and I have gone through every possible scenario to keep you safe, and this is the best option."

"I still don't see how you're going to just… magically poof me into the most secretive and brutal college on the planet," I protest.

"The Ares Academy is notoriously difficult to get into," he agrees. "I know our parents never discussed this with you, but there was interest in you when you turned eighteen. Do you remember Vladimir Adamovich?"

Frowning, I vaguely remember a big, white-haired man with a mustache that made him look like a walrus.

"He came to dinner at the house several times," I said thoughtfully, "and I remember him at some of the bigger celebrations."

"He was an old friend of Father's," Ilia agrees, "but he's surprisingly progressive. He is the president of the Board of Regents for the college. He'd suggested at the time that you would be a good candidate."

"Really?" I'm shocked. "I don't think I've ever spoken to him."

"Father, of course, immediately dismissed the idea," he said wryly, "which I thought was a shame. Roman and I believed you could have flourished there."

"You're kidding." I said bluntly, "I'm majoring in Literature."

He shrugged, smiling a little devilishly. "Ah, but you're still an Aslanov. In any case, since the Ares Academy's origins over two hundred years ago, the first, unbreakable law is that it is neutral. There is a permanent détente between all factions. No murders, no attacks against another student."

"What happens if someone just… snaps?" I ask.

"They're put to death," his expression is solemn. "It's ugly. Very ugly. But it's only happened three times in nearly two centuries, so those odds are good. Not to mention that all families who send a student there are required to defend the school against any attack. That has never happened. Do you see why this is the safest option for you?"

"I understand your reasoning," I agree, "but it doesn't change the fact that there's no way they're going to admit me. Particularly since the school year has already started."

"It's already done." Ilia leaned back, unbuttoning his suit jacket, and finally taking a sip of the drink the flight attendant had made for him. "Adamovich messaged me an hour ago. Lev will take you to Inis Mór and see you safely to the Academy."

"I'll stay in Kilronan Village on the island," Lev adds, "it's close to the Academy in case you need me, and I can keep an eye out for anyone coming to the island that shouldn't be there."

I'm grateful for that, but it feels selfish. "If I'm safe in this impenetrable fortress of gangsters, maybe you should be helping my brothers?"

Ilia and Lev exchange a glance, and my brother smiles at me. "What's the Aslanov family motto?"

"*Vsegda dvoynoye nazhatiye*. Always double tap?"

His brow raises, "Uh, a good way to make sure your enemy stays down, but no."

"Don't go stingy with the bullets?" *Nice, ten points for the dark humor, you idiot.*

"That's a subset of the former motto," he corrects, but there's a slight smile playing around the corners of his mouth.

Sighing, I drop my head. "Always watch your back?"

"That would be the one," he says, no longer smiling. "Lev will be there to help you if you need him, but he's not allowed on campus. You're going to have to do that for yourself."

"Didn't you just make a case for how this is the safest spot on the planet for me right now?"

Ilia shakes his head. "You'll be safer there, but you're still among our kind. Don't ever let your guard down. There are some people you can trust, your friend Mariya Morozova is there, and her affianced Konstantin Turgenev."

He hands me a silver necklace with a small charm.

"What's this?" I ask, turning it over to find a button, a bit recessed on the other side.

"No outside forms of communication are allowed on campus, though..." he grins a little, "there's always some enterprising student making money by selling illegal cell phones."

Rolling my eyes, I laughed, "You, most likely."

"Maybe," he allows. "But this device won't get picked up on their scanners. I want you to always keep it on you. If you're in danger, hit the button. Kilronan Village is still about ten minutes away, so no matter what is happening, you must stall for time, all right?"

Studying him, I feel the ache in my chest grow. We look the most alike of the Aslanov siblings, with blonde hair and dark green eyes. But while he's tall and confident, and walks with a swagger, I'm the one who stays in the background and watches everyone. It's easy to see how he ruled that campus.

"You will stand tall, *Malen'kaya iskra,* my little spark. You're an Aslanov. Just like anywhere else in our world, any sign of weakness can be dangerous." Ilia's thumb brushes my wrist and

I know he can feel my rabbiting pulse. "This is hard, I know it. Losing our parents..." his head drops for a moment until he regains his composure. "You can do hard things. You have before."

His thumb brushes over the thick scar on my back and I twist my body away. Lifting my chin, he forces me to look at him. "You will again."

Lucca...

"Who the hell is *that*?"

I turn to look at whoever sparked Mateo's idiotic wolf whistle. She can't be a student; this campus is small enough that everyone knows everyone. She's gorgeous. Lean, long legs, and blonde hair flowing down her back. Petite. She wouldn't even come up to my shoulder. She glances over briefly at Mateo's whistling, rolls her eyes, and continues into the main building.

"Oh, I am fucking that." Mateo's such an asshole, though he does well with the women on campus.

"Don't you mean her?" I said.

"No, *that*," he grins, "I just need her pussy. The rest of her is hot, though."

"You're a charmer," I said dryly, walking away from him. I don't want his asshole stink to rub off on me. I'm meeting with Professor Fukumoto, so I pass Dean Christie's office as she's entering it, shadowed by some big bastard who stares at me suspiciously.

"Tatiana Aslanova, a pleasure to meet you!" Dean Christie's warm greeting is standard for new students. Until you get to know her and she scares the everloving fuck out of you. I don't see her table saw in her office but I pick up the pace until I'm past her door anyway.

"Ah, Mr. Toscano, come in." Professor Fukumoto is one of my favorite instructors, and he looks up with a smile as I knock on his open door.

"Professor, how are you, sir?" Seating myself when he nods at the chair in front of his huge, cluttered desk, I rack my brain for anything wildly against the rules I might have done lately. He doesn't seem angry, though.

"Quite well, thank you." He settles back against his chair and examines me. I'm less bitter and sullen than I was when I arrived here two years ago. It didn't take long to realize being the biggest asshole on campus required a lot more effort than I was willing to put in. I'm still bitter as fuck, though. Mainly at my brothers.

Fukumoto is my "academic advisor," which is hilarious when you learn he was one of the senior men in a powerful Yakuza syndicate. No one's certain why he would step down from that position to work here at the Academy. Or they know better than to talk about it.

"I called you in because we will be meeting with Dean Christie in a moment," he says, watching me closely.

Raising one brow, I wonder if this is an interrogation technique designed to make me panic and spill information about some infraction. There have been plenty, and I'll never confess to a single one. "Oh?"

His smooth skin breaks out into a thousand tiny wrinkles as he chuckles. "Yes. I wanted to speak with you first. How do you feel you've been performing in your major?"

Frowning, I try to figure out where this is going. "I've learned a great deal. I feel like I've honed my craft."

"Agreed," he nodded, "your work is excellent, both academically and in practical application. However, over the last two years, the Dean and I have been watching you grow, and we are questioning your original placement."

It feels like he just punched me in the throat. Everyone in my family who came through the Ares Academy was assigned the Assassinations major. As the eldest brother, Dante would have been placed in the Leaders major, but he was denied admission. He was furious when Gio and Dario received their admissions letters.

"This... Professor, this is what I will do in life. This is my family's primary source of power and wealth. You trained both of my brothers in this major," I said, forcing myself to sound calm.

He inclined his head. "It was a primary source. Giovanni's been moving the Toscano empire into more mainstream endeavors. You might find yourself without a purpose in your family's organization."

My calm, cool exterior is wilting, and I can feel beads of sweat at my hairline. "The only reason you'd be telling me this is if you have an alternative," I say. "Have you been in communication with my brothers?"

Fukumoto's eyes are nearly black; endlessly dark pools that drown a multitude of sins and secrets. There is a soft buzz from his laptop, after glancing at it, he rises to his feet. "The Dean is ready for us."

We pass the blonde leaving the Dean's office, her mouth is tight like she's trying to hold back a torrent of screams or tears, and she hurries past me without looking up. The guy behind her looks at me though, like he wants to tear my spine out through my neck. Fuck this asshole and his posturing. I smile menacingly and lean in just slightly as he passes by.

"There we are, right on time!" Dean Christie says cheerfully, "Come right in, gentlemen."

She's lounging behind a desk so huge that it could swallow her and three more like her. Having been called into her office before,

I know the two seats in front of the desk are uncomfortable enough that they could be classified as instruments of torture.

"Mr. Toscano, have a seat. Professor? I just picked up some excellent Scotch if you'd care for a drink. The chair next to the bar is quite comfortable," she said sweetly.

Taking my seat as ordered, I try not to shift around as a spring digs into my left ass cheek.

"In the last two years, you've settled in well here at the Academy," the Dean says, looking over something on her computer monitor. "Excellent scores, particularly in poisons and knife work. You're good with other students, you take the lead naturally in group projects."

They're both looking at me, so I offer up a polite thank you.

"Here's where I feel things have shifted," she says, "while you're certainly on track to graduate in the Assassins major, Professor Fukumoto and I feel that your talents would be better used in a different major."

Frowning, I try to make sense of her words. "I have never heard of a student switching majors once you have assigned them, Dean Christie."

"It *is* highly irregular," she agrees, "but it has been done before when we find that a student begins to show an aptitude for something else. While we are *never* wrong in our initial placements, room must be made for change and growth."

Professor Fukumoto hastily takes a drink to hide a slight smile when the Dean emphasizes 'never.'

"After some consideration, we've decided to change your major to the Leaders program with a specialty minor," she says, watching my surprise before I hastily school my expression.

"With all due respect Dean, Professor," I nod politely to both while resentment starts churning my guts. It's a familiar feeling, honed by years of being the fuck-up of the family, and then the invisible son. "My brother Giovanni is the Don of the Toscano Mafia, and my brother Dario is the Underboss. There's no room in the organization for me with a Leaders degree."

The two exchange another glance that makes me want to sweep everything off her desk and yell at them both to stop fucking with me.

However, I value my life and all my limbs intact, so I don't.

"I know you have questions about this change," the Dean says, "and I fear we can't answer all of them at this juncture. But here's the paperwork for the change in majors. Professor Fukumoto will continue on as your academic advisor. He'll delve into your new major and specialty minor in more detail over the next few weeks. Now, I fear that's all the time I have for now. You are excused, Mr. Toscano."

Finding myself out in the hallway with an envelope of papers and a pat on the shoulder from Fukumoto, I try to understand what the fuck just happened.

CHAPTER THREE

In which Tatiana discovers that there is no such thing as a warm welcome. At least not at the Ares Academy.

Tatiana...

Earlier...

"Tatiana Aslanova, a pleasure to meet you!"

Dean Christie was not at all who I would expect to be running a college for criminals and assassins. She was short, maybe 5"2 or 5"3, and dressed in a soft black suit that looked like it was chosen for comfort rather than high style.

The drive up to the gates of the Ares Academy is beautiful; the harsh, windswept landscape and sheer cliffs looming over the Atlantic. Kilronan Village is charming, with pretty, painted cottages and a bustling harbor. The Academy, however, rises over the flat lands surrounding it, casting a long shadow in the sunlight. Tall black iron fencing and stacked stone walls surround three-quarters of the estate, the fourth faces the towering cliffs the Aran Islands are famous for.

All the buildings are Gothic style, with steep slate roofs and ominous towers and spires. It looks like an extremely exclusive Ivy League college until I see the guards at the main building and security cameras in every tower facing outside the campus. Like... they're bracing for a rampaging horde of Vikings, bellowing and swinging their axes as they descend upon the campus. It makes me remember what Ilia said, that in case of an attack, every crime family is obligated to protect the school.

Safe from the outside world, I think, *but I'm not so sure about inside these walls.*

"I wish I could photograph every inch of this and put it on my Dark Academia board on Pinterest," I whisper to Lev as we're escorted to the Dean's office. The only reaction I get from him is a slight upward curve of one corner of his mouth.

"So, Miss Aslanova, while it is highly irregular to admit a new student when we're already into the school year, special circumstances can, upon occasion, warrant a slight bending of the rules," Dean Christie says, pushing her shoulder-length hair back. It's brown and wavy, and I can see glimmering shots of silver through the brown.

Not surprising, I thought, *running this college could turn your hair white overnight.*

"I appreciate your willingness to accept my late admission," I said, trying to sound responsible and calm and not like the weepy mess I am inside.

She eyes me for a moment, eyes narrowed and suddenly she doesn't look like the "fun aunt" anymore. Her unblinking focus on me is more like a hawk searching for a tasty rodent in the underbrush. "I need to be very clear with you, Miss Aslanova. While I understand you have been through a traumatic experience, no allowances will be made for it. We expect you to work even harder than the other students to catch up. Your stay here is not guaranteed."

"How long..." I sputter, "How long do I have to catch up?"

The Dean runs her fingernail along the shining surface of her desk. "I will meet with your department head and instructors in early January and we will evaluate your potential to continue here at the Academy."

"That's three months!" I protest, "Surely-"

"Here are your admission papers and major placement," she interrupts. "You'll have a chance to go over them after you're escorted to your living quarters. You will need to say your goodbyes to Mr. Khorkina now and give him your phone. No outside means of communication are allowed here."

Dean Christie stands and it's clear our little conversation is over.

Lev gently takes me by the elbow and walks me out of her office and to the massive wood, iron, and glass doors in the entryway. There's a bored-looking student there who rolls her eyes as she spots me. She has short dark hair and a gorgeous olive complexion.

"She looks fun," he murmurs, trying to make me smile. He watches my pathetic attempt and squeezes my shoulders gently. "You can do this," he said, looking me in the eye. "As the *Sovietnik* says, you have done hard things before. You must stay here, Tatiana, it is crucial."

"Failure is not an option?" I try for breezy and confident, and it comes out more like a gurgle, like the last of the water circling the drain. The girl waiting for me gives a very loud sigh and looks pointedly at her watch.

My bodyguard of ten years suddenly hugs me. He hugs me like a brother and I am stunned. Aside from general directional nudges or abrupt moves when he thinks I might be in danger, Lev has never touched me. "Stay strong," he whispers, "remember who you are, and always wear that necklace. Always."

Letting my forehead drop to his shoulder, I give myself five seconds to mourn everything that's lost to me before stiffening my spine and giving him a determined smile. Lev has enough to worry about without me turning into a boneless chicken and flopping on the polished wood floor, wailing loudly, which is really what I want to do. "Thank you, Lev. For everything."

Giving my tour guide one hard look, he pulls away and heads out to the SUV without looking back.

"You're Tatiana, right?"

It's the bored girl. "Yes, hello. Tatiana Aslanova. What's your name?" I ask, trying to look friendly instead of weepy.

"Your roommate," she snarls, heading out the door without checking if I've followed her. My new roommate is tall, her stride eating up the path. She's charging ahead to the next closest building, also built with tall, leaded-glass windows and multiple towers and turrets. There's a huge stone entryway that does not look in any way welcoming, nor does the group of guys lounging in an outdoor seating arrangement on the terrace.

"Look lads, fresh meat!"

"I'll be your tour guide, honey."

"Hey Dukakis, who's this?" This specific cat-caller is handsome in a sharp, dark way and he knows it, preening as we both glance in his direction.

"No one who will ever likely be desperate enough to fuck you, Mateo," drawls my tour guide.

"Why do I get the feeling you just did me a favor?" I ask her as we climb a flight of stairs to the second floor.

"Because Mateo Costa is a fucking prick and there is no woman on this campus who hasn't had to deal with his special brand of asshole behavior," she snaps, turning to her left and heading down a long hallway with a huge, floor-to-ceiling window at the end of it.

"I appreciate the warning," I said. I am grateful for it. My experience with the opposite sex was always conducted under the scrutiny of my family or my bodyguard, which means nothing more exciting than a handshake and some polite conversation. The concept that I'm going to have social interaction with men - and without the looming presence of Lev - is both giddy and terrifying.

"This is us," she says, opening an ancient oak door. "Until two hours ago, I was the only student on this floor with my own suite," she adds sourly.

"I'm sorry," I offered weakly. The suite is startlingly luxurious for student housing. There's a large main room with a fireplace flanked by two windows and comfortable leather couches. The first door to the left leads to what I assume is my bedroom because the large bed is stripped bare. There's another huge window with an amazing view of the cliffs and the ocean, a good-sized desk, a chair, and a lovely oak armoire.

"That's your bathroom," she said crossly, opening another door. "Don't use mine. Ever. Basic rules, don't fuck anyone in the main room, at least have the common courtesy to use your bedroom and keep it down. Don't leave a mess where I have to look at it. I have to actually graduate from here, so I study. A lot."

This sets me off. "I have to graduate too, Dukak- wait, what's your first name?"

"Athena," she says reluctantly.

"So Athena, I'm sorry you have a roommate now. But my presence here isn't specifically to ruin your life," I said, trying to sound firm and confident. "I'm a nice person, you might actually like me if you give it a chance."

"Uh, huh," she says dubiously. "Anyway, the grand tour is over. Dinner starts at five and ends at seven. Bye."

"Wait, where's-" Athena's closed her bedroom door and our conversation is finished.

Sitting on the floor in front of the window, I watch the whitecaps on the Atlantic and wonder if I've somehow stepped sideways into a parallel world, one where my mother and father are gone and my brothers are an ocean away and completely unreachable.

"You can cry and completely lose your shit," I lecture myself, "or you can just keep moving." The sound of my voice is a little jarring in the silent room, but I can see why people talk to themselves. It sounds authoritative. It's soothing.

Pulling the manila envelope toward me, I wonder where they placed me. There are four majors at the Ares Academy; Leaders, always the first-born in the family. Then there are the Warriors, who usually head up the organization's soldiers and security, the Assassins, who do most of a crime family's dirty work, and the Spies, who gather information and analyze threats.

Seems like the Aslanov Bratva's spies weren't doing their work. An attack on the scale of what was just launched against our family surely couldn't have gone undetected like this. Knowing my brother Roman, there are already heads on a pike somewhere as a warning.

Reading down through the Admissions letter, I see I've been placed in the Spies track. I stand up, rubbing my face and pacing some more. Tatiana Aslanova, the Spy. It would be hilarious if it wasn't so sad. But where else would they put me? The Warriors? The vision of me in body armor and wielding a bloody sword is just entertaining enough that there's still a smile on my face when there's a knock on the suite's door.

A woman in an honest to god's old-fashioned maid uniform is standing there holding a pile of bedding in her arms and boxes stacked behind her. I knew Ilia had his personal shopper set me up with a new wardrobe and necessities since everything I own is still back at our family's home in Vancouver. The speed of delivery, though, is impressive since I've only been here a couple of hours.

"Hello, I'm here to make up your room?" She's got a nice smile, even though her eyes dart everywhere but at me.

"Oh, thank you," I said. Suddenly, the thought of anyone in the room with me seems like too much. "I'll take care of it myself." I put my arms out, smiling expectantly, and this seems to alarm her.

"No, Miss Aslanova, I'm required to do it."

"Oh, I insist," I said, smiling widely in a way that I know is super creepy but it's all I can manage right now. "I'll tell them that you did it and you are an amazing bed-maker."

Her pretty face scrunches up a bit, but she nods reluctantly and hands over the pile of sheets and towels like they're the Crown Jewels of England.

Dinnertime has come and gone but I can't seem to leave my spot in front of the window. Somehow, having all these bags and boxes of clothes piled in the corner makes this too real. My entire life has been narrowed down into this one room, surrounded by things I don't recognize and with no way to reach the few people left who care about me. All the girls I'd made cautious friendships with at the University will never know what happened to me. Will they care? Will anyone try to reach me?

Wrapping the comforter around my shoulders, I do none of the things on my to-do list. Instead, I cry, staring out at the ocean until I fall asleep on the floor.

CHAPTER FOUR

In which Tatiana is introduced to the Infamous Jankowski Beatdown. And Lucca.

Mike Posner - Not Dead Yet

Tatiana...

The alarm jolting me awake brings back a vivid memory of the night Lev hauled me out of bed and away from everything I'd known.

Covering my face, I swallow back the sobs trying to force their way out of my throat. No crying. Tears are weaponized against you at the Academy, I know that much from my brother's horror stories.

Forcing myself from my warm blankets with a groan, I paw through the unpacked boxes until I find some leggings and a tank top. My first class is Combat Instruction and I'm going to need something I can run in. Preferably, run away.

Lev taught me some Krav Maga and basic defense moves when I was in my early teens, but my mother put her foot down when she heard about it, insisting that he stop. Apparently, it's "unladylike" for a woman to know how to protect herself. I've tried working on what he taught me with the help of some YouTube videos, but I'm not fooling myself into believing I could take out the ancient gardener that I just passed who is laboring in the greenhouses, much less one of the savages enrolled here.

Still, it's my first day. Surely, the professor would give me some time to catch up.

The building that houses all the classes dedicated to beatings and murder is the farthest from the main hall, the path winds through a series of limestone boulders and for a moment, I'm alone in the mounds and jagged shards of rock. The frigid wind tears through the gaps and I shudder, moving faster until the combat building is back in sight.

There's a little shower of pebbles and dirt that just misses me, and a little scuff of a sound, like someone stepping down from a boulder.

Well, that's creepy, I think, walking faster. Was there really someone up there? Watching me?

Just making it into the gym at 8:59 a.m., I smile a bit in relief.

"You're late, Miss Aslanova." The cold tone of Karl Zimmerman stops me mid-stride. The rest of the students are sitting in a circle, staring at me contemptuously.

"I'm sorry, Professor Zimmerman, but I thought class began at nine a.m.?" I look at my watch again, as if seeing the correct time is going to make a damn bit of difference. He's out to Make An Example Of Me, I can tell.

"It's ten after nine," he lies, "and I do not tolerate the disrespect of being late to my class."

Waving my hand awkwardly like I'm leading the Symphony of the Bullied, I try to apologize again. "My watch must be off," I offer, though we both know it's not, "I will make sure I'm early to your next class to show my respect."

Apparently, my apology comes out wrong, because the beefy German's expression hardens. He's a giant; almost seven feet tall with close-cropped blonde hair and muscles bulging out alarmingly in every direction.

"You're first on the mat today," he says, looking over the other students, who are clearly enjoying this far too much.

"Oh, well, this is my first day and I haven't had a chance to catch up with-"

Cutting me off, he snaps, "Get on the mat or get out."

Dropping my backpack, I step into the center of the circle, rubbing my sweaty hands against my leggings. *He's just going to have one of these meatheads knock me off my feet to embarrass me, and...*

"Miss Jankowski," he says sharply, "join your opponent on the mat."

Oh, crap... The girl he's picked out is maybe six inches taller than me and better muscled than half the men in the class. She steps in front of me, rotating her shoulders to loosen up. She is completely expressionless, I can't tell if she's going to tear my head off or just push me down.

Clapping his hands, the professor shouts, "Begin."

The next thing I see is a fist heading for me and I'm on the mat, staring up at the ceiling, and my face is on *fire.* It feels like she shattered my cheekbone. Rolling painfully to my side, I get up, darting at her and trying to land my elbow in her abdomen. She's in a slight crouch, arms out and still looking completely indifferent as she dodges my pathetic attempt and then barrels toward me, kicking my legs out from under me with a strike to my right thigh.

I land face down this time, and my blood is dripping in a crimson stain on the blue mat. My thigh is screaming in agony. Gritting my teeth, I'm up again, surging toward this Polish machine of death like I have the slightest chance of getting out of this match alive. An explosion of pain under my chin sends me backward and as I hit the ground, everything goes black.

"Your skills are abysmal."

Opening my eyes, I realize they've dragged me over to the side of the room and left me there with an ice pack on my face. There's blood on the pack and when I wipe my eyes, my hand comes back smeared with more. My blood. I didn't land a punch anywhere near Jankowski. I have never been in this much pain, even when I broke my arm in two places on our skiing vacation in St. Moritz. My left eye is already swelling shut and I'm pretty sure I bit my lip on that last punch because there's blood running down my chin.

Everyone else is sparring in pairs, ignoring me as the professor crouches next to me. "You must practice," Zimmerman says, "a great deal. We don't slow down or hold back for weaklings. You must learn how to keep up."

Chuckling even though this is not the slightest bit amusing, I nod. "My mother ended my Krav Maga lessons because they were unladylike."

He shrugs, standing up. "Mr. Toscano, attend to me."

A man almost as tall as Zimmerman halts his sparring and walks over, clearly unhappy to be selected. He ignores me, rubbing his hands together as he nods to the professor.

"I want you to train Miss Aslanova," Zimmerman says, "she's essentially useless. Bring her up to speed as quickly as possible."

The guy is definitely unhappy with this plan. He's beautiful in an almost unseemly way, with dark hair and pale golden-brown eyes, almost an amber color, which are currently settled contemptuously on me. I'm mesmerized by his tattoos. Blazing up his bare chest, cascading down his arms and up his neck, they're all beautiful and vividly colored. "Sir... perhaps it would be better if you picked a female to-"

"You're my best fighter in this class," the professor cuts him off. "Work with her every day for a month." Looking down at my pathetic, bloody self, Zimmerman adds, "We'll take another look at your skills then. If you can't pass muster, you're out."

"Of this class?" I ask hopefully.

Leaning down, he stares at me. "Out of the Academy."

Putting the ice pack back on my face, I hope it hides my wet eyes. I *have* to stay here. There must be another way other than getting the living hell kicked out of me every day.

An alarmingly large, tattooed paw is shoved in my face. "Get up," orders Toscano - I think that's what Zimmerman called him.

Begrudgingly taking his hand, I stifle a yelp as he briskly hauls me off the floor and into his broad chest. Making an exasperated sound, he lifts me off of him.

"Sorry," I mumble, "gravity is not on my side."

"Come on," he sighs, striding out the door and clearly assuming I'd be trotting after him, like an obedient Shetland pony.

Which I am.

"Where are we going?" I wheeze, trying to ignore the stabbing pains in my thigh and face.

"To the clinic to make sure there's no serious damage," he said, eating up the path with his long legs and forcing me to keep trotting, trying to keep up.

"Could you just- please slow down!" I said, grabbing his arm.

Looking down like I'd just infected him with typhoid or syphilis with my mere touch, he pulls loose. At least he had the common decency to shorten his stride a bit.

"So, I guess Jankowski is a 'hate at first sight' kind of girl, eh?" My feeble attempts at conversation were met with a slight flaring of his nostrils.

"Don't flatter yourself," he said dryly, "it was nothing personal. In combat, it's always the last man standing. You won't get any special consideration out there in the real world just because you don't know what the fuck you're doing."

"Well, I'm sorry that I didn't arrive here as a world-class ninja," I snarl, feeling the cut in my lip open again, blood trickling down my chin. Wiping it away, I continue, "No one here can be an expert in *everything*."

Stopping suddenly, he grabs my arm to keep me from crashing into him again. "Really," he looks me over slowly, head to toe, and clearly finds me lacking. "And what are you an expert in? Anything?"

I am very, very good with computers, but I'm not telling this arrogant dick a thing about me. "Nothing, I guess." I snap. "Why don't you just point me in the direction of the clinic and I'll-"

Curling his thick fingers around my upper arm, he sighs irritably. "Keep walking. And stop talking."

"You started it," I mumble, instantly sorry because that sounds so stupid. What is it about this man that reduces me to the eloquence of a toddler?

The medical clinic looks reassuringly professional, though the ancient doctor looks like a stiff breeze would blow him right off the cliff and into the ocean.

Pulling down his reading glasses, he looks at me disapprovingly. "What happened here?"

"Combat practice, Dr. Giardo," my unwilling guide says.

"Hmm," the doctor scowls. "Very well, you can leave, Mr. Toscano." Looking sternly at me, he points to an exam table, neatly covered in a pristine white sheet. "You. Over there."

As he walks off, I look back to... Toscano, right? "Hey," I call. He stops, one hand on the door. "What's your name?"

He turns slightly, looking me over one last time. "Lucca."

"Lucca? Nice to meet you, I'm-"

He's already gone, the door shutting firmly behind him.

"You slept through dinner."

Opening the eye not swollen shut, I look at Athena, who is staring down at me like I'm roadkill.

Shrugging, she says, "I'm only bringing it up because the medication you've got on your bedside table needs to be taken with food. Call down to the kitchen and order something, they'll bring it up pretty quickly."

"How do you know that?" I groan, wondering if it would just be easier to curl up in a corner and die quietly.

Giving an inelegant snort, she rattles the bottle at me. "Dr. Giardo gave you his famous "night-night" pain pills. You'll puke them right back up on an empty stomach and believe me, you don't want to waste these little gems."

Trying not to whimper like a wounded animal, I sit up and reach for the Academy iPad, used for messaging throughout the college.

"I heard Lucca Toscano carried you down to the medical clinic," Athena says casually, lounging on my bed and showing more interest than she has for the last two days.

"Carried?" I laugh, "He dragged me behind him like I was a deer he'd just shot, but whatever."

Shrugging, she stood up, ambling into the living room. "Every girl in this college has been after Lucca. He's a 'thanks for a good time, see you later' kind of guy."

"Given that he looked at me like I was something he'd stepped in, I doubt that I'll be following the pack on this one," I said coldly. Athena is putting in her Air pods and no longer listening.

Stifling a gasp at the size of the bruise on my thigh, I groan quietly. How am I going to handle a month of this arrogant dick telling me how much I suck at everything?

Lucca...

"So? What does she feel like?"

Kon will not shut the fuck up. After hearing the campus gossip that I'd be training Tatiana, he's been nonstop with the idiot questioning. "Is she soft? Silky skin? How about her breasts? Are they as perky as they look?"

"Exactly what the hell did you think I was doing with her?" I snarled, rubbing my eyes. "I scraped her off the floor after Ania Jankowski kicked the shit out of her."

"Zimmerman paired her with Ania for her first match?" Kon flinches, "*Podonok,* what a fucker! He must have hated her at first sight."

"Like I told Aslanova," I shrug, "it was nothing personal. If anything, Jankowski was holding back. What is a soft little princess like her doing here at the Academy?"

"The Aslanov Bratva is one of the Six Families in Russia," he said, "I don't know any of the details on how they got her a placement here two months into the school year, but they wield a lot of power."

I put my hands behind my head, looking up at the skylight and the pale clouds scudding over the night sky. "Tatiana's completely unprepared for this place, she's never going to make it."

"Ah, you're on a first-name basis already?" he leers, "Nice. Are you sure you're telling me everything that happened this afternoon? Did she thank you for taking her to the infirmary? A little hand job, maybe?"

"*Tu stronzo,* you asshole," I laugh, "she has a fat lip and a black eye. Not remotely sexy, unless you're really into blood."

"I haven't seen her for years," he says, pulling off his shirt, throwing it, and as always, missing the laundry basket. "I know the Aslanov Bratva does business in Moscow, but they're mainly based in Canada. Vancouver BC, and spreading down into Seattle. Something's definitely off about it all."

Turning off my light, I stare up at the night sky. I'll pull my highly illegal cell phone from its hiding place tomorrow and look up Tatiana Aslanova and see what's happened with her family. Not because I give a shit. But if I'm forced to deal with her every day, a little history might just be useful.

CHAPTER FIVE

In which Tatiana opens her big mouth. A lot.

Cavetown - Devil Town

Tatiana...

Meals at the Academy are a special exercise in torment.

I never dealt with the awkward hesitation in the cafeteria at school, wondering where I should sit and who I should avoid, so I have no idea what to expect here. Of course, comparing the dining room at the Academy to a school cafeteria is like comparing a golf cart to a Maserati. The dining room here in the main building is more elaborate than most of the Michelin three-star restaurants I've visited, with a full bar - a shining mahogany monstrosity with a bartender and hundreds of bottles of liquor - on one end of the massive room and white-coated servers taking meal orders. The arched mullioned windows look out on the ancient rock remains of Black Fort.

I survived on granola bars and the Academy's room service menu until my fifth day, when Athena casually mentioned that everyone thought I'd sustained some sort of brain damage from the infamous Jankowski beatdown.

"Suck it up," I tell my reflection, trying to shake the tension out of my hands. "You're twenty, not twelve."

Still, walking into the gorgeous room at lunchtime is terrifying. The tables can seat anywhere from four students to twenty, and I can feel the stares as I glance around the room, hoping for a nice single spot somewhere.

"Tatiana!" Mariya Morozova bounces up to me with her arms wide, giving me the traditional Russian three kisses. "I just heard today that you were here at the Academy, I'm sorry, I would have come to find you sooner if I'd known."

"It's so good to see you," I said fervently, returning her embrace. "Knowing you were here was one of the very few selling points for this place."

"Here, come sit with us," she says, pulling me over to a big table with a scatter of girls, three or four I vaguely recognize, and five guys. They're all staring at me like I'm a particularly interesting lab experiment and I'm rethinking room service and my cozy bedroom.

"Everyone, this is my friend Tatiana Aslanova," she announces happily, briskly going through introductions so quickly that I only catch every other name or so. Looking down at the pristine white tablecloth and shining cutlery makes me want to laugh. The ridiculously high-style ambiance juxtaposed with these already battle-scarred and hardened twenty-somethings is sort of hilarious.

"I hear you're training with Lucca Toscano," ventures one girl - Camilla, I think? "That must be fun." There's a frisson of giggles around the table, while the guys groan.

"If this is going to be another session of the Toscano Slut Club, I'm leaving," growls Aleksandr Rostova. I've known him since spending time during a couple of meetings in Moscow ten years ago when the Six Families got together for a Bratva summit. I suspect my father included me in the gatherings to… I don't know, show me off as a potential match, or something. But Aleksandr was always nice.

"Well, that's rude," Camilla scolds him.

"We don't slut shame at this table," Mariya says primly.

Laughing behind my fancy cloth napkin just brings the

attention back to me. "What?" I said defensively, "He could not make it more clear that working with me is about as pleasant as having his face smashed in with a brick. Trust me, other than barking commands at me and criticizing my feeble efforts in sparring, there is nothing happening. What's the attraction here? Are you all blinded by his shiny white teeth and glaring toxic masculinity?"

The table's gone silent and I feel a presence behind me.

"Get up," Lucca says coldly, "we're scheduled for gym time in ten minutes."

Lucca...

I want to spank her ass so bad, my fucking palm is itching. Tear those tight yoga pants right off her and slap her perky little ass bright red until I make her cry. Lick the tears off her face and stick my fingers inside her and-

Fuck. What the hell is wrong with me?

Tatiana is walking with me as ordered, keeping her gaze firmly fixed on the path. Gleaming white teeth and toxic masculinity? She definitely needs a lesson in respect today. The bruising and swelling around her eye are nearly gone, though that vicious-looking blue-black bruise I'd seen on her thigh is going to take a while.

She's a terrible fighter, still flinching every time I come at her, and taking her down is painfully easy. I have to admit though, she won't give up. Maybe it's her Russian stoicism, but she gets up every time I knock her to the mat.

"Get in position," I said sharply. The four guys leaving the gym suddenly decide to hang around when I bring in Tatiana.

"I'm sure you've got something better to do," I glared at them.

"No, not really," shrugs Mateo, "maybe she could use a hand. I could teach her a couple of moves." The douchebags with him chuckle.

This is the time Tatiana chooses to be brave, which is a huge mistake.

"I already know about the dangers of STDs from manwhores and the heartbreak of premature ejaculation, so thanks, there's really nothing you can teach me."

"Whoa…" cackles the entourage of assholes.

"*Cagna,* you bitch! Who do you think you're talking to?" Mateo hisses.

Shit, I groan silently, *she's ridiculed him in front of his friends, and this isn't good.*

He marches toward Tatiana until I clothesline him with my forearm across his chest. "Mateo?" He glances at me, furious. "Fuck off."

"You sure you want to be on my bad side?" he says, grinning with his teeth clenched tight enough to crack a molar.

"Go smoke something and calm down," I said quietly, "or find a girl from your harem and get a blowjob. This isn't worth getting worked up."

"Wrong choice, *compagno,*" he hissed. Throwing his shoulders back, he chuckles, strutting back to his little group of ass-kissers. The only students here who can tolerate Mateo enough to hang out with him all have families connected to his father's mafia in Sicily.

When the door shuts behind them, I grab Tatiana with my hand on the back of her neck, pulling her closer to me. "Do not fuck with Mateo Costa. Do you understand me? If you embarrass him, he will make your life hell for the next two years. The little prick never forgets an insult."

She stares up at me, and from this close, I can see the little flecks of gold in the forest green of her eyes. That she smells of jasmine and something spicy. That the heat coming off her skin makes me want to run my tongue down her throat and between her breasts and-

Fuck. Me. Get it together, you asshole!

"Do you understand me?" I persist, giving her a little shake.

"Yes! Just take your hands off me!" Tatiana snaps.

I let go of her and walk off, hands on my hips as I try to control my temper. Why should I care if she insists on making an enemy of Mateo? The first answer is obvious, that miserable prick shouldn't be here at the Academy, he's done some brutal shit without being caught, and she is no match for him.

The second answer is harder to accept. I want to protect her.

Her parents were just murdered and instead of keeping her with them, her brothers sent her here to sink or swim. There's a lot of chatter between the families about the attacks, but no one seems to know who's behind them. Why would the Aslanov Bratva send her here? Tatiana's gentle and reserved, she's not meant for the cutthroat environment of the Academy.

She's not your problem, I try to convince myself, *train her, and move on.*

Sucking a deep breath, I clap my hands. "Get into position on the mat."

Taking her place, she plants her feet. Her lips are pressed together tightly but she forces herself to look at me, eyes narrowed.

"One of your weaknesses is not using momentum in your favor," I said. "You are rarely going to match an opponent in size, so you need to use their height and bulk against them. I'm going to charge at you, when I'm almost within arm's reach, I want you to pivot right, get your left arm against my chest, and your right behind my head. The second my chest touches your arm;

pull with everything you've got against the back of my head. Visualize me flipping over and landing on my back."

"I'm not strong enough to flip you," she said, already looking miserable.

"That's why you're using my momentum to do the work for you," I said patiently. "Let's give it a try."

Taking a deep breath and shaking out her hands, Tatiana nods firmly.

"I'm going to do this in slow motion the first time to let you get the sense for your foot and arm placement," I coach her, "then I'm coming at you. Ready?"

"Yes…" she agrees hesitantly.

As always, she flinches when I move in on her, but since I'm going slowly it gives her a chance to focus again. Her arm placement is perfect, and I correct her foot positioning with a tap to her ankle. "Good. Let's try it again for real this time."

We work on the move six times and she still can't make me flip, but she doesn't want to stop. "Again," she says, panting.

"We'll take a water break," I said.

"Once more," Tatiana insists.

Cracking my neck, I take my place and charge her, a little faster this time because her stubbornness is both irritating and impressing me. This time, she does every move perfectly and I'm flying, flipping, and landing on my back on the mat.

"It worked!" she shrieks, jumping up and down. "Hah! I did it!"

Leaning back on my elbows, I chuckle at her little victory dance. "You did," I said, "that was a slick move."

"Wait," she pretends to be shocked. "Did the Great and Untouchable Lucca Toscano just tell me I didn't completely suck at something?"

"Shut up and grab some water," I grouse, picking myself up off the mat.

CHAPTER SIX

In which Lucca is a complete dick. And his gets punched.
Cavetown - Boys Will Be Bugs

Tatiana...

Two weeks later...

"So, how's it going with Mr. Dark and Dangerous?" Mariya asks one day at lunch. I have my poisons notebook open and I'm trying to review my notes for the "practical applications" test this afternoon.

"There is nothing reassuring about the phrase 'practical applications' when it comes to poison," I sigh. "What does that even mean?"

"You're avoiding the subject here," Mariya grins.

"Lucca will never admit it, but I think he's not actively hating our training sessions as much," I said. "At least he doesn't look at me like I'm a used litter box anymore. I've noticed he's also taking more time with me than the required hour for our training sessions."

"Oooo, extra sparring time with that tasty morsel?" Mariya nudges me. "Just how hot do these training sessions get?"

She's a tiny thing, even shorter than me but wiry. I've seen her spar and take out someone twice her size. She has the same controlled savagery as her brother Maksim. They look the most alike of all the Morozov siblings, with dark hair and icy blue eyes. But she has a warmth her brother doesn't. She pulled me into her friend group effortlessly, and they welcomed me like I'd always been there. Her roommate Camilla Boucher is one of my favorites, a relentlessly cheerful redhead from a French crime syndicate and in the Leaders division.

It's nice to know that *some* crime families have given up their misogynistic views against female leadership.

Aleksandr also made me feel welcome immediately. He's tall and lean, without the overly bulked-up look most of the men have here. He's slow to anger, though I can tell by the way other students look at him that he's held his own in a fight before. There are twins in our circle - Meiying and Jun Chen - from a Chinese Triad organization so notorious that even I knew all about them before I came here. Meiying is far more terrifying than her brother. She's also the most persistent.

"Come now, we want details, Tatiana," Meiying pokes me in the ribs, "does he pin you down on the mat? A few full-body contact moments? Does he get hard when you're sparring? Does-"

"*Bozhe moy*, my god! What is wrong with you all?" I laugh, though there is a humiliating red flush blooming on my cheeks. "Lucca has absolutely no interest in anything but getting through his commitment to Professor Zimmerman and then removing my presence in his life."

Aleksandr shrugs, "Lucca's not the type to spend this much time trying to please a professor. If he really hated you, he would have found a way to break your leg or something on the first day he trained you."

"Very inspiring, Aleks," I said dryly, "I feel so much better now that my leg has remained unbroken. Has he always been this..." I flounder for a moment, "This surly?"

They all laughed. "Worse," Mariya says, "He came to the Academy with a huge chip on his shoulder. He was in a lot of fights."

"He didn't start many of them," Aleksandr adds, "but he definitely finished them. After a few legendary drubbings, everyone left him alone."

Camilla leans in, lowering her voice. "My father has a trade deal with the Toscano Mafia. He told me that Lucca did something the *famiglia* found unforgivable, so they set him aside."

"What does that mean?" I frown. It sounds archaic.

"It means he fucked up so seriously that they don't view him as family," Camilla said, "he has to redeem himself here at the Academy. He doesn't even go home for those two months during summer. My best guess is that they'll accept him back into the family based on his performance here."

My gaze wanders over to a table by one of the windows, where Lucca's surrounded by his friends. One of them is Konstantin Turgenev, Mariya's fiancé. I've always thought it was odd that he and Mariya don't ever sit together, considering that they're getting married after they graduate.

Konstantin is talking and laughing, gesturing wildly with his hands - more Italian than Russian - having Lucca as his roommate must be influencing him. Lucca's leaning back, arms folded, listening to his friend's story with a slight smile on his face. It's genuinely startling because I don't think I've ever seen him smile. Not once. It's a shame, too, because his smile is beautiful, his full lips curved up and his eyes are softer, more relaxed.

My brothers are hard men, they've had to be. But I can't think of what I could do that would make them throw me out of the family.

Have sex with someone they haven't chosen for me? I think bitterly. *Virginity is still a currency in arranged marriages.*

My gaze goes back to Lucca, wondering what he'd be like in bed. With that body? He's like an X-rated anatomy lesson in physical perfection. He's never taken off his shirt when we work out, but just in basketball shorts and a t-shirt, he's ridiculously sculpted. His ass is...

Wait. What the hell am I doing? I'm perving on *Lucca?* What is *wrong* with me? Of course, just then, he looks over at me and his smile drops. Sighing, I turn away, focusing on some story that Jun is telling involving a baby tiger, too much sake, and a kidnapping.

Lucca...

Later that day...

Tearing through the underbrush, the same phrase circles my brain.

I'm an uncle, not an uncle. Not an uncle.

Fucking Gio and his wife Ekaterina had a baby.

This discovery came from the Google search I do on my family every few weeks. There it was, an article from an Italian magazine about the huge donation the Toscano *Famiglia* made to the Pausilipon Children's Hospital in Naples, where apparently, my sister-in-law delivered my nephew *(not* nephew) a few weeks ago.

I didn't even know she was pregnant.

There's a big picture of Giovanni and Ekaterina standing in front of a new wing in the hospital, she's holding a blue blanket-wrapped bundle, and next to them, Dario and his new wife Cora, and my sister (*not* sister) Francesca and my nephew (*not* nephew) Alessio.

What's left of the Toscano *famiglia.*

They all look so fucking happy in the picture, standing close together as some fawning hospital official thanks them for the donation. There's no space there for me.

I laugh harshly as I bound over a limestone outcropping. "Family is everything," as my father loved to remind us. "Family will always come first." Somehow, this bit of news is the last punch to crush my pathetic hope that I am still a Toscano son. It doesn't matter what I do or don't do here. They've cast me out.

"Lucca?"

Blinking, I look around and realize I'm in front of the gym, and Tatiana is waiting for me with a concerned expression.

"Are you okay?"

"Just... get inside," I snap, trying to pull myself back together.

It's not fair, how I'm yelling at her tonight, I know that. I can't stop mocking her efforts and irritably tapping her feet and hands back into position. Tatiana keeps her mouth shut, working harder to get the moves right and I keep ridiculing her efforts.

After the eighteenth time of knocking her on her back, I stand over her, irrationally furious. *"Gesù Cristo,* why are you wasting my fucking time?" I shout down at her, enjoying her shock. "Why are you here? Everyone else is years ahead of you in these skills! Why don't you go home and stop pretending to be anything other than a useless Bratva princess?"

I've never been punched in the dick before.

Fuck...

The next thing I'm aware of is lying sideways on the mat, knees up, and breathing through my clenched teeth. *When I get up, I'm throwing her off the cliff, I swear to fucking-*

"Go to hell! You have been a complete asshole to me since day one! Do you think I *wanted* to work with *you?*" Tatiana's screaming at me, fists clenched and looking like a warrior princess. "Why do you think you're God's gift to this place? What do you get out of trying to make me feel like nothing?"

"You shouldn't be here," I hiss between gritted teeth, "you're not tough enough for this place. You're fragile as fuck."

"I am not fragile!" she shouts back. "Do you really think you're the worst problem I've had this year? You're not even in the top three, *ty pridurok*, you dick! I'm not going anywhere!"

The crippling agony has receded just enough to let me get to my feet again, looming over her. "Face it, you're not going to make it through the next month, much less the year. Go home."

"Shut up!" She pushes me away from her but I keep following her.

"Go home, Bratva princess," I snarl, so fucking furious and knowing I'm not angry at her, but she's here, right in front of me, and flinching as I yell at her.

"No! I'm not going anywhere!" She goes up on tiptoe, shouting in my face.

"You don't belong here!" I'm bellowing back at her and she's holding her ground, then her furious little face crumples and she hits my shoulder as hard as she can.

"I don't have anywhere else to go!" Tatiana screams.

Stumbling backward, she sits down abruptly, drawing her knees up, tears pouring down her face. "There's nowhere else for me to go." Her head drops to her knees and she's sobbing like her heart's been torn out and I am such a bastard.

Running my hands down my face, I take a deep breath. Sitting down next to her, I almost smile as she scoots away from me, still crying.

"I'm sorry... about your parents," I offer awkwardly.

"Don't talk about my parents."

"My parents died together, too." Why am I telling her this? "They were in an attack at a New Year's Eve party. My mom died that night and my father held on for a little while... I think someone told him mom was gone, and then he was, too."

"I'm sorry," she said, still hiccupping sobs. "That's horrible."

"Yeah," I chuckle humorlessly. "Finally, something we can both relate to."

That, and the fact that neither one of us has a home to go back to...

We sit together in the gym, the last rays of the sun disappearing over the cliffs. When it's too dark to see, I stand with a groan, feeling a vicious twinge from my cock, which is still holding a grudge about that punch. Holding my hand out, I wait for her to take it. She eyes my outstretched fingers suspiciously for a moment before accepting my help getting up.

"Sorry about punching you there..." she says, gesturing awkwardly at my crotch.

"No, you're not," I'm laughing, even though my dick doesn't think it's even remotely amusing.

Trying to hide her smile, she shrugs.

"We have another ten days before Professor Zimmerman evaluates your fighting skills," I said. "I'll reserve one of the gyms for longer sessions, they're usually not in demand later in the evening."

The hope on her face unnerves me, like she really thinks I'm someone she can count on. "Oh?"

"There's some tricks I haven't shown you yet," I admit, rubbing the back of my neck. "It's not about who's the biggest in a fight, it's about who's the smartest. We'll start again tomorrow, all right?"

Nodding, she smiles cautiously. Her eyes are red and her cheeks are wet, but she still has a smile for me. "Okay. That's really...

thank you."

"C'mon," I said, "I'll walk you back to your place."

CHAPTER SEVEN

In which Tatiana learns that guns are helpful but never there when you really need one.

Tatiana...

There are ten different buildings within the Academy's high stone walls, a few smaller outbuildings, and a lovely, huge greenhouse where a lot of the food served in the dining room comes from. Then, there's the lighthouse. It's right on the tip of the grounds jutting forward on a jagged outcropping of rock, and while it once guided sailors safely home, it's primarily used as a seedy spot to get high and have sex. Maybe I'm too conservative, but having sex on a grimy stone floor in a rickety structure seems extremely non-erotic.

I'm heading to the Digital Arts building, which is the closest to the lighthouse, making it somewhat secluded. It's five minutes before my Dark Web lecture and Mateo and his three little chuckle buddies step out from behind a shed.

"Where's Toscano?" Mateo says with a smirk that seems permanently affixed to his face, "Doesn't he usually have his mouth buried in your pussy?"

Sure enough, his posse of scumbags starts chortling on cue.

"Get out of my way," I sigh, trying to walk around him.

Grabbing my arm, he leans in, "Why don't we spend some quality time together? I think we had a bad start. That *puttana*, that bitch Athena tried to poison you against me."

Granted, Athena doesn't seem to like me any more than when I moved in with her, but it didn't even take her warning to let me know what a pig Mateo is. Still, he's oddly popular with the girls here, so I have no idea why he's bothering me.

"Yeah, calling my roommate a bitch really shows the respect you have for women," I said, yanking my arm away. When his eyes narrow to dark slits, I try to soften my comment. "I hear you've got a dozen of my fellow classmates begging for your time, so I'll let you go-"

"Let *me* go?" he said incredulously, "I don't think you know how things work here, *puttana*,"

"I'm going to be late for class," I said wearily. "I get it. You're in charge. You're the top dog. Have I covered it?" He's still blocking the path and his creepy buddies have formed a half-circle behind me.

"Not until you give me a kiss with that pretty pink mouth of yours," he goads me. "Kiss me sweet and I'll let you go."

Lev always reminded me to find at least two or three ways out of anywhere I happened to be. The exterior stone wall of the Academy blocks me on one side, and there's a little grove of trees on the other.

Trees it is.

Leaning closer, I whisper, "Let me tell you a secret."

Intrigued, he bends down a bit and is slightly off-balance on the rocky path. "Yeah, baby?" He's grinning, the smug little prick. I swing my backpack hard and nail him in the side of the head. He hits the ground with a satisfying "oof!" as I dart through the trees and onto a more traveled path, students looked at me in surprise as I burst through the trees. I can hear him screech *"Puttana!"* as I head into the Armory building.

He's such a dick, but I know I've made a serious enemy here.

"Take a breath, hold it, squeeze the trigger on the exhale," I whisper, focused on the target, shooting carefully, precisely until the clip is empty.

"Miss Aslanova, that's impressive!" Professor Suarez hits a button, bringing the target closer to get a look at my shot placement. "That's a solid cluster of shots for twenty-five meters."

He's a short man, but brawny with thick forearms and capable hands. I caught a glimpse once of his chest when his shirt gaped, he has six puckered scars on his chest. Bullet holes. He was a legendary sniper for the US Special Forces, I'm not quite sure how he ended up here.

His keen brown eyes examine the target as he pulls the empty clip out of my Glock and loads another one. Putting a fresh target sheet on the line, he sends it back down the range. "Let's try thirty-five meters, concentrate on keeping that tight grouping."

Going through my mantra again, I take the first shot. It's wildly off the mark, but the next fourteen bullets all hit the target. Holding my breath, I wait for Suarez to bring the paper target in. He's examining the shot pattern and whistles. "You really have had no training in firearms?"

Shrugging awkwardly, I can see other students cluster in to see the target. "No. I mean, my brother took me out for target practice a couple of times when I was younger, but…"

Nodding, he folds the paper target and hands it to me. "That's worth pinning on your wall as a bragging point. Well done."

Beaming, I feel ridiculously happy for something so small. But Professor Suarez rarely says "well done" to anyone.

"I want to try you on sniper rifles next," he said. "On Monday, we'll go through the various weapons and find one that suits you."

"Thank you, Sir. I would like that," I'm still grinning like an idiot. For the first time, I feel like I belong here.

CHAPTER EIGHT

In which Tatiana discovers the allure of the lighthouse.
Calum Scott, Tiesto - Dancing On My Own

Tatiana...

As a Russian, it is almost unseemly for me to feel optimism, but I do.

In most of my classes, I am catching up with the curriculum. I just passed my exam in Extortion with an A, which seemed to surprise my professor, since he went through it twice before handing it back to me with a sour "Congratulations."

My skill in marksmanship was not a fluke. Professor Suarez seemed to enjoy taking on the role of mentor for me, introducing me to some spectacular weaponry, like the Barrett M82 sniper rifle and the SAKO TRG 42. However, I was not prepared for the recoil and was now sporting yet another black eye from the scope smacking me painfully on my eyebrow.

"At least it's the other eye," Mariya's trying to cheer me up, "now your blunt force facial trauma is at least symmetrical."

"Thanks, bestie," I said dryly. I'm attempting to put some coverup on the bruising while she vigorously brushes my hair. "Why is it that we're going to the lighthouse? It looks like it's one good windstorm from crumbling and toppling over the cliff, crushing screaming students in its path."

"Because everyone is going tonight," she said, "two of the seniors, Louis and Marcel Fournier, are throwing a proper rave, with booze-"

"We can keep alcohol in our rooms and there's a full bar in the dining room," I remind her.

"Great music," Mariya continues, ignoring me, "their father owns nightclubs all over France and Italy, so the sound system they smuggled in is amazing. Plus, there's party favors." She winked at me, pulling half of my long and unmanageable hair up and leaving the rest down in waves.

"Not my thing," I say dismissively, "plus, it's against the rules and if I get kicked out of here, I won't have to worry about an unseen enemy, my brothers will kill me themselves."

Mariya's one of the few people who knows the real story of why I'm here. The Turgenevs and the Morozovs have aligned with my brothers, believing in this case that a threat against one of the Six Families could be a threat against all.

"You've been here a month," she reminds me, "and so far the only thing you've done is study and get beaten up a lot. Though when it's Lucca, you don't seem to mind as much, hmm?"

"If he can teach me enough to get Professor Zimmerman to keep me in his class, I don't care what he does to me," I said, pulling on a thick green cashmere sweater.

"Who does what to you?" Camilla comes into Mariya's bedroom where we're getting ready, "What did I miss?"

"Nothing!" I said.

"Lucca, and doing anything he wants," Mariya chirps happily.

"Details, *s'il vous plaît?*" Camilla urges, lounging on the bed. She's wearing an elegant combination of sleek black trousers and a blue silk top that's going to freeze her half to death in the November weather.

"Nothing," I repeat, exhausted with their endless questions about Lucca. "There's nothing to tell other than he's really helping me enough that there's the possibility that I might pass Zimmerman's test next week." They share a skeptical glance and it makes me cranky. "How are you two finding the time to socialize? How is this schedule not crushing you?"

"You get used to it," Camilla promises, "it does get harder though when they start the challenges."

"The what?" I croak, "It gets harder?"

"Don't scare her!" Mariya scolds her roommate, who shrugs. Even her shrug is elegant because the woman is quintessentially French. They haul me out of the building before I can ask any more questions.

There are other students winding through the boulders and small groves of trees on school grounds that lead to the lighthouse. The trees are stunted by the winds that tear across the flat island, but they're stubbornly clinging to the rocky soil. The memory of the towering pines that surround our estate in Vancouver makes me acutely homesick. Will I ever be able to go home again?

Mariya must sense my misery because she links her arm with mine, giving me a big grin. "Lighten up, you're going to have fun tonight."

To be fair, the Fournier brothers have done a spectacular job. Blue, yellow, and green lights blaze out from the cracks in the tower and if I didn't know I was partying in a fifty-foot-high deathtrap, it could be considered a proper rave. We hand over our money to go inside, and the glow from a huge bonfire competes with the cleverly arranged club-style lighting.

"Ladies," Marcel manages to leer equally at all of us, which is oddly gracious because I know he follows Camilla around like a lovesick puppy, "can I offer you anything special tonight?"

"Where's the bar?" Camilla is looking over his shoulder and I feel a twinge of sympathy at his obvious disappointment.

"Over by the stairs," he says, turning to meet the next group and take their money.

Other than a bottle or two of wine that I'd saved for my crying binges, I haven't had anything to drink here at the Academy. Navigating all the little dangerous currents I swim through every day is hard enough sober. Still... When Mariya hands me a cup of something purple, I take it.

It's just one night.

"Here are the hottest women on this island!" Aleks drapes his arms over my and Mariya's shoulders. He's clearly ahead of us in drink consumption.

"Thank you for your beer goggles assessment," I say dryly, but give him a squeeze anyway. Aleks may be one of the best students in the Leaders division, but he's still kind in a way most of the First-Born students are not.

"We are dancing!" Mariya shouts, draining her cup in three gulps. Knowing I'll likely regret this, I finish mine and let Aleks drag me into the writhing mass of bodies.

There are a lot of girls looking our way, and I laugh as he spins me around. "You have quite the fan base, my friend."

He glances over to a gawking cluster of Juniors and shakes his head. "I met someone in Europe last summer."

"She must really like you if she's willing to wait another ten months to see you," I said, "is she someone you could marry? I mean, your father hasn't arranged a marriage for you yet, so... possibly?"

His warm brown eyes are bleak as he looks down at me. "No. My father would never agree to the match. But... you never know, right?"

"Exactly!" I nod firmly, "Nothing's set in stone."

He looks down at me with an expression I can't identify, and his arms wrap around me in a crushing hug. Touched, I squeeze him back. "Guess I shouldn't have done that," he says with a grin, "he really looks pissed off."

"Who?" I turn to look over my shoulder and see Lucca standing by the bar, glaring right at us. "What's he upset about?"

Aleks squeezes me again. "Tell me you're really not that blind, Tati. I'm going to go get a drink before Lucca stabs me."

Watching him walk away from me, I wonder what it's going to take to prove to my friends that Lucca Toscano feels nothing for me.

Hands wrap around my hips in a tight grip and I wince as fingers dig into my skin, yanking me backward. Before I can pull away, someone licks my neck and I yelp, clumsily shoving them away.

"I'm going to let you apologize for all your disrespect with a blowjob," Mateo makes a sleazy flicking gesture with his tongue.

"You're disgusting," I hiss, wiping furiously at the spit with my sleeve. "Don't touch me again, you pig!"

Mateo's unhinged entitlement is extremely creepy. A lot of the guys here probably are like that, but at least they hide it better. His friends are crowding closer, trying to herd me away from the others and it's seamless enough to make me think they've done this before. The music's so loud that I'm not sure anyone will hear me if I start yelling.

A new set of hands pulls me away from Mateo's little circle of predators and against a hard chest. "Give it the fuck up, Costa. She's with me."

It's Lucca, and I sag with relief.

"This is the second time you've come between me and my meat, asshole," Mateo's fists are clenched, though I can tell he's hesitating to come closer, even with his buddies behind him.

"Meat?" I snarl, "Who the hell-"

Lucca moves me behind him so smoothly that I don't realize it until I'm staring at his broad back. "She's not meat, and she's not yours, motherfucker," he said viciously, "if you touch her again, I will beat you into a pulp of broken bones and blood. Are we clear?"

"You're making a big mistake, Toscano." Mateo's grinning, and it's unnatural, showing all his teeth, his skin is stretched tight over his features.

Like a skull, I thought, shuddering.

Dragging me along like I'm luggage, Lucca stalks out of the lighthouse.

CHAPTER NINE

In which Mariya and Konstantin fight. Tatiana and Lucca do not. Fight, anyway...

Eve 6 - Here's to the Night

Tatiana...
"Wait- Lucca, just-" He's hauling me along the exterior stone wall of the school grounds and I'm tripping over tree branches and rocks. Stubbing my toe, I yelp and dig in my heels. "Stop! What the hell was that?" I almost pitch backward when he abruptly lets go of my wrist.

"Goddamnit! How many times do I have to rescue you?" He's shouting in my face and I really want to punch him in the dick again.

"I didn't ask you to rescue me," I scoffed, "I don't need you-"

"Apparently, you do." Lucca cuts me off, amber eyes blazing, "because every time I turn around, fucking Mateo is all over you! Do you want to get hurt? Is that it?"

"He keeps popping up like a fungus everywhere I go!" I protested, "Believe me, I don't want anything to do with him." Remembering his disgusting tongue on my neck, I shudder and wipe at the spot again.

"He's been following you?"

"If I'm walking alone, he always seems to show up with his little douchebag entourage," I admit, "I try to stay with a group between classes. He's just a creep. He'll get tired of his game and go harass some other poor soul soon."

This just seems to make him angrier. "Has that fucker hurt you? Is that where you got that black eye?"

Laughing, I shake my head. "No, that's from a rifle scope, I wasn't prepared for the recoil, that's all. He hasn't touched me." I try not to shudder again but I do, remembering his slimy mouth. "Not until tonight."

"Mateo is a psychotic asshole from the nastiest family in the Cosa Nostra," he says, rubbing the back of his neck. "No one wants to do business with the Costa Mafia because they're backstabbing pieces of shit, and their main source of income is the Red Trade. He despises women, especially the ones who reject him."

The Red Trade. Human trafficking, women, and children. Specifically for sex work. Even in the world of organized crime, any mafia, bratva, or cartel who traffic these poor souls are the lowest of the low.

"Well, just in case I needed another reason to hate him, that would do it," I said. The autumn wind picks up, rushing around us and sending another scatter of leaves flying from the last few clinging to the trees. Shivering, I pull my sweater down to cover my hands.

"Here," Lucca says crossly, pulling off his leather jacket, "put this on."

"I'm fine." He ignores me, sliding it over my shoulders. I love this jacket, made from battered brown leather, the best kind that only looks better as it ages. He helps me slide my arms into the sleeves.

"Do you want to go back in?"

Honestly? No. I want to keep walking with Lucca. I want him to talk to me about something other than combat techniques. I miss the night I broke down in front of him because at least for that moment, he was open. When he was emotionally raw, like I was, and he shared part of himself with me.

Lucca absently straightens the collar on the jacket, pulling me closer in the process. "You look good in my jacket," he says.

"You just said something nice to me," I grin, "is your head going to explode now?"

"I've said nice things to you before!" He looks so offended.

"The phrase, 'yeah, that move wasn't pathetic, try again,' is not exactly sweet talk, Toscano," I laugh.

His amber eyes narrow and in the moonlight, he looks decisively wolf-like. "What would you like me to say? That you're much stronger than I thought? That you're brave, even after they threw you in the deep end? You keep dog-paddling your way out of trouble, and-"

"Did you just compare me to a dog?" I said incredulously.

"No, I-" For the first time, Lucca Toscano looks flustered. "I admire your strength and your courage. It's safer to focus on those qualities of yours, instead of your eyes. They're green, like pine trees with golden flecks. Or your gorgeous, pouty mouth."

"Those are pretty good compliments," I croak.

His hand slips behind my neck. "I keep vacillating between wanting to spank you, I mean, turn that ass *red,* or kissing you."

Why did I just feel like he plugged me into a light socket by mentioning spanking me? Everything below my waist is suddenly tingling and my face is as red as the shade he wanted to slap onto my ass. "Maybe... uh, maybe we could just start with the kissing?" I ask awkwardly.

Lucca Toscano, the man I've been sure despises me suddenly smiles, and it's beautiful. He's beautiful, with his sharp, high cheekbones and gorgeous mouth. When he leans down to kiss me, I let out an embarrassing little moan but *bozhe moy*, my god, his lips are so warm.

"Beautiful," he murmurs, pulling back long enough to cup my cheeks, running his thumbs over my skin before kissing me again. His tongue traces the seam of my lips before slipping inside, and his hand moves into my hair and gripping a handful, pulling my head back and kissing me thoroughly.

Just then we hear the furious bickering from two voices we instantly recognize.

Slipping past a bush and a bit closer, I see Konstantin holding Mariya's arm, pulling her along. "What was that *mudak*, that fucker doing rubbing up on what is mine?" he shouted at her, "Is this the first time?"

Mariya hauls off and slaps him across the face and I smother a yelp. "Oh, screw you! I follow all the rules of the marriage agreement - as stupid and archaic as they are - because I won't disrespect the Morozov name. But you, oh, you get to fuck around all you want, don't you? Ronan and I were just dancing, he wasn't even touching me!"

Konstantin took the slap without a word, still staring down at her in fury. My feet are already moving. I won't let him hurt her. I don't care if our families are allies, I'll gut him before he can touch a hair on her head. Mariya's done more for me here than anyone, I wouldn't have made it this long without her and he can't hurt her...

Lucca's arm wraps around my waist, his hand flat against my stomach and holding me still. I'm about to dig my elbow into his solar plexus when he whispers, "Stop. Kon won't touch a hair on her head. He's not like that." Nodding, I sag back against him with relief.

"You need to remember who you're promised to, and it's not that Irish prick," Konstantin grits out.

"Oh, don't worry," Mariya's still yelling in his face, and I can tell he's not used to that. "How could I possibly forget? You're always lurking around like a creep, sneering at me."

"Then you shouldn't have come to the Ares Academy," he snarls, "we could have had four years of freedom away from each other, but you just had to show up, didn't you?"

"Did you think I would turn down being accepted here just because you'd be stinking up the place?" I know Mariya's on a roll now, there's no stopping her. "I'm the first woman in the Morozov family line to be accepted here!"

He pulls her closer, "Ronan Cox is a sleazy prick who's been sniffing after you since you came here. He'd love to get you in bed just to fuck with me."

"Of course," she scoffed, "because everything is about you, isn't it?"

Lucca's warm, rough palm flexes on my stomach, and his other hand goes over my mouth to stifle my startled yelp. His fingers are sliding under the waistband of my jeans, instinctively, I try to move away from his hand, which ends up pressing me against his chest. There's something hard poking me in the small of my back. Very hard. And large. Maybe it's a really big wallet?

I am such a moron, I think, cringing, *a wallet…*

Sucking in a desperate gasp of oxygen when his hand loosens over my mouth, I wheeze, "What are you-"

"Shh…" his perfect, full lips are tickling my ear. "You don't want them to see us, do you?"

Lucca Toscano's long, calloused fingers are in my undies and I can't seem to process this. One finger slides lightly up and down the seam between my lower lips and I can feel myself getting wet, embarrassingly, eagerly slick and he's using it to circle my clit with the lightest, most infuriating touches.

He tightens his hand over my mouth as my hips make an executive decision and push forward against his hand. "Do you want me to stop?"

Did I? I should. I should want him to stop but the feel of his hard, roughened fingers is just... I shake my head.

I can feel his grin against my cheek. "You're going to be quiet; I know you can do it." The heel of his hand slides down and grinds gently against my clitoris as his fingers stroke and pinch me. "When you come, you're not going to make a single fucking sound."

My flailing hand somehow ends up pressing on the outside of my jeans, right over where this man is touching me. He chuckles quietly. "You'll come when I tell you to come. You're not going to hurry this along."

What is happening here?

I'm trying to form some kind of logic in my brain that would make Lucca's hand inside my undies my sense. He tolerates me at best. *Oh, god this feels so good.*

The warmth of his skin soaks into me and I can barely feel the chill in the air, his stubbled cheek rubs against the thin skin of my neck as he whispers something filthy-sounding in Italian.

The sound of Mariya and Kon's squabbling fades away and my head drops back against his chest. I can feel the rumble from his silent chuckle as the heel of his hand keeps circling my clitoris, hard, then softly, not keeping a rhythm that will let me get close to coming but *bozhe moy,* my god, my fingers could never do this. The heat and roughness of his hand are so foreign and wildly erotic.

His palm slides from covering my mouth to resting lightly against my throat. "Not a sound, understand?" Lucca whispers, "I'll stop if you even open your mouth and you don't want that, do you?" He squeezes my neck lightly when I don't answer him and I nod rapidly, pressing my lips together.

Later, when my brain has rejoined my body, I'll think about this and most likely torture myself with guilt and question why I allowed this arrogant man with the looks of a supermodel and all the charm of a serial killer to *do* this to me. Later. But right now he's unbuttoning my jeans to give himself more room and the tip of his forefinger slowly slides up into my channel and I stiffen. His movements pause for a moment, and then the finger withdraws, circling my entrance instead.

His fingers swirl and slide faster and my legs are shaking. "So close, aren't you, baby?" he whispers diabolically and I can feel him grin against my neck before biting the skin gently. Two of his fingers pinch my clitoris and tug and then I'm flying, I'm coming, and before we can test my ability to keep my mouth shut, Lucca's lips descend on mine, kissing me greedily, his hand sliding up from my neck to my jaw, turning my head so he can push his tongue and his breath into my mouth and he swallows the moans of my orgasm and his teeth scrape my lip.

We stand hidden in the little grove of trees, I'm shaking as Lucca buttons my jeans and then puts his wet fingers into his mouth, tasting me. It's not until sometime later that I notice Mariya and Kon's argument is over and they're long gone.

CHAPTER TEN

In which Lucca questions his sanity and employs diversionary tactics.

Lucca...

What the fuck did I just do?

Tatiana is thankfully silent as I straighten her clothes and take her back to the steps of the student housing building. She blinks and seems to come back online, slipping off my jacket.

"Thank you. I mean, for the jacket- for keeping me warm- *der'mo!* Shit! I meant warm because of your jacket..." She's so mortified that she can't even look me in the eye. It's a shame because I'd like to see her green eyes, the flecks of gold that make them shimmer. She licks her lips and I want to kiss her again, steal more of her breath and orgasms to live inside me.

"Well... goodnight Lucca," she says, nodding firmly, concluding this conversation.

Leaning down, I kiss the curve of her neck. She smells like me; old leather and wintergreen, with a hint of her jasmine scent. "Goodnight."

She hurries up the steps like I might chase her, disappearing through the doors.

Bringing up my fingers to smell her one last time, I walk in circles around the campus for the rest of the night.

"Where were you?"

Konstantin is acting especially pissy this morning, slouching on the couch, clutching a cup of coffee, and the fireplace blazing away with enough wood to build a new tree.

"How many times have you set our suite on fire?" I ask, using the fireplace poker to even out the blazing logs.

"The key clarification here is almost. I *almost* set the suite on fire," he corrects me haughtily, moving his foot to cover a burn mark on the oriental rug. "So where were you? Wait. Let me guess. Dragana Stojanovic's room? She's been chasing you for over a year. Did she finally get her hands down your pants?"

Remembering how it felt to have *my* hand inside Tatiana's panties, it took me a minute to answer him. "No. That will never happen. I shouldn't have slept with her cousin."

"Ljubica, in the Assassins division?" Konstantin asked.

"Yes, they tell each other everything," I said. "Dragana already offered me a threesome with her and Ljubica."

"And you said no?" Konstantin's sitting up now and clearly outraged.

"You'd sleep with Dragana and her cat and would count it as a threesome, wouldn't you?" I'm laughing and it's just enraging him more.

"I've had plenty of threesomes, you asshole!" he snaps.

"Yeah? Were you the meat in a sandwich last night?" I goad him. I know he wasn't. He fought with Mariya behind the lighthouse and then the two of them disappeared for the rest of the night. Is he going to admit that he is finally fucking his Bratva intended?

A muscle flexes in his jaw. "No. And you're not going to distract me. Who were you with? It's not like you to be so secretive."

"I didn't know we were going to do each other's hair and makeup and talk about crushes," I said, walking to my bedroom and pulling off my shirt. I throw it at the laundry basket and it lands inside perfectly. With a sigh, I hook a couple of Kon's shirts lying right next to the goddamn basket on the floor and throw them in, too.

"You're not turning back into a grumpy asshole again, are you?" he asks, "Because I almost killed you six times during our Freshman year."

"I was the only reason you got laid Freshman year. I'd charm them and then pass them on to you."

"Fuck you, Lucca. Have you been taking too many punches to the head? It was definitely the other way around, *ty mudak!*" Konstantin throws his shoe at my head and I bat it away.

"For real though," I said, "are you and Mariya okay? If you keep this shit up, you will convince her that you hate her. We both know this is an act, brother."

"We got into it last night," he says, running his hand through his short blond hair, making it stick up in uneven spikes. "She was dancing with Cox, the sleazy prick."

"Unless they were fucking on the dance floor, what's the problem?" I asked. "You know she's not going to let anyone else touch her and let's be honest, I know you haven't been with anyone since she was admitted to the Academy."

"I'm not going to dishonor her by having sex with someone when she's right here," he snapped, "but damn it, I thought I'd have more time."

"Brother, the tension between you and Mariya is painfully obvious," I said. "You don't have to wait until you're married, for fuck's sake. Just do it. You'll be a lot more pleasant to live with once you let off some steam and stop being so paranoid and controlling."

Konstantin is as tall as I am, with muscles honed from years of sports and combat lessons. So, when he leaps up and stalks over to me, I have to stop myself from clenching my fists, instantly ready to take the first punch.

"Do you know what Maksim Morozov would do to me if I slept with his sister before the wedding? Do you know what my *otets* would do?"

"Yeah, because you two will be the first arranged Bratva couple in history who slept together before the ceremony," I scoff, rubbing my eyes. The lack of sleep from last night is catching up with me. "If it's what you both want and you manage not to knock her up before you're married, what's the problem?"

He puts his hands on top of his head, walking in a circle around the room. "I… I can't. I can't do that."

Patting his shoulder, I head for my room again. "I know you're conflicted as hell about this, but we've got two years left here. Are you really going to spend the next twenty-four months yelling at your fiancée, beating the shit out of anyone who looks at her and ending up with the worst case of blue balls in history? Think about it. Maybe talk to Mariya. Not yell. Talk."

Pausing in my doorway, I look back at him. The Konstantin I know is always quick with his decisions and so certain about them. This indecisive shit is going to make him a nightmare until he decides to take his thumb out of his ass and court Mariya.

Getting into my shower, I groan with relief as the hot water hits my back. Working up Kon like that guaranteed he'd be too distracted to insist on asking about my night. I'm not ready to talk about what happened with Tatiana. I don't even know why I did it. She was pressed against me, so warm and soft. So worried about Mariya. The feel of her skin as I slid my hand into her pants…

Bracing one hand against the tile wall, I take my cock in the other and begin to stroke it, thumb flicking over the piercing on the head. The thought of how it would feel to rub the metal over her G spot and feel her pussy tighten around me like it did last night… *Fottere*, fuck! When she came, she was so slick… I grip myself tighter. The grip of her virgin cunt on my cock would be…

Stifling my growl, I come, still thinking of being buried inside her pretty pussy. Rinsing off, I rub my face.

What the fuck was I thinking?

This is Tatiana Aslanova. A sweet virgin Bratva princess. Worse, she trusts me, I can see it. I have no fucking business putting my hands on her. Professor Zimmerman is testing her new skills on Monday, it will be easier then. I can keep my distance. Bringing my fingertips to my nose, I swear I can still catch a fleeting scent of her.

I turn the shower knob to as cold as it can go.

CHAPTER ELEVEN

In which Tatiana and Lucca spar. A lot.

James Bay, Alesso - Chasing Stars

Tatiana...

What the hell did I just do?

As I change into some sleep shorts, the memory keeps repeating in vivid detail. We're kissing like kids, sweet and soft, and then suddenly Lucca's hand is cupping my center and he's making me come and it's incredible and I am such a *durak,* such a fool! Back in Vancouver I never progressed further than a quick above-the-neck makeout session with a guy from my Economics class and now, I jumped right into getting fingered into an orgasm with his hand on my mouth?

Worse, I loved it. I want more.

I hear Athena come in, stomping around the main room and then, the low murmur of a man and a drunken chuckle. *Oh, please go into your room,* I groan silently, *please don't make me hear this. Not tonight.*

Thankfully, her bedroom door slams but it's not enough. My roommate is a screamer. She ramps up quickly and extends far beyond what is surely normal.

Putting my pillow over my head, I try to block out her wailing, "Yes Christos, like that! Just like that!"

Probably Christos Gataki. He's in my Bitcoin and bank fraud class. Sort of a lumbering, hulking kind of guy but pleasant enough. Also, apparently blessed with impressive stamina because they are not finished.

"Yes! Just like that, you *panémorfo gamiméno,* you gorgeous fucker!"

"Please let it stop," I moan.

Even though Athena's orgasmic screaming didn't stop until she kicked Christos out at around 4 a.m., I still wake up when the sun rises. After staring at the ceiling for a while, I drag myself out of bed to put on some leggings and a fleece-lined hoodie. I may as well go for a run before my training with Lucca.

My fingers get tangled in my shoelaces as I ponder that. Will he pretend it never happened? Will he throw me down on the mat and give me a replay? What the hell was wrong with me for hoping it's the second option?

It's freezing outside, any pretense of lingering summer is gone. Zipping up my hoodie, I head for the rock-paved path that circles the outer rim of the campus. I always make a point of waving to the guards when I pass them. They never wave back, but I know a lot of the students here act like they're servants, which seems like a deeply ill-advised way to treat someone who carries weapons.

This running path is safer than most of other ones laced through the campus. There are no hidden spots, no trees, or boulders where predator scum like Mateo can hide themselves. I suspect this path is kept clear for a reason, so that the guards can spot any potential threats from outside the college. Still, there are dangerous spots where the rock crumbles close to the sheer cliffside. I always wondered why Dean Christie didn't insist on putting up fencing, but I'm sure it goes back to the unofficial school motto, "If you let it happen to you, it's your fault."

By lunchtime, I'm a mess, thinking about training with Lucca in less than an hour.

"What's going on with you?" Mariya asks, eyeing me suspiciously as she digs into her stroganoff.

"Nothing," I try for a breezy response and end up more in the range of an anxious croak. Pretending to cough, I drink half a glass of water. "Just a little stressed. I have a long afternoon of training ahead of me."

"That's right, your big combat test is on Monday, isn't it?" she says, looking genuinely concerned. She's the only one of my friends here who knows just how crucial this performance for Professor Zimmerman is going to be. "Hey, you've got this, I know you do!" Giving me a hug, she nods reassuringly.

Anxious to change the subject before my anxiety turns into nausea, I ask, "How was last night? Did you have fun?"

Mariya instantly scowls. "No. Konstantin was being a creeper again and dragged me off the dance floor."

"Why?" I feel terribly guilty because, of course, I know why but I can't tell her without admitting what I was up to out there behind the lighthouse.

"I was dancing with Ronan and that idiot Kon came charging across the room and acted like we were dry humping, or something," she says angrily. "*Etot glupyy zasranets*, that stupid asshole is determined to ruin my social life! He can have sex with half the female population of this school and I'm not allowed to dance? I know everything about this arrangement is the Bratva at its misogynistic best, but this is ridiculous!"

"I'm sorry," I said. As angry as she is, I know Konstantin's rudeness is hurting Mariya. Their marriage was arranged between the Morozov and the Turgenev Bratvas when she was only fourteen, and she and Kon have bickered ever since. But this aggressive meanness from him is new. "If it's any comfort, I don't think he's sleeping with anyone else."

"How do you know?"

"Lucca mentioned it," I admit, "I'd asked him why Konstantin was being such a dick to you." Seeing Lucca nod at me across the dining room, I put down my napkin. "I have to go, *moya podrug*a, my friend. If anyone can straighten Kon out, it will be you."

Lucca's expressionless face doesn't give me any comfort as we head into the training room. I'm guessing he's going with pretending it never happened. Then he insists on making this worse by pulling off his shirt, something he's never done in front of me.

Damn him, he has a six-pack that I would have believed could only be achieved with some serious photoshopping. He's all hard, sculpted muscle and suddenly, I wonder what it would be like to trace every one of those colorful tattoos with my tongue. Abruptly yanking my gaze from his chest, I flush.

Then his mouth is on mine in a hard, hungry kiss and when he pulls back, I'm weak-kneed and panting. "Well, that blows my theory out of the water," I wheeze.

"What theory?"

"That you were just going to pretend last night didn't happen," I said, loving the feel of his bare skin against mine.

Raising a brow, he asks, "Did you want me to?"

"God, no!" I blurted, wanting to smack that cocky grin right off his face.

"Good," he said hoarsely, kissing me again, one hand sliding down to the small of my back, pushing me harder against him. Resting my hands on the sides of his neck, I raise on tiptoe to get closer to him.

For the first time since I walked through the gates of the Ares Academy, I feel safe.

"Have you talked to your brother since you came here?"

We're lounging on a pile of mats, watching the sunset through the dirty gym window. We've done a little sparring, stopped to kiss, a little more sparring, much more kissing… Lucca has his arms wrapped around me.

"You know that as per Academy rules, we are only allowed to contact family members once a month from the phone bank in the main building," I reply primly.

His silent laughter jostles me a little. "It's interesting. The school's best hacker and purveyor of illegal phones lives next door to Kon and me. Mark Tanner, do you know him?"

"I think I've seen him a couple of times, an American? He's in the Assassins division?"

"Yeah," Lucca's fingers are idly stroking down my arm, as if he's acquainting himself with all the bits and pieces of me. "He was in a panic last week because there was a new digital signal for a server that just popped up somewhere here on campus. Not an Academy-approved one."

"Hmm," I hum noncommittally.

His amusement is obvious. "He was scared it was going to set off the Academy sensors and get his little network shut down, but it seems like it's impossible to trace. It's patched into Skylink and the VPN changes every couple of minutes when it's active."

"Is that so?"

"Funny how it popped up right after you came here, isn't it?" He's goading me now. Lifting me easily, he turns me around to straddle him.

He's watching his hands smooth up and down my thighs, his dark lashes are a thick fan against his cheekbones. "You know, it's so unjust that you were given those eyelashes," I complain, "you're never going to appreciate them the way a woman would."

"My eyelashes?" Lucca starts chuckling again. "That's what you feel is unjust? Not genocide or... say, dengue fever. My eyelashes are the ultimate injustice?"

When I crossly attempt to climb off him, his long fingers slide down to my ass, gripping me tightly. My hands are on his shoulders, about to shove myself away from him when I feel the thick bulge in his shorts growing, pushing against my center. It makes me suck in a deep breath, and he goes still. His chuckle drifts away and he watches me closely. I feel the muscles in his shoulders flex as his hands squeeze my ass, dragging me closer against his dick, already hard and thick and separated from me by just scant bits of cloth.

There's a weird sense of something slipping into place, a precise fit like a key to a lock. My spread legs fit perfectly around his, and Lucca's hands curved over my ass as if they'd always belonged there.

He lifts me just slightly and drops me against his cock again, then a slow slide back and forth, and the friction is almost enough to make me combust. Sliding my hands over his shoulders and down his chest, I trace his sculpted pectorals, his chest hair brushing against my sensitive palms. Lucca doesn't speak, just watches my face as my breath grows shorter with each slide across his hard thighs and back against his cock. It's hot, I can feel the burn of it through his thin shorts and mine and I'm already so slick that I'm afraid I'm going to leave a wet spot on his lap.

Leaning forward to kiss me, his teeth latch onto my bottom lip, tugging slightly. "I think you can come, just like this. What do you think, *piccolo bacio?*"

"I... uh..." The ability to form a coherent sentence has apparently been lost and all I can focus on now is the very real need to come, rubbing shamelessly against his clothed cock. He's pushing it against me, his hips tilting up to make sure it rubs over my clitoris on each downstroke.

"Your nipples are rubbing against my chest," he whispers diabolically, "so stiff. I want to suck them into my mouth. Bite them. I think you'd like that too, wouldn't you?"

My hips are moving on their own, pressing hard against him, and I think he's right, damn him. I'm going to come on his cock and it's not even inside me and when I do, my thighs tighten convulsively and my nails dig into his skin. It must hurt but he doesn't stop me, he just keeps whispering dirty suggestions into my ear as I gasp and shake, the warmth threatening to sear through me and it's so much better, so much stronger than anything I've ever managed to achieve on my own.

Lucca groans, his hands tightening enough that I know I'll see bruises tomorrow, and I'll silently gloat over each one. "So pretty when you come," he says, biting my shoulder.

When he lifts me off him, I see, to my extreme embarrassment, that I have not only left a wet spot on his shorts I have soaked them. And also, that he's still hugely hard. "Can I help you, um…" I gesture at the very obvious bulge, "Can I take care of you?"

Kissing me, he helps me up with a groan. "I'll handle it later. Our reserved time is up and no one is going to see you like this but me." He pulls his shirt on, an act I watch with some regret because I have so many questions about his tattoos and it seems like a crime to cover a chest so perfectly sculpted.

We're almost to the student housing building when he asks, "Why didn't your father make an alliance with an arranged marriage for you?"

"I'm not really sure," I said slowly, "after all, Mariya was only fourteen when she was promised in marriage to Konstantin. I always got the sense that I was…" I'm waving my hands, trying to think of the right phrase, "An asset he held back, like a royal flush to pull out at the end of a game of poker, or something."

He's frowning and I feel like he's judging my parents.

"My father and mother loved me," I said a little defensively. "I know I was never a key piece on the Bratva chessboard. They did love me though, and my brothers do, too."

Lucca chuckles bitterly, and it makes me sad to hear it. "We're all fucking pawns on this chessboard. Just pawns."

He stops just out of view of the building, light blazing from the windows against the early night. "One more practice session tomorrow, I am confident about your skills. You're smart, and you're strategic. I don't want you to worry tonight. Get some sleep."

I know him well enough now to know that he does not give out compliments freely. If he says he's confident about my skills, then I must be, too.

"Okay," I take a deep breath. "Okay. Thank you, Lucca."

Kissing me on the forehead, he gifts me with one last, gorgeous smile. "Goodnight, *piccolo bacio*."

CHAPTER TWELVE

In which Tatiana goes low.

No Doubt - I'm Just A Girl

Tatiana...

The sun is breaking through the typical Irish cloud cover and the bright rays feel like they're mocking me. If the weather matched my mood, we'd be in a violent storm with lightning strikes and a vicious downpour. Zimmerman has never hidden his contempt for me. If this isn't a decisive win, he'll have an excuse to kick me out.

It feels like I'm walking to my execution.

"Take a deep breath and let it out," Lucca leans in, almost whispering in my ear. "Do it."

Shakily doing as he says, I feel the tightness in my chest loosen, just a bit.

"Do it again."

Blowing the breath out between my pursed lips, I force my shoulders to relax.

Lucca puts his hand on the back of my neck, squeezing gently. "This isn't a fight to the death," he said, "you just have to prove you're capable of holding your own." He kisses the top of my head. "And you are capable, okay?" We pause in the middle of the path as he puts his hands on my shoulders. "Say it."

"I don't-"

"You fire with the accuracy of a military sniper, you're already ahead of your class in computer hacking and the dark web, you-"

"How did you know all of that?" I interrupt.

"The point here," he said patiently, "is that for someone who got dumped onto this campus four weeks ago, you're moving ahead, not falling behind. Physical combat may not be your strength, but you've made more progress in a month than anyone I've seen. You can do this."

Staring up into his amber eyes, I feel oddly grateful. I know Lucca well enough now to know he wouldn't sugarcoat it for me. If he thought I was going to get my ass kicked, he would tell me. As ego-crushing as it would be.

"Okay," I nod, "thank you."

"Say, 'I can do this,'" he persists.

Rolling my eyes, I repeat, "I can do this."

"Just for that eye-roll," he whispers, "I'm turning your ass red tonight."

I make an incoherent, whiney little noise and he laughs, urging me down the path to the combat class.

"Miss Aslanova," Professor Zimmerman stands in the middle of the gym, arms folded and biceps bulging in his clean white t-shirt. "You were given a month to develop even the most basic combat skills. Let's see what you've learned from Mr. Toscano."

My blood pressure is so high that it's a miracle I'm not having a stroke. "Yes, Professor," I manage, after clearing my throat three times.

"Mr. Tanaka, join Miss Aslanova on the mat."

A murmur flows through the group like leaves scattering in the wind. Hiroto Tanaka is the second son of one of the most dangerous leaders in the Yakuza. He's already sporting dozens of tattoos indicating his rank. I know from watching him that he's not the strongest fighter in class, but he's definitely a step above Ania Jankowski, and even she is looking at me with concern.

That bastard Zimmerman. What did I ever do to him? Why does he want me out of here so badly? Squaring my shoulders, I stare at his expressionless face. I can still sense his smug satisfaction.

Lucca casually walks behind the professor so that my gaze moves to him. His mouth curves into a gorgeous smile as he nods at me.

Bringing up my fists to protect my face, I plant my feet. Lucca taught me countermoves for most of the fighting styles I'd seen in class. I'll never take down Tanaka with his martial arts skills, so I have to go dirty.

"You never stop fighting until they're down," Lucca had told me. "The fight is not over until they're incapacitated."

My only advantage here is that Hiroto hasn't really seen me fight at all. I've only practiced a few moves in class, so he's probably assuming I'm nearly as helpless as I was on that first day. He's eyeing me calmly as he takes his place on the mat.

Please let him underestimate me, I prayed.

Swinging his elbows back and forth, loosening up, he watches my stance. I hope I don't look as terrified as I feel. Realizing I'm not going to make the first move, he gives the slightest of sighs and charges me. This time, I don't flinch. I watch his eye movements as he looks down at my ribs and I know he's going for a kick to incapacitate me right away. He probably thinks of it as merciful.

As his foot comes up for the blow, I surge forward, sliding to my knees and punch up at his crotch with everything I have. My fist lands solidly and I hear a chorus of "Oh, *fuck!*" from the male portion of the class. Hiroto's face pales as his mouth drops open, but I can't trust that this is enough. As he bends over, clutching between his legs, I bring up my elbow and slam it into the back of his neck, and he blacks out for a moment, dropping to his knees.

I'm feeling horrible about this, but I cannot lose. Keeping my fingers as stiff as I can, I slam them into his unprotected throat. *Oh my god, that hurts so much!* I'm pretty sure I broke at least one finger, but his pale face abruptly goes brick red and he falls sideways onto the mat, out like a light, still clutching his privates.

There's no applause, not even a polite round of golf claps. I get it. This was all dirty, even here in combat there's some code of honor about not trying to permanently damage anyone. But… there's also not anything specific about *not* fighting dirty. Backing away, I hold up my rapidly swelling fingers.

Definitely broken.

"I told you to keep your fingers stiff on the throat punch," Lucca whispers, holding my wrist and looking at the damage.

"You should check on Hiroto," I said, feeling like pond scum right now. He's still on the floor in the fetal position, but he's groaning as he regains consciousness.

"Those kinds of moves are contemptible, Miss Aslanova," Professor Zimmerman Is Not Pleased.

"I know, sir," I said, "but you told me I had to be the last one standing. With a month's preparation. Isn't it one of your favorite sayings, to do whatever it takes to get out alive?"

His gaze travels from me to poor Hiroto, who's writhing slowly, like a turtle flipped on his back.

"You pass," he says reluctantly, and now there's applause. Not a huge amount, but definitely there and I notice that Ania Jankowski is the one that started it. She nods to me and gives me a brief wink.

This might be the best day of my life.

CHAPTER THIRTEEN

In which Tatiana and Lucca celebrate. Hiroto eats muffins and cradles ice packs.

Lily Allen - Fuck You

Lucca...

I don't think I have ever seen anything as fucking hot as sweet Tatiana decimating Hiroto. And watching Zimmerman's smirk slowly die was the second-best highlight of the day. He knew he couldn't match her up with one of the very best fighters in class, it would have made his bias too obvious, but I'm sure he thought Hiroto would take her out within thirty seconds or so.

She's trying not to wince or grin and failing at both as the class breaks into applause. Based on how badly her hand is swelling, she's broken at least a couple of fingers, but I'm so damned proud of her.

"We should probably go get your hand looked at," I said, grinning at her. "Keep your fingers rigid, remember?"

"Believe me," she says, "I was trying."

"You did so well, *piccolo bacio,* I'm proud of you." I know we've just outed ourselves to the class, and with the gossip network as well-defined as the one here at the college, every student will know we're together by dinner, but I can't stop grinning as I kiss her forehead. If we were alone right now, I would have already ripped those tight bike shorts off her with my teeth and my face would be buried in her pussy.

"I think you should check on Hiroto," she says, looking genuinely sorry as she gazes at him, curled up like a potato bug on the mat. Zimmerman's already barking orders to a couple of his friends to pick him up off the floor and help him get checked out by Dr. Giardo.

"Let's go ice your hand, maybe you won't need to go to the clinic for a splint," I said.

"Good," she whispers, "because I feel bad enough about punching Hiroto in the groin. I don't think he's going to want to see me for a while."

"Well, we both know the dick punch is your signature move," I agree, making her slap her hand over her mouth to smother her laugh.

Tatiana...

"Behold our champion!" Mariya shoves open my door without knocking, holding up a bottle of champagne. "Our conquering hero!"

"Shhh..." I laugh, pulling her in and closing the door. "Taking away Hiroto's ability to father children doesn't seem like something we should be celebrating."

"Don't you dare!" She sternly points her finger at me. "Believe me, he would have given you the mother of all thrashings if he'd had a chance and you know it."

"Probably," I admit, "I asked one of his friends about his favorite things and he said that Hiroto loves these muffins the Emerald Bakery makes in Kilronan Village, so I got them to deliver a box of them here. Will you come with me to drop them off?"

"Yeah, he's probably afraid to be alone with you right now," she agrees.

The male students are in the other wing of the massive building, and I wonder which door is Lucca's as we walk up to the fourth floor. When Mariya raises her middle finger to the second door on the right, I have my answer.

"Have you made up with Konstantin yet?" I ask as she turns, walking backward so she can keep flipping off the door. "Never mind, I think your actions speak for themselves."

At Hiroto's door, I suck in a deep breath before knocking.

"I hope he doesn't keep a gun in his room," Mariya mumbles as the door swings open.

His roommate gives us a long look, grinning. "Which one of you is the crazy bitch who knocked my boy's nuts up into his throat?"

Wincing, I said, "Is he here? I have a peace offering."

"Yeah, he's on the couch," he opens the door wider and I see Hiroto sitting there glumly, an ice pack on his crotch and one on the back of his neck. I wince when I see the huge purple bruise spreading across his throat.

Glancing up, he groaned. "What the fuck do you want?"

"I, uh, I wanted to apologize," I said, thrusting out the muffins awkwardly. "I heard you like these, so…" When he doesn't reach out for them, I put them on the coffee table in front of him. His roommate grabs one as Hiroto glares at me. "Really, I'm sorry. I had to pass that test, and I-"

"I get it," he interrupted. "I do. But fuck you."

"That's fair," I nod rapidly. His eyes are glassy and I lean closer. "Did Dr. Giardo give you his night-night pills?"

"Yeah," he said, "and fuck you."

"Um, I have some left over from when Jankowski gave me that beatdown." Pulling the bottle out of my pocket, I set it down next to the muffins. "In case you need more."

"Okay," Hiroto is rubbing his eyes. "Fuck you."

"Understood," I said, backing towards the door, "I'll just see you later, then."

"Thank you for the muffins," he groans, "and fuck you."

"That went well," Mariya said brightly.

"I appreciate your optimistic nature," I said sourly, heading back down the hall. As we pass the second door on the right, it opens, Lucca steps out and picks me up, throwing me over his shoulder.

"Do you mind if I borrow Tatiana?" he calls over to Mariya, who is grinning at this new development.

"No problem," she chuckles, but her smile drops instantly as Konstantin holds the door for Lucca, who is still carrying me like a sack of flour.

"Great. Konstantin is going to walk you back to your suite," he says, shutting the door, which is not thick enough to muffle their instant bickering.

"Smooth, very smooth," I laugh, "can you put me down? All the blood is rushing to my head." When he does, I find a table in front of the fireplace, nicely set with room service silver, crystal goblets and two covered plates. "What's all this?" I ask.

He gifts me with another one of his beautiful smiles. "We have to celebrate, what you did today was fucking amazing."

Why does praise from this man make me feel like there's nothing I can't do? "You've already done so much for me," I said, "I should be making a celebration dinner for you."

"Oh, you'll be doing something for me," Lucca leers meaningfully. Laughing, I let him seat me at the table and pour me a glass of wine. "To the dirtiest fighter in Ares Academy history," he raises his glass in a toast.

"Don't say that!" I groan, "I feel bad enough for what I did to

Hiroto."

"He's fine," he shrugged, "trust me, it's not the worst injury he's had here at the Academy. But you! Less than one month and you've turned into the toughest woman on campus."

"Doubtful," I said, taking another sip of the wine, a delicious red that is bright and wonderful on the palate. "I just had the element of surprise, that was the only reason it worked."

"Don't diminish this," he said, "how's your hand?"

"Better," I said, "I waited until Hiroto left the clinic to go in. Dr. Giardo said two of the fingers were sprained, but that's it. I just need to keep it wrapped and iced for a couple of days."

"Good," he gifted me with another smile and lifted the covers on the plates. "Solyanka to start."

"It's my favorite comfort food!" I said happily, as he ladled the sausage soup with vegetables and extra pickles into my bowl.

"So, I hear," he said, "and then Pirozhki and Shashlik for the main course."

"You are amazing..." I sighed. "Wait. You're being too nice to me. Am I dying? Do I have incurable cancer? Is there something you're not telling me?"

Lucca laughs, he actually laughs and it is beautiful. It's the first time I've heard it and the sound is so joyous that it breaks my heart that he doesn't laugh more. That his brothers crushed this part of him.

"No *piccolo bacio*," he said, "I know your suspicious Russian heritage tells you that good news is followed by bad. But not here. You should be proud of yourself."

"You know I couldn't have done it without you," I said.

"I know," he modestly agreed.

"Thank you." Impulsively, I took his hand resting next to mine and kissed it softly, watching the surprise on his face soften to something else. "So, what's next?"

Look at me being all brazen.

"Next?" Lucca grins at me devilishly and it is not at all reassuring. "I'm going to feed you. And then fuck you. So, you'd better start in on those Pirozhki because you're going to need your strength."

CHAPTER FOURTEEN

In which it starts with a kiss...
Julia Michaels - Lie Like This

Tatiana...

It starts with a kiss. A spectacular kiss.

It's hard, slanting over my lips as Lucca's tongue slickly moves between them. I can feel him hum in appreciation as he traces over my teeth and tongue, the sound vibrating against my mouth. One hand is fisted in my hair, just hard enough to let me know he means business without really hurting me. At the same time, his arm slides around my waist and hoists me abruptly onto the desk in his bedroom, necessary, because like most humans of normal size, I have to crane my neck back uncomfortably to look at him unless he finds a way to put us on the same level.

After savaging my mouth with clear relish, he moves to my neck, running his teeth gently along the line of my jaw and then, placing a sharp bite into the thin skin of my throat, he leans over me, blocking out the light. All I can see is his long and powerful body, hovering, ready to pounce and shred me to pieces.

"I want to fuck you, *piccolo bacio*," he said, voice turned guttural and greedy, jaw tight. "We haven't talked about it, but I know you feel... whatever this is between us. I can stop here. If you tell me no."

My eyes are wide, I know I look shocked. But not frightened. Finally, I took a deep breath. "You don't have to stop. I want to. I want... I want you."

Groaning, he sweeps me up in his arms and moves to his bed with a flattering amount of haste, not quite throwing me on his mattress, and quickly covers me, pulling my tank top and bra away from my breasts as he bites one, then sucks the nipple of the other, enjoying how I jump, then moan holding his dark head to my chest. Lucca plays with my breasts, not giving me time to feel self-conscious, pushing them together so he can suck one and then the other. My legs suddenly tighten against the small of his back, my heels digging into his gorgeous ass.

He pulls back and harshly yanks one leg straight and then the other, pulling down my shorts and undies, baring his teeth and grinning at my yelp of alarm before delicately gliding those even, white canines against my calf, my inner thigh, and then straight to my heated center.

"Oh! OmigodLuccawaitstop!" I'm desperately trying to recover, lost in this melee of his lips and mouth, and then his teeth and tongue against the thin skin of my inner thighs. And now... am I really about to let him go down on me? I've heard guys joke about it and act like it was a chore and I'm terribly shy about the whole concept anyway. But Lucca is already there, eagerly licking and sucking my lips, running the harsh point of his tongue in the sensitive furrow between them, dipping into my channel, and grinning when I stiffen and gasp, holding my legs open.

I nearly come when Lucca's beautiful face looks up from my pussy, chin shining with my slick and his gaze feral. "Delicious. Be still and let me enjoy you."

Oh, and he *did*, pushing his stubbled chin into my opening and making me nearly scream with the intensity, then sliding up to fasten his lips around my clitoris and suck it just a bit harder than was comfortable. The shock nearly sends me upright as my stomach muscles clench.

One broad hand pushes between my breasts, shoving me back onto his mattress. The combination of his prickly chin and slick tongue are too much, tipping me into an orgasm even stronger than the one he'd given me in the gym that afternoon.

He was *so* perfect... thick thighs and a taut ass, his muscles moving sleekly under smooth skin as he bares himself to me. When Lucca lifts his hips to pull off his shorts and throw them on the floor, I blush at how loud my gasp is. Of course, the arrogant bastard hears it, a wide grin spreading across his face as Lucca chuckles. "It's for you, *piccolo bacio*. All for you. I'm going to make you feel so..." he places a hard kiss on one nipple, then moves to suck the other, "...*so* good. You're going to come screaming for me. I can tell."

Sitting up, I touch the tip of his shaft. "Is that a *piercing?*" I can't imagine the pain of piercing such a sensitive spot. There's another smug chuckle, I'd punch him but I'm too fascinated and intimidated by the silver ring glinting up at me.

"Yes, and when I rub it against your G-spot I promise you're going to appreciate it." He kisses me again, and I hear the crinkle of a wrapper and his fingers swiftly rolling a condom down his shaft.

I hold my breath as the wide head of his cock first breaches my entrance and I grip his shoulders, nails digging mindlessly into his back as his agile hips swirl, easing an inch or two in, out, then in again, just a bit further each time until I can feel the heat and weight of him take over everything. My body, my mind, my soul. There's no room for anything but the feel of him inside me. I never understood how overwhelming this could feel, to be connected to someone so deeply.

"Just- just- god, Lucca! Slowly... okay?" I'm moaning, not sure if it's pain or neediness or both, and I try to force myself to concentrate. What did Camilla call this? "Cock-drunk." Oh, I am so cock-drunk. I'm inebriated by this lovely, thick thing pushing inside me and spreading my slick walls wide to accommodate him.

This beautiful, terrifying man is the perfect combination of cruelty and kindness - quite aware that his cock is hurting me, but holding himself still - muscled arms shaking with the effort, to let my strained body stretch to accommodate him.

"Such a sweet girl," he whispered, hot breath on my skin and making me shudder, "let me in, now. Open wide." Grunting approvingly at the sudden, shocking amount of slick inside me, he began moving his hips, pushing, and pulling with some force and effort still as my body struggled to hold him.

Finally, he adjusts by going back onto his heels and pulling me up to straddle him. Circling his hips as his big hands went to my ass and squeeze, he smiled devilishly. "I'm going to rip you in half, baby. And you're going to thank me for it. Are you ready?"

A sharp scream flies from my mouth as Lucca drives his hard shaft up so high that I choke, he's deep enough inside me that I have no room left for breath. He slows a bit, squeezing the globes of my ass as he hoists me up and down on his cock, grunting each time he bottoms out inside me.

Wrapping both arms around his shoulders, I try to hang on as he continues driving inside me, the sweat from us both slipping against our skin as he moves those cruelly agile hips faster. I can feel that ring of metal rubbing me inside and it feels like a series of electric sparks, my nerves firing with each pass. My nipples are wildly oversensitive from rubbing against the hair on his chest and finally, I bite into the thick muscle of his shoulder, trying not to scream.

He laughs breathlessly against the pain of my bite. "You're going to come now, you juicy, dirty, girl. Do you hear me? You will come right..." I scream in shock as he lifts and drops me, the head of him slamming into my cervix, sparking off shocks that blaze through me. "The. Fuck. Now."

Each word is punctuated by another harsh thrust and this is so good and I will remember this forever. His scent, the warmth of his skin, the guttural groan he gasps into my ear, and the shocking heat tearing through my sore channel and overheating me into a wild, painful, wonderful orgasm. I scream, just the way he told me I would. I shudder and gasp and he laughs breathlessly as he forces me up and down again, prolonging our finish until I clench so violently that it nearly pushes his cock out of me.

Lucca's long arms wrap around me tightly, sealing us skin to skin as we mindlessly rock back and forth, faces buried in the other's neck as we ride out the last shudders of our finish.

Lucca...

What the fuck did I just do?

I seem to keep saying that when I'm around Tatiana, but I can't resist her. I don't want to, even though I know she's not meant for me. But I want her. More than I've ever wanted anything. Even more than getting back into my family's good graces.

She's slumping against me, relaxed and almost boneless. With a final, gentle squeeze I lift her off my cock with a mutual groan. "Relax," I tell her, laying her against the pillows with a kiss. Discarding the condom in my bathroom, I wet a cloth and bring it back to her. When I touch her with it, her knees slam shut.

"Oh! I'll just..." That pretty pink flush I love is coloring her cheeks.

"Shh, I'm going to take care of you *piccolo bacio.* Relax." Wiping her center gently, I'm uncomfortably aware of the amount of blood there is. I must have been too rough for her first time. "Are you sore?" She covers her face with her hands and I peel them away. "We just had sex. I think you can look me in the eye."

"I'm fine," she smiles up at me, still blushing, "a little sore, but it was worth it."

I finish cleaning her and press a soft kiss to her clitoris. "Here, drink this." Handing her a bottle of water, I cup her head and watch her finish about a third before she pushes it away.

"What does it mean, *piccolo bacio?*" Tatiana asks sleepily when I get back in bed with her.

"It means 'little kiss'."

"Oh, that's pretty," she murmurs, her green-gold eyes are already drooping.

"You had a big day," I said, turning on my side and pulling her back against me. She unconsciously nestles her ass against my cock and I groan silently, feeling it already rising hopefully again. "Get some sleep."

"I should go back to my place," she mumbles, but with a grin, I note she doesn't move.

"Shh… I'll walk you back later," I promise, dropping a kiss on the top of her head. I listen to her deep, slow breaths and try to will my cock to go back down. When she shifts slightly, I see a scar on her back, just under her left shoulder blade. It's thick and a little puckered, about three inches long. When I touch it lightly with my fingertips, she pulls away, groaning in her sleep. Pressing my chest against her back, I think about that scar and who could have given it to her.

CHAPTER FIFTEEN

In which we learn why Lucca is the Invisible Son.

Tatiana...

Waking with a gasp, I don't need to check the readout on Lucca's alarm clock to know it is 3:36 a.m.

The time Lev had ripped me out of bed on the night my parents died.

The time that I usually wake from a nightmare now, or some push from my paranoid subconscious.

It's gotten a little better over the last couple of weeks, due mainly to the exhaustion from Lucca's ruthless combat training.

Sitting up, careful not to jostle him, I settle against the pillows and enjoy my chance to stare at him like a creep without him catching me. Those thick eyelashes I covet, resting on his sharp, high cheekbones. All the parts of Lucca are sharp and angular, his jawline, his nose, his hard sculpted body, everything but those lashes and his full, soft mouth. I love the way my lips sink into his plush ones. With the white sheet only half covering his gloriously naked body, the parts bared to me are like living art, the moonlight slips over his colorful tattoos like ghostly fingers.

I tiptoe into the bathroom, trying to tidy up a bit before my walk of shame back to my suite.

My walk of shame. Why would that make me smile? It feels like such a normal thing. Something that a girl not raised in a Bratva would do. A girl who can make choices for herself.

His bathroom is spotless, his towels crisply folded, and no soap smears on the granite counter. Opening a drawer, I find his cologne, the scent of cedar, rum, wintergreen, a sharp bite of coffee. Very him, though there's always something slightly salty in Lucca's scent, too, like seawater.

Creeping back into the bedroom, I try to dress silently over by his desk. There's a scatter of framed photos there, a few with Konstantin, and just one of a younger Lucca and a beautiful woman, his mother, I'm guessing. She has a warm smile, exactly like his when he chooses to offer it. She's hugging him with an arm around his shoulders and he's leaning away, playfully, like boys do in their early teens when getting embraced by a parent is just so mortifying.

"I look more like my mother," his voice is deep and a little raspy from sleep. "My other brothers are all the spitting image of my father." I hear the rustle of sheets as he rises, walking across the room to me, flagrantly naked.

"She's really beautiful," I offer, "you have her smile."

He takes the photo from me, looking down at his mother. "I'm pretty sure my father already considered me a disappointment by the time they died, but she didn't."

I'm silent, barely breathing while I listen. The way he speaks… looking down at his mother, long gone except for the echo of her in the photo, I don't think he's ever talked about this with anyone else.

"She told me it takes some people longer than others to find their place." He chuckles mirthlessly, "She told me I was a leader. Giovanni told me I was a fuckup."

Instantly, I despise Giovanni. "He's your oldest brother?"

"Yes, now that Dante's gone." His amber gaze moves to me. "Giovanni killed him."

"What?" It's not like fratricide was unheard of in our world, heck, it was more commonplace than anyone wanted to admit. "Why did he kill him?"

Lucca puts the picture of his mother down gently. "Dante was part of the group that killed my parents at that party. They were trying to kill the heads of some of the other families, too. Mariya's brothers almost died there."

"Oh... I'm so sorry. It must have gutted you to discover that."

He shrugs, his expression indifferent. "He was trying to pull our *famiglia* into the Red Trade. He deserved it. He left a long trail of fuck-ups behind him for my brothers to clean up. I wasn't much help."

"That was... what? Four years ago? Five?" I asked, "You were a teenager trying to deal with losing your parents."

"Oh, I was an asshole," he said, walking over to the window. He has a view of the waves crashing against the cliffs, too. "A couple of DWI's, once I fucked one of our Capo's daughters. I didn't know who she was at the time. The only reason I wasn't forced into an arranged marriage with her was the fact that she was cheating on her boyfriend."

"Do you think that's what she was trying for?" I said.

"Probably," he said, staring at the waves. "I got kicked out of my prep school for running an on-campus gambling ring."

This time, I dared to laugh a little. "In our families, that's usually a point of pride. I don't even want to know half of what my brother Ilia did here."

"However, the breaking point for Gio and my other brother Dario was some financial records our Consigliere discovered. It looked like I'd been siphoning money from three *famiglia* accounts. That's when Gio called for me, Dario standing by him, looking all stern and disappointed. They set me aside."

"What does that mean, exactly?" I asked.

"That's as bad as it gets in the Mafia, the only thing worse would have been to kill me." He looks at me, his sharp gaze glinting, wolf-like. "They sent me here to make something of myself," his tone is viciously sarcastic, "and at the end of four years, they would *consider* allowing me to be a Toscano again."

I try to picture a younger Lucca, standing in front of his brothers, his identity taken from him. "Why do I not believe that you embezzled that money?"

His fists are clenching, knuckles bulging and white. I'm not sure he knows he's doing it. "Because I didn't. It was Dante, my oldest brother. I caught him funneling money from my trust fund just before our parents were killed. He told me he was trying to create a side business that would make our father proud of him, he said he couldn't get the money any other way, but that he would pay me back. I always knew he was a fuck-up, but everyone thought I was, too. I told him to go ahead and pay it back later."

"That's pretty noble to forgive your brother for stealing from your trust fund," I said, my disgust for his family growing.

"He must have started using my identification and bank accounts to siphon money from some of the other Toscano accounts." He's still staring at the ocean. "When our Consigliere found it years later, it looked like my work."

I lean in, trying to catch his gaze. "Why didn't you tell your brothers this? Dante stole from you and left you to take the blame."

"Because fuck them," he said viciously, "if they could really believe that I'd do something like that, they don't know me at all. Fuck them both. They've both gotten married since I've been gone, Gio has a baby, there are pictures all over the fucking internet of the happy, growing Toscano family and none of them mention me because I'm invisible."

Putting my arms around him, I rest my head on his back. I don't know what to do besides hold him, so I do. After a while, he puts his hands over mine and we watch the waves beat futilely against the indifferent face of the cliffs.

CHAPTER SIXTEEN

In which there is girl talk.

Tatiana...

"What are the five primary weak points we look for when infiltrating an organization?"

Professor Campbell is one of my favorites here. She's younger than most of the other educators and doesn't seem to have the same need to intimidate her students, most likely because her coursework is fun and challenging. But today, I can't pay attention. There's a dull ache between my legs that doesn't seem to lessen, though I'm trying to subtly shift position every few minutes.

Meiying nudges me. "What's wrong with you? You're wiggling around like someone stuck a weasel down your pants."

The image makes me want to laugh, but I smother the impulse. "Just tired," I lied. That ache feels good in a way I can't explain, it's lingering proof that Lucca and I had an incredible night together. The sex was everything I could have hoped for, and the fact that he was willing to trust me with something as intimate and painful as his family's cruelty means so much to me.

That reminds me that I need to talk to *my* family. Roman and Ilia both knew about yesterday's test in Zimmerman's class, I should let them know how well it went. Calling Lev was the first thing I did when I got back to my suite yesterday, and he was exuberant at my news in a way that was almost non-Russian.

The day before...

"I'm so proud of you," Lev said warmly, "how's your hand now?"

"Not broken," I told him happily, "that's all I care about."

"Nobody likes a dirty fighter," he agreed, "but it was the right move for the moment and you know those skills will come in handy in the real world, too."

"Why do you think my mother wouldn't let me take self-defense lessons from you?" I asked. I'd swallowed down the anger and resentment at the time, but those few hours when Lev taught me to protect myself helped pull me out of the misery after what had happened to me.

"I don't know," he said, choosing his words carefully. Even now, Lev was so cautious about what he said about my parents. "Maybe… maybe the lessons made your ordeal too real for her. The realization that your child can be hurt is terrifying, I'm sure."

"So, her denial was more important than teaching me how to protect myself?" I blurted. I was shocked at my bitter tone.

Lev was silent for a moment. "The point is, you're learning now, and you're doing beautifully. Is the Toscano kid as annoying as he was at the start?"

I feel guilty because there is no way in hell that I can tell my bodyguard that I've been doing all kinds of naughty things with Lucca and very much wanted to do more. So, I lie. "It's fine. I know he's looking forward to being done with me. He was a good teacher, though."

"Excellent," he said, "even the *Pakhan* can't complain about your unsupervised association with him since he's helped you keep your place at the Academy. Have you spoken to him yet?"

Oh, good. More guilt. "No, I called you first," I admitted, "but I will call Roman, I promise."

"Thank you," he said with relief. "He worries about you. They both do."

"I'm certainly learning enough in the Spies division to know that we had a catastrophic intelligence breach," I ventured, "what do they know so far?"

The weariness in his voice tells me that he's been as relentless in searching for clues as my brothers have. "Multiple threats from different directions," he said, "they're constantly shoring up our defenses from one attack after another."

"There has to be something I can do," I said, "it's so frustrating to be sitting here when everyone I love is in danger."

"There is something..." he allowed. "I'm sure your brothers wouldn't want you to put yourself in danger. But the families of some of the students there are likely involved. Is there anyone who's aggressive toward you? Seems to hate you for no reason?"

My first thought is Mateo, though I suspect he's just an equal-opportunity asshole. As for everyone else, it feels like the standard indifference. "I'll keep an eye out. I haven't had a chance to get to know anyone outside of my circle while I've been training so much."

"This is a good time to put those spy skills to use, then," he encouraged. "Just be careful."

"I will," I promise. "Are you all right, Lev?"

"Me?" He seems surprised. "Of course."

"It feels like this has to be frustrating for you. You're on the outskirts, not able to protect me directly, not able to help my brothers." I hesitate. "I feel guilty, you should be protecting them."

"I'm right where I'm supposed to be," he says warmly. "You keep your focus on your studies, all right?"

"I will," I promise. "Please stay safe."

Currently...

After class, Mariya drags me into her suite.

"Tell me." She has a tight grip on my arm and I'm pretty sure she's ready to beat the information out of me if necessary.

"I... we..."

While I'm not promised in marriage like she is, we both know that Bratva princesses are expected to keep their virginity. Sucking in a deep breath, I meet her gaze. "We had sex. And it was amazing."

Smiling tremulously, she said, "I'm happy *and* sad, if that makes sense. This is such a serious choice, Tati."

"I know." Sitting down on her bed, I pick up her ragged stuffed bunny by her pillow, gently straightening an ear. In many ways Mariya has far more life experience than I do, even if she's two years younger than I am and still took her stuffie to college. "This is one of the very few choices I've ever been allowed to make," I said. "I wanted it to be with Lucca."

"What if Roman makes an arrangement for you?" she said, her worry is clear and touching. It's been a long time since I've had someone to talk to like this.

"If it happens, I'll tell him the truth."

"How do you think he'll react?" Mariya asks.

"Honestly? I don't know," I admit. "My virginity, this thing- this relatively insignificant bit of tissue was still in *my* body. It still belonged to me. I decide who I give it to. So, they'll have to live with it. If not being a virgin makes me unmarriageable, maybe I can help the Bratva as a spy."

Studying my expression, she finally smiles. "You're so confident in your decision. I'm happy for you." Then, her grin turns sly. "So, it was amazing, eh? Tell me more! Does the inhumanly-sized man have an equally inhumanly-sized dick?"

"*Bozhe moy,* my god, woman! I'm not talking about his equipment!" I laugh, and she scoots closer to me on the bed.

"Oh, yes you will, *moya podruga,* my friend and there will be details!" Mariya demands, laughing with me. "I must live vicariously through your sex life and I already know it must be spectacular, so talk to me! Besides, with the BDE Lucca radiates like a beacon of sin, I knew he had to be legendary in the sack."

I'm laughing too hard to answer for a moment and she shoves me. "Tell me something! Anything!"

"I know I'm going to regret this but okay. One thing! One, and then you promise to change the subject?" I ask.

"It depends on how juicy it is," she says unrepentantly.

I lean forward, blushing uncontrollably. "He's got a piercing."

"Get. Out!" she screams. "Where? What! Like a barbell, or-"

"I looked it up," I said, "it's called a reverse Prince Albert? It's a silver ring on the top of his... you know."

"You can say penis," she says, rolling her eyes, "or dick, or cock, or whatever. But if you fucked it, you can say the word."

"Shut up!" I'm laughing so hard that I'm wheezing, "Stop the dick talk, please!"

"Whose dick?"

Camilla is Mariya's roommate and she bounces eagerly into the room. "Seriously, catch me up. Whose dick are we talking about?"

"One I saw in a porn video," Mariya lies flawlessly, "we were wondering how a piercing would feel during sex."

"*Oh, s'il te plait,* oh please! If you find a man with one of those, you've got a professional cocksmith in bed!" Camilla said. "I would let a man like that do anything he liked with me."

"Except for butt sex," Mariya says wisely, "you should definitely talk about butt sex first."

I wonder if it's possible to dislodge an internal organ from laughing too hard.

CHAPTER SEVENTEEN

In which there are sexytimes.

Ariana Grande - Bad Idea

Lucca...

"Welcome to your first challenge of the year, gentlemen."

There was a not-so-quiet snort from the woman sitting next to me. Lauren Birch is the firstborn from a crime family settling into a position of power in southern California. She's one of only six women in the Leaders program. I may have just transferred into this major but I can already tell every one of them is sick of the stubborn misogyny of teachers like Professor Fukumoto.

He ignores the provocation and continues. "You'll pick a team of nine men. And... women," he adds an afterthought. "They must be evenly selected from the other three divisions. You know I'm not allowed to give you advance notice of what to expect, but you will need students with qualities like strength, strategizing, and a strong knowledge of firearms." He looks around the room before his gaze settles on me. "This challenge is a crucial part of your scores for the first semester here. You do not want to fail."

"Who are you picking for your team?" Konstantin reaches over and takes half my sandwich.

"I'm not telling you, asshole!" I said, watching him bite into my lunch.

"Yeah," he muses, mouth full. "It's going to be hard to have to keep secrets from each other now that we're both in the same major."

"No problem, since I'll never tell you a thing," I said pleasantly, "who are you selecting for yours?"

"I was thinking maybe Tatiana," he grins, "she's a hell of a shot, right?"

"You know, there's a high possibility that I'm going to punch you in the throat." I smiled back, showing all my teeth.

"So wrong," he said with faux shock, "so very, *very* wrong to hurt your best friend. We better get to it right after lunch, are you noticing that Mateo and Aleks are already making the rounds?"

He's right. Mateo, that little bastard, is already heading across the room to Tatiana and Mariya's table. Shoving my chair back, I get there seconds after he does.

"You can't say no when you're selected for a Leader's team, *bambina*," he leers at Tatiana, who looks mildly nauseated.

"She can when she's already been selected," I step in, interrupting her. "She agreed to be on my team right before lunch."

"Is that right," he sneers, looking her up and down but his gaze never getting higher than her breasts.

"Yes," Tatiana says firmly.

"There'll be other challenges," he tells her tits, "I'll still get you on my team."

"Can't wait," she said dryly.

Before Mateo can turn to Mariya, Kon is there. "Hey, come over to my table," he tells her, "we're going to start strategizing."

It's clear that she's only slightly more enthused by being stuck with Kon than Mateo, but she forces a smile. "Thanks, oh mighty leader! I'll be right there."

Seating myself next to Tatiana, I smile malevolently at Mateo until he turns and leaves with a huff and a mumble of Italian curses.

"Thank you for that," she whispers, "what's going on?"

She's smiling, looking so pleased to see me. "I want to kiss you," I blurt.

"Okay?"

"If I do that," I lean closer to whisper in her ear, "two things will happen. First, everyone on the entire campus is going to know we're together. Second, one kiss will not be enough and I will drag you back to my place and I'm going to bury my face in your pussy."

A high, inarticulate noise escapes her, like air leaking from a balloon.

"Is that a yes?" I ask solicitously.

As an answer, she leans forward, offering up her mouth and with a groan, I kiss her.

"Well, you do keep your promises, don't you?" Tatiana laughs breathlessly as I slam my bedroom door shut and push her against it.

"How sore are you?" I ask hoarsely.

"Only a little," she lies.

"Not for long," I said, throwing her onto the bed hard enough to make her bounce twice and send the pillows flying. She laughed, a high, clear sound and for a moment, I just drink her in, how beautiful she is. She'd been as guarded as I was when she came here, shipped off because her family didn't know what to do with her.

Just like me.

Now she's in my bed with that sweet smile and she looks happy. Happy to be with *me.*

She eyes me curiously. "What are you staring at? Do I have something on my face?" She laces her hands behind her head, smiling at me cheekily.

"You're fucking gorgeous," I said, wincing internally at how awkward that sounds. From the way she lights up, she doesn't mind. She's wearing a long skirt today and nothing could make me happier, throwing the fabric up over her chest and kneeling at the foot of the bed, slinging her feet over my shoulders.

She jolts when I rip her panties down each side, pulling them off and stuffing them in my pocket. "Is this the big meeting we're supposed to have for your Leader's challenge?"

Wrapping my forearms around her thighs, I yank her forward, enjoying her squeal. "Of course it is," I said, running the flat of my tongue from her clit to her ass and back again in a long, slow lick, rubbing my stubbled chin against her soft opening. I remember how she moaned last night when I'd done that. My thumbs spread her wet lips wider and I enjoy the sight of her, pink and glistening. As I gently rub my thumb on her clit, I wonder how she'd look with a piercing there.

Fastening my lips over the stiff little nub, I suckle it until her fingers slide into my hair, tugging it. It's like a crackle of electricity from my scalp to my cock and I groan as it stiffens rapidly. She takes this as encouragement and tugs lightly again.

"I love your hair," she sighs, "so thick and silky."

"Pull it again," I'm talking with my mouth against her pussy, but she gets the message and the sparks from my scalp are making my balls ache. If I don't get inside her soon I'm going to lose the power of higher thought. I'll turn into a grunting mess and pummel her with my cock.

Sliding one, then two fingers inside her, I stroke them along her walls, pressing sensitive spots and making her slick and slippery in the best way. Her pussy is squeezing my fingers tight enough that I'm hoping I can get my cock back inside her.

With some effort, Tatiana sits up, pulling at my t-shirt and sweater. I lift my arms to help her just long enough to get them over my head before attacking her center again. My palm slides up her stomach, feeling her muscles clench as I drive her into an orgasm, humming with my lips around her clit again.

"Good girl, keep coming," I gloat, watching my fingers slide in and out of her clutching pussy. "So pretty when you come for me." I'm enjoying myself so much that it takes a while to realize her heels are drumming on my back.

"Please, you have to…" she's trying to drag in enough air to form a full sentence, "you have to stop. Give me a minute…"

Resting my chin on her soft mound of curls, I play with her breasts, lightly tweaking her nipples as I watch her chest heave, trying to recover. "These would look incredible with piercings," I said, rising to suck one of them.

Too soon? Her wide, alarmed gaze finds mine. "I don't… that's never been a thing, seriously, that sounds really-"

Chuckling, I kiss her. "Suck on my tongue. I want you to know how sweet you taste when you come." When she does, pulling my tongue into her mouth and playing with it with hers, I groan, yanking her legs wider.

Rolling on a condom, I pull away from her lips just long enough to watch my cock sink into her. "Fuuuuck," I groan, my forehead dropping to her shoulder for a moment as I force myself to get back under control. It feels like I'm fourteen again, trying to keep from coming the minute I got into my first woman. "You are taking my cock so fucking good," I whisper, biting her earlobe. Tatiana surrounds me, arms and legs wrapped around me, and the heat and grip of her pussy is the most intensely erotic thing I've ever experienced.

Angling my hips so that my piercing rubs against her G spot, I watch her gasp and then moan as she tightens around me, strangling my dick.

"Baby, you have to loosen up," I groan, "I can't move." I gently rub her clit with my thumb, bringing it down to circle her entrance, straining around my cock and back up, keeping still inside her until I felt her relax a little. *"Bellisima, così dolce,* so sweet," I murmured against her lips, moving my hips from side to side, trying to make some room for me.

When she lifts her hips in an invitation, I thrust in and out again, shuddering at how good it feels to be inside her. "Being inside you is like being wrapped in hot, wet velvet," I said, kissing her, "I could stay like this all day and it still wouldn't be enough."

"That's going to make walking to class a bit awkward," she said, grinning and kissing me back.

I laugh, feeling my cock vibrate inside her, pushing higher and she groans and giggles too. I never thought of sex as something warm, where there is laughter along with the driving need to bury myself deep. Pulling on her left knee to bring her leg higher, I move faster, my thumb still strumming her clit.

"You're close, aren't you *piccolo bacio?* I want you to come for me," I said hoarsely, "you juicy, perfect *tesoro,* my treasure." Her eyes are closed, her mouth open and I take her chin in my thumb and forefinger. "Look at me. I want to watch you soak my cock."

Her knees tighten around me, her fingers digging into my back. *My girl likes the dirty talk,* I thought, *I can work with that.*

"You're going to let me do anything I want to your delicious body, aren't you, baby?" I whisper to her, thrusting faster. "I'm going to spank you and fuck you. You're going on your knees to take my cock down your throat. I'll tie you up, blindfold you, and stuff your panties in your mouth to keep you quiet when you come. And I am going to make you come so much and so hard you're going to be addicted to my cock, the way I'm addicted to this perfect, tight cunt."

Her sharp little nails are going to leave some marks on my back. I wince slightly, pounding harder and losing my mind, feeling nothing but her heat and the snug fit of her pussy, and when my sweet girl lets out a strangled shriek, she clamps down on my cock the instant it swells to spurt inside her. It is like nothing I've felt before and far past pleasure.

The room is silent, aside from our harsh breaths, and I stroke my fingers along her skin, kissing her while she recovers. She's so beautiful, my Tatiana.

Mine.

CHAPTER EIGHTEEN

In which we are introduced to the Leader's Challenge. Most of it is painful.

Tatiana...

How is he still hard?

Lucca's panting, holding most of his weight off me with his arms braced on the mattress. He's still inside me, hot and hard and even as weak as I am right now, if he started moving I'd probably come again and I don't think I have any fluids left in my body to do it.

His nose is buried in my hair, and his chest expands against me as he breathes in.

"Are you huffing me?" I laugh weakly, "Like glue, or something?"

"Maybe," his voice is muffled. "You could be my drug of choice."

You're already mine, I think, stroking the back of his hair.

Three days later...

"I think we can all agree that Professor Fukumoto is a sadistic swine and whatever he's planned for the challenge is going to be horrible."

Liam O'Neill is a sour and superstitious Irishman who is often right about how bad things are going to be, according to Lucca. But he still wants Liam on his team because he's exceptionally strong, and Fukumoto warned that strength would be important.

This makes me question what I have to offer if everything is based on muscle mass.

"Liam, it's not just Fukumoto," Lucca says, "Dean Christie's in on this one, and that woman can be evil in a way that even the male professors don't have the imagination for."

There's some uneasy stirring from the group at that observation.

This is my first time meeting some of these students, several are juniors and seniors, but their obvious respect for Lucca makes me proud of him. He's also picked Ania Jankowski who still scares me a little, and Jun Chen.

We're crowded into Lucca and Konstantin's place, Kon having taken his team elsewhere to make a plan. Lucca confidently goes through the group, discussing everyone's greatest strengths. We're all wearing black suits, some kind of tough mesh-like material that's easy to move in, and some sturdy boots. I've pulled my hair back in a tight braid to keep it out of the way and I'm terrified. Not exactly about getting hurt during the challenge, but failing Lucca. This is his first real test as a Leader. I don't want to be the reason he loses the competition.

"Go grab some breakfast," he says, "we'll meet out on the north field in one hour."

Everyone bolts out to carbo-load in the dining hall and Lucca looks back to see me still huddled on his couch. "You need sustenance for this challenge," he scolds me, striding over to haul me up.

"Maybe you should have let Mateo put me on his team," I blurted, "I could have sabotaged him with my lack of experience."

"Not every student at the Academy has participated in one of these challenges," he said. "Relax. Even if I wasn't having sex with you, I would have picked you for your sniper skills, I know we're going to need you."

"Even if you weren't boning me, huh?" I said dryly. "You smooth talker, you."

Lucca's hands slip to my waist and he lifts me, feet dangling, so he can stare at me, eye to eye. "If we don't win this challenge, I'm going to edge you for a week and not let you come. For a week. So go find your confidence and get moving."

Staring at his narrowed gaze, I nod a little too fast. "I'll just go grab a granola bar or something."

"What do you think they'll do for the first part of the challenge?" I'm whispering to Ania, who's standing tall in the chilly wind whipping over the flat plains of the island.

"Probably something very uncomfortable," she says placidly, "if not acutely painful."

"Oh," I put my hand on my stomach. I will *not* throw up. At least right now.

"Welcome, students!" Dean Christie shouted, looking alarmingly cheerful. The rest of the college has gathered to watch, probably hoping someone will die in a terrible way.

"This is a three-part challenge," she continued, "the first team to get to their flag wins. The Leader can direct their team but cannot participate."

Glancing over at Lucca, I can tell he doesn't like that.

"One of the key qualities to being a great leader is being able to direct your people successfully and trust that they'll handle the job." Professor Fukumoto says. "Even if you know you're sending them into danger."

No, Lucca really doesn't like this. His mouth is a thin, flat line as he listens to the instructors.

"Your first task," calls the Dean, "use these logs to create a bridge over the ravine and have a team member cross it successfully." She fires a pistol in the air. "Go!"

The ravine she's talking about is a deep split in the rocky surface of the field. The bridge that's usually there is gone, and the pile of cut logs she's pointing to must weigh two hundred pounds each. The rest of the teams are picking their biggest players, but Lucca's picked two muscled Seniors I don't recognize and Jun, who's very lean. He gives them a quick series of directions and they race off to the logs.

"Brilliant," murmurs Ania.

"Please explain," I ask, leaning closer.

Our three are moving slower than the others because Jun can't carry one of the logs on his own. He's still helping where he can and I see him directing the other two on where to place the logs.

"Do you know what Jenga is?" Ania says.

"The game with the wooden pieces and you stack them until they fall?" I said.

"Yes. Jun is the campus champion for the life-size Jenga pieces on the grounds by the main building."

"I've never seen them," I admit, marveling at the creation of our team's bridge. Two other log spans were finished before ours, including Mateo's team. But when his team member tries to cross it, one of the logs slips almost instantly, sending him plummeting onto a safety net stretched out ten feet below. The next team is doing better, their man is halfway across, but his weight is unbalancing their log bridge and he falls, too.

"Go!" Lucca roars, "You've got this!"

Jun's creation looks haphazard, but he's traversing it effortlessly. When he reaches the other side, the Dean blows her whistle.

"First round goes to Toscano!"

Professor Fukumoto doesn't give any time for gloating or celebration. "The second task is at the grotto," he shouts, "get moving."

I exchange glances with Lucca as we run past the combat gym. I've swam in the grotto before, but it's not my favorite thing. I've always thought a college swimming pool would be well-lit and nicely heated. The Ares Academy uses a cenote. It's a deep cavern created by collapsed rock that fills with rainwater. Picking our way down the carved stone stairs, I'm already hoping Lucca doesn't pick me for this challenge. It's not as brutally cold as the Atlantic surrounding the island, but no one can stay in for long, aside from the two Norwegian students who insist on swimming every day.

Neither one of them, unfortunately, are on our team.

"This task is two-pronged," Dean Christie grins, and it's not the "fun aunt" smile, it's the leer of a sociopath. "You must retrieve your team's bag from the water. It might be on a ledge, or at the very bottom. At the same time, you must attempt to take another team's bag as well. Your members may not leave the water until both objectives have been achieved. Of course, the other team's players will also attack to retrieve their bag from you. You will need a team member for retrieval, one for defense, and one for offense. Leaders, you have five minutes to pick your people and have them enter the water."

Lucca looks over the remaining six of us. His gaze pauses on me for a moment and moves on. He picks Ania and two of the men. When the pistol goes off, they all dive in. One of our team members is a sturdy-looking blond guy, circling the water and looking for the yellow bag with a "T" on it. They all look heavy and lumpy, I suspect they're filled with rocks. Or lead. This administration is that sadistic.

The blond swimmer spots our bag and heads for it at the same time as three swimmers from other teams. Apparently, no one likes us for winning the first challenge. Ania glides through like an orca, effortlessly knocking aside two of the challengers as our third member goes for the bag with an "R" on it.

"Crap, that's Aleksandr's," I said nervously.

Lucca glares at me. "Whose team are you on?"

"Yours," I said, squeezing his arm, "always."

Several of the students are writhing underwater like eels, battling each other for the bags.

"Hey!" I shouted, "What the hell!" I point to where Ania just got hit in the back with one of the bags, and it's heavy enough to knock her into the side of the rock wall.

"Ania!" Lucca shouts, "Are you okay?"

She looks up long enough to nod and dives down again. There's a trail of red through the water from a cut on her back.

When our team finally makes their way back to the entrance, they have our bag and the one belonging to Miguel Herrera, a short, powerful-looking Leader who's set to take over his father's cartel. Unfortunately, we are also the fourth team to finish. Mateo, the little slime, places first after his swimmers knocked competing players unconscious with their bags of rocks.

"Good work," Lucca says warmly, "we're still in a strong position for the third challenge."

"Leaders," shouts the Dean, "gather your last three players and meet us at The Barrens." She smiles with all the happiness of a rabid coyote catching a ground squirrel.

"*Merda,* shit," mutters Lucca. "The Barrens."

There's a row of rifles waiting for us at the next stop, and I'm feeling some cautious optimism. I can shoot well. I can help Lucca win this. Eyeing the boulders scattered across The Barrens, I wonder what the plan is. They're all massive; some nearly twenty feet high, left over from some prehistoric glacier.

Konstantin and his team are standing next to us, and I give Mariya a smile. She's covered in blankets because she took part in the last challenge. "I had no idea how vicious you were," I whisper, "I have never admired you more."

She'd stolen another team's bag and fended off an attacker by biting him hard enough to make him let go of it.

"Thank you, honey," she says demurely.

"Here's your third and final task," shouts Fukumoto, "your team will be armed with rifles. They may shoot members from any other team. If they accidentally shoot one of their own, the team is automatically disqualified. The first player through the course wins for their team."

"That's not so bad," I whisper to Lucca, "like paintball, right?"

"The rifles are loaded with percussive paint capsules," the professor continues. "If you are hit, they will knock you off your feet, expect it. Since a shot to the head could be deadly, you will all wear helmets." He smiles, and I wonder if everyone who teaches here is fresh out of a hospital for the criminally insane. "The helmets have a heavily shaded visor that will reduce your vision by 75% or so. You will need all your other senses to make it through this obstacle course."

Lucca pulls me and the remaining two players aside. "Get a good look at each other," he says, unzipping my jacket and peeling it off me.

"Hey, what-"

He cuts me off impatiently. "Take off your jackets. It'll make it easier to distinguish you from the other teams." We're all wearing black tank tops, and while the ever-present wind is tearing through the boulders, my adrenaline buzz is keeping me from feeling it.

We're handed our rifles and I check to make sure mine is loaded, then adjust the sight. "Our capsules are green," he instructed, then grinned savagely. "Cover every one of those bastards. Paint this course Toscano green!"

I can do this, I think, tightening my grip on my rifle. *This is so much better than the underwater fight to the death.*

Lucca fastens the straps of my helmet under my chin. The professor wasn't kidding. The visor is so heavily smoked that I can hardly make out the shape of the boulders, and the other players are just blobs of black. Seeing the bare arms of my teammates will at least help me tell them apart from our opponents.

"Mateo's guys are looking over here," Lucca warns, "I'm sure he told them to target you. But you're quick, and he's picked a couple of his biggest idiots to run the course. Be careful of Schmidt, though. He's smart and a real bastard."

I know that guy. He's one of Mateo's most irritating hangers-on.

Nodding, I try to sound firm and not like I'm about to wet myself, "I have this."

"You get through this course unscathed and I will eat you out for an hour tonight," Lucca whispers, "I won't stop until you come six times." He gives me a filthy grin before giving me a pat on the top of my helmet.

Oh, I am so winning this thing, I think, fingers tightening on my rifle.

CHAPTER NINETEEN

In which there are dirty tricks and oral sex. Not at the same time.

Lucca...

Tatiana leaps into the boulder field like a fleeing deer after hearing the pistol shot. We've run through The Barrens before when I was training her, but I don't know how much she remembers about the layout. Since she's essentially running blind and holding a rifle, I'm cursing myself. I should have put her on the first challenge. She's so light. She could have scampered across those logs like a spider monkey. Instead, I've sent her out into a minefield with a group of rifle-toting assholes who won't let her out of there unless she's covered in contusions and paint.

The Leaders have access to a platform above the course, so we can watch our teams, but we can't shout any instructions. I can see Liam racing through the south end of the boulder field, Freddy Martinez, my third player, just shot three paint bullets, one hitting a member of Alek's team square in the chest. He yelps, leaving the field.

Scanning the boulders, I can't see Tatiana and I curse under my breath. Then she pops up behind a limestone outcropping and deftly shoots an opponent in the shoulder. I suck in a sigh of relief until I see another player creeping up behind her. She dodges his paint bullet and it splatters against the rock. The color is purple, Michael Doyle's team. He's just behind us in the rankings, so it looks like he might have had his team target my players, too.

Tatiana darts around another rock outcropping and nails the Doyle player in the chest. He flies backward, dropping his rifle and she takes off for the end of the obstacle course. Just then, Liam gets hit in the neck, the orange paint splattering across his jacket and then a streak of red, too.

"Dr. Giardo!" I shout, he looks up and I point in Liam's direction. "It's O'Neill, he took a hit to the neck and he's bleeding."

The doctor looks over to where Liam is slumped against the rock. "He'll be fine until the task is over," he says dismissively.

"No!" I head for the stairs, "He's bleeding from a neck wound." One of the security guards steps in front of me.

"No entering the challenge field," he recites indifferently. I'm about to punch him and take a leap over the side of the stand when Aleks shouts over to me.

"Toscano! Hold up." He points to The Barrens and I see Tatiana veer off course, running over to Liam. She takes an impressive side shot, knocking over another player without breaking stride. Kneeling next to him, she pulls off her tank top, pressing it against his neck.

"*Der'mo*, shit!" I groaned, "She's trying to drag him out, she's going to get pummeled with paint bullets."

"That's pretty cool, though," Aleks says, "didn't you do something similar last year during the mid-winter challenge?"

"That was different," I said tersely. Folding my arms, I try to look calm, like a leader though I want to vault over this fucking stand and knock the heads off two of Mateo's players. They're creeping up on Tatiana, who is still dragging Liam. They step into the path at the same time, one behind her and the other in front.

At first, I'm not sure if Liam collapsed and knocked Tatiana down until I realize she dropped to the ground so that Mateo's two players would shoot each other in the chest. They're both flat on their backs and Tati's back up and heading for the finish.

She knocks another player out of their way with a shot to the thigh and they're across the line. I'm about to roar in triumph when Schmidt races up, shooting Tatiana in the back, knocking her forward into the dirt.

A chorus of shouts and booing rises from the stands as I push past the other students, trying to get to her and Liam.

"Are you all right?" It's that slick bastard Ronan Cox, dropping his rifle to kneel by Tatiana, trying to help her up.

"I'm fine," she shrugs, self-consciously wiping at the blood streaming from her nose. "Liam needs help, though."

Cox hasn't bothered to look at her bloody teammate, still holding her shoulders.

"Move, both of you." Dr. Giardo pushes between them to get a look at Liam, still holding Tatiana's tank top against the wound on his neck. I realize that my girl is standing there in her sports bra and pull off my jacket, putting it over her shoulders.

"Toscano wins the first Leaders challenge of the year!" Dean Christie shouts, firing off her pistol again. Five times. The woman loves her bullets.

"That's bullshit!" Mateo shouts, "Aslanova was disqualified! You can see my team's paint color all over her back!"

Professor Suarez steps up. "I saw your player take the shot," he said coldly. "She was almost two meters past the finish line when he shot her in the back."

"I didn't see her pass the finish line," Schmidt says with a grin that I'm going to punch off his fucking face.

"You lying asshole," I snarled.

"It's okay," Tatiana interrupts us. "Lucca, can you help me give our equipment back to the groundskeeper?"

"Let Dr. Giardo check you first," I said, softening at the grin on her dirty face.

"It's okay," she shrugs, then winces. Those paint bullets hurt like hell, and she wasn't wearing her jacket, which would have at least given her some protection.

"How are you doing, brother?" I ask Liam, who's tilting his head so Dr. Giardo can clean the wound.

"I'll be fine," he groans.

The rest of the team crowds around us, cheering, and slapping each other on the backs. Tatiana sidesteps a back-slapping attempt by Jun, who puts up his hand in apology. "Sorry!"

"Drinks at my place tonight!" I shout. I say it just to get them the hell out of my way so I can get Tatiana somewhere quiet and check her back.

Tatiana...

Lucca should be happy that we won the challenge, but he looks furious, glaring at Mateo, Schmidt, and even poor Jun who just tried to slap me on the back to congratulate me.

"What's the matter with you?" I ask as he's hustling me down the path. "We won!"

"That fucking prick shot you in the back," he snarls, "you were over the finish line and halfway across the fucking campus before he fired on you."

"Okay, wait- Lucca- I'm serious, stop dragging me!" I have to yank on his arm before he's willing to look at me. "You can't be surprised that Mateo's people are back-stabbing, I mean, back-shooting dickheads. That's part of the deal here. I'm going to have a huge bruise and based on my recent injury inventory, that's not too bad." He's staring down at me, brow furrowed. Putting my hands on his shoulders, I shake him gently. "We won! This is such a great thing!"

"You got hurt," he insists, shaking his head.

"How are you going to send your people into danger if you freak out every time they're injured?" I said. "Part of being a leader is picking the best man - or woman - for the job and knowing they might get hurt."

"I'm not-" he presses his lips together.

"You *are* a leader, *velikolepnyy*. You may not be first-born, but they see you for what you are here, a leader," I insist. "So change your thinking."

A slow smile spreads across his full mouth. "You're calling me gorgeous?"

"You know Russian?"

He chuckles, kissing me, "I've been roommates with Konstantin for over two years. Of course, I had to learn it."

"Good, *velikolepnyy*, because you are," I said, beaming up at him. Feeling a little daring, I add, "Didn't you promise me something if I won today?"

Lucca bursts into laughter, which does not make me feel sexy and daring at all. "I plan to spend most of tonight with my mouth and my cock buried in that tight pussy," he purrs, "but first, why don't we get the blood off your face and make sure you didn't break your nose in that fall, eh?"

CHAPTER TWENTY

In which justice is served. With a side of power tools.

Tatiana...

The moment I open my eyes, I really, really wish I hadn't.

Someone is jabbing a screwdriver into my skull and something smells like a dumpster, and I suspect that something might be me.

"I think a rat crawled into my mouth and made my tongue its final resting place." It's Mariya.

Rolling over with a moan, I find her next to me in bed. She's wearing clothes, thank god, and so am I. "This isn't my bed," I whine.

"We're in Lucca's bedroom, I think," she groans, "I'm going to have to renounce my Russian heritage. I'm so hung over. I want to die."

"There was... we won, right?" I touch my finger to my tongue which feels too big for my mouth and dry. Dry as dust. "Where is he?"

"He went out to pick up some pain meds for everyone." A hoarse voice pipes up from the floor on Mariya's side of the bed.

"Who's that?" I said.

"Kon," the disembodied voice says, "I wasn't going to let my fiancée sleep in another man's bed."

"What's wrong with your bed?" Mariya's almost unintelligible, her face smushed against the pillow she's too weak to move from.

"Fucking Liam O'Neill hosed the entire bed with puke," he said, finally sitting up and trying to focus on us. "Fucking Irishman, 'I can hold my fuckin' liquor' O'Neill!"

I want to laugh but I know it would hurt so much.

The door opens and in strolls Lucca. He looks rough, like he's been rolling around in the woods wrestling wolverines.

God, he looks so hot right now.

"Hey baby, how are you doing?" I can tell he's trying not to laugh and I want to hit him but that would involve moving which might kill me right now. Opening a bottle, he taps three pills in my hand and holds a water bottle up to my mouth. "C'mon, you'll feel better once these get in your system."

He holds the bottle for me until my pathetic self can swallow enough water to get the pills down. I sigh with relief when he cups my cheek. "You feel nice and cool. Please don't move."

Lucca's gaze travels from me to Kon and then to Mariya. "Are you sure you're Russian?"

"Shut up," Mariya said weakly.

"We still did better than the fucking Irish," Kon says from the floor.

"Yeah," Lucca nods, "I saw the state of your bedroom. Not to sound like a bad roommate, but get out of here. I kicked everyone out of the main room. You can nurse your hangovers on the couch."

Grumbling, Konstantin hauls himself off the floor and reaches down to help Mariya off the bed. "I can get up on my own," she said, slapping his hand away.

Gently sitting on the bed to keep from jostling me, Lucca watches them bicker as they shut the bedroom door. "How are you doing, baby?"

"I'm questioning my Slavic heritage," I moaned. "I'm so ashamed." He has the nerve to smother a chuckle while he helps me sit up. Running my hand down my chest, I notice I'm wearing his t-shirt. "Oh… did we have sex? Did I miss it?"

Lucca bursts into laughter and I cringe, holding my hands over my ears. "No, baby. You… tried. But I'm not going to fuck you when you're drunk. I want you fully aware of what's happening."

"This is very embarrassing," I moan.

"Go back to sleep for a little while," he whispers, "give the paracetamol a chance to work."

It takes most of the day to recover from our deeply ill-advised victory party, but by late afternoon, I feel well enough to drag myself out of Lucca's bed to take a run. He's in a meeting with Professor Fukumoto, so I leave him a quick note and head over to my suite to change.

The sun's rays are stretching across the flat landscape of the island, lighting the insanely sheer cliffs to a golden shade. As usual, I take the outer running path, wanting to be close to the cliffs, to see Mother Nature's late autumn show.

When I was first sent to the Ares Academy, I never thought there would be a day when I would not only be happy, but happy to be *here*. But maybe Vladimir Adamovich was right, when he approached my parents when I was eighteen, maybe I was a good fit for the Academy.

Breathing in deep, letting the ocean air fill my lungs, I push myself a little faster on the path, waving at the guard always stationed by the lighthouse. This time, he nods to me, which feels like a breakthrough.

The shadows are looming over the path as I hit halfway through my route, and I slow down, thinking about cutting through the campus to get back home. As I catch my breath, I hear the footsteps.

"*La mia piccola puttana,* my little whore, there you are." Mateo steps out in front of me, he must have been hiding behind one of the sheds attached to the greenhouse. Schmidt stands next to him, fists clenched. Glancing over my shoulder, I see two other members of his gang of assholes.

"I'm meeting Lucca," I say flatly, trying to come up with an escape route. They've learned from their last attempt, hemming me in from the front and back, the thick glass wall of the greenhouse on one side and on the other…

I'm so screwed.

Unless I take a dive off the cliff or break through the glass wall of the greenhouse, I don't have a way out of this. Can I scream? Can I scream loud enough for anyone to hear me? The roar of the waves beating against the sheer rocks is so loud that I don't catch the next thing this evil prick says.

"I beg your pardon?"

His face flushes an angry red. "I said, *puttana,* that I'm first in line for your magic pussy. Has Lucca fucked you yet? It's going to be impossible for your *Pakhan* to marry you off to someone now, isn't it? Maybe there will be some nasty old fuck that won't mind that we all screwed you first."

This isn't happening. I clench my hands, trying to hide that they're shaking, I feel violently cold, then hot, sweating, and clammy.

You just need to take out two of them to run, I hear Lucca's voice. *You scream and charge them; they won't expect it.*

"You're not getting away with rape, asshole," I said coldly. "Even the Academy's not going to overlook that."

They all laugh, and the ugly sound swirls around my brain. Mateo pulls out a phone and holds it up, the flash clicking madly as he takes pictures of me. "Schmidt, you got the video rolling?"

"Yeah." The blonde who shot me in the back is almost giggling with excitement.

"I don't think you want these pictures sent to your big brother, the *Pakhan*, do you?" Mateo grins, "Maybe I'll put a video together, put it online, featuring you creaming on my dick, you little whore? You're going to-"

Screaming so loud that my vocal cords vibrate, I charge at him, slamming the heel of my hand into the bridge of his nose, hearing a deeply satisfying 'crack!' as it breaks. Driving my elbow into Schmidt's throat, for a second I think *I'm getting out of here, I'm going to make it-*

A hand digs into my ponytail and yanks me back violently, throwing me onto the limestone path. Mateo straddles me as one of the others holds my arms down. I'm still trying to buck him off me, still screaming as he slams his hand down on my throat, squeezing viciously.

"I offered you the easy way," he sputters through the blood gushing from his nose. "You might have even enjoyed it. But now..."

The flash blinds me as they keep taking pictures, his blood is dripping onto my face as my scream turns into a croak.

There's a blur, and Mateo's off me, and then the hands holding me down are gone. I roll to my side, coughing.

"You motherfucker! *Ti ammazzo, maledetto bastardo!* I'll fucking kill you, you bastard!" Lucca slams his fists into Mateo's face and I see the guard who nodded at me pull his gun on them.

"Get off him, Toscano! We'll take him to the Dean. Stop!" The guard's shouting at Lucca but he keeps smashing one fist, then the other until two more men race over, pulling him off a limp and bloody Mateo.

Lucca yanks away from their hands and turns around, looking

for me. "I'm sorry, I'm so sorry," he whispers, scooping me up and heading for the medical clinic.

"It's not your fault," I sobbed, "I thought I was safe."

"I should have been with you," he said, shaking his head.

"Take me back to your place," I beg, "I don't need the doctor. I just want to take a shower or something."

"They hurt you." The sound that comes from him is painful to hear, anguish, and self-loathing.

"Stop. Lucca honey, look at me. Just put me down, okay?" Stepping into the shadow of a building, he does, cupping my face, running his hands over my clothes. "See? I'm not hurt. They just yanked me down onto the path. They didn't touch me, not really."

His mouth twists. "There are marks on your neck from that fucker. You're going to bruise."

"Thank you for coming," I croak, wrapping my arms around his waist.

A guard joins us. "Dean Christie requests that Miss Aslanova get checked out by Dr. Giardo. The Dean understands that she might like to take a moment to recover, but she has set a meeting for 8 p.m. in her office."

Resting my head against Lucca's chest, I focus on my breathing. *"In, out. Another deep breath, hold for five seconds, out. Deep breath in..."* Lev taught me how to regulate my breathing when I started having panic attacks the year he was assigned as my personal bodyguard.

"Fine," Lucca gritted out. "We'll be there."

"The request is for Miss-"

"We'll be there," he corrected the guard, picking me up again and heading for the clinic.

I sat through a quick, deft examination with Dr. Giardo, who patched up my skinned elbow and gave me some arnica cream for the bruising forming around my neck. Luca texted Mariya to bring me some clothes and put me in the shower in his room.

"Do you want me to stay?" he said, running the back of his hand over my cheek.

"No, just… give me a minute," I try to smile, nodding firmly. I'm going to cry, and I don't want him to watch me. Lucca's taken the responsibility of this completely on himself, and I won't make it worse.

Standing under the hot water, I can feel my back itch and throb. The huge bruise on my back from being shot there by Schmidt is still aggravating my scar. Getting thrown on the rock path just made it worse. I remember so vividly when the monster shoved the knife in my back. I remember the shock, and then the pain.

"I'm alive, I'm still alive," I whisper. "They didn't get me. I'm still here." Sitting under the shower spray until it runs cold, I repeat my mantra, over and over until my teeth start chattering from the frigid water.

"What happens next?"

"We go see Dean Christie," Lucca says. He looks like he really wants to keep carrying me around. However, after the shower, I dressed in the sweats and hoodie Mariya brought me, put my wet hair up into a bun, and pulled myself together. We would walk into the Dean's office and I would look that piece of shit right in the eye and tell her what he and his sick little buddies planned to do to me.

The main building was quiet, it was late and everyone was gone, aside from the guards who came to my rescue. Lucca and I seated ourselves in the waiting area. Dean Christie is taking a call and has put the person on speaker.

"How can you prove the little bitch wasn't wanting it?" A man with a coarse, ugly voice shouted.

I couldn't see the Dean, but her crisp, cold voice was quite clear. "Because your son and his friends were filming the attack on cellphones - illegal here, as you know, but hardly the main offense - and he bragged about it on the video. He was quite descriptive."

Lucca squeezed my hand, "Are you all right?"

Nodding, I tried to catch the rest of the conversation.

"She must have provoked him," the man hissed, "Mateo is a strong, responsible young man."

"We beg to differ," she said. "Regardless, after he and his friends receive their punishment, you are welcome to bring him home."

"Punishment?" Now, his nasty voice switched from spiteful to alarmed.

"Yes, Signore Costa. Of course, there will be repercussions for his actions. He will be allowed to call you tomorrow and you can determine how to proceed from there." There is a long, unintelligible string of cursing in Italian, and she pleasantly cuts him off. "Have a good evening."

After a moment of silence, she calls out. "Ivan, is Miss Aslanova waiting?"

The guard pokes his head into her office. "Yes Dean, accompanied by Mr. Toscano. Shall I keep him out here?"

"As a witness, he should be questioned as well," she said placidly. "Bring them in."

Dean Christie is lounging behind her magnificent desk, but she's wearing coveralls of some kind and looking distinctly un-academic. There's a grease stain on one shoulder.

"I do hope you didn't hear that unpleasantness," she said, gesturing to the chairs in front of the desk. I'm sure she intended on having us hear the conversation with Mateo's father, so I shrug.

"Miss Aslanova, I would like to begin by commending you for your courage in the face of such an ugly situation." She picks up a remote and turns on a monitor on the wall. "While we do not believe every inch of the campus should be under surveillance, the outlying running path is covered quite well with our security cameras, as well as the guards' scrutiny. It could be considered a point of weakness to a potential exterior threat."

"I see," I said, watching the monitor. The footage is grainy, but it clearly shows Mateo and his band of assholes getting into place, waiting for me.

Lucca's holding my hand, rubbing his thumb over my wrist. He must feel my pulse speeding up because he says, "We don't have to see this."

"It's okay," I interrupted, "I want to."

He frowns at me, concerned, sitting back in his chair, and putting his arm over my shoulders.

The moment I see myself in the footage, I start to shake, but force myself to keep watching. My expression is furious, not terrified, the way I felt, and I attacked Mateo and Schmidt with a swiftness and force that was pretty strong.

"I'm so proud of you," Lucca whispers.

Within seconds, he's in the camera frame, tearing Mateo off me and pounding his face into unrecognizable mush. Ivan, the friendly guard arrives just after him, pulling his gun on the other three as they try to run away.

"They were so stupid that they held onto those highly illegal phones," the Dean said in disgust, "they could have just thrown them over the cliff and destroyed the evidence." Clicking the monitor off, she turns back to us with a professional smile. "I would like to get your statements, of course, though really, this case is quite clear."

"What happens now?" Lucca said coldly. "Eye for an eye, isn't that the justice standard here at the Ares Academy?"

Like the last time I'd seen her, Dean Christie's smile slips from Fun Aunt to something chilling, almost feral. "If those little bastards had managed to hurt Miss Aslanova, I would have cut their dicks off. As it is, they will regret their actions for the rest of their lives."

After giving our statements, I offered my hand to Ivan. "Thank you for what you did for me. I am so truly grateful." Lucca told me that Ivan had directed him to where I was on the running trail. He might not have found me in time without his help.

Ivan slowly takes my hand, shaking it gingerly. "You are most welcome."

Lucca says the oddest thing to him. "Does she have the table saw in her office?"

The guard's eyes darted back to the building. "In the basement. In fact, I should return."

"What was that about?" I said, appreciating the warmth of Lucca's arm around my waist.

"I'll tell you tomorrow," he said, kissing the side of my head. "You've been through enough tonight."

As we walk up the stairs of the student housing building, I see Dr. Giardo making his way to the main building, a large medical bag slung over one drooping shoulder.

Lucca...

"How's she doing?"

Konstantin is standing behind me, looking at the view.

"She's asleep," I said, ashing my cigarette out the window.

"Considerate of you to leave the window open," Konstantin drawls. "Do you have another one of those?" Chuckling softly, I hand him the almost empty pack. Lighting up, he eyed me. "I thought you were quitting."

"I am," I said, watching the two lights burning in the main building. One is from Dean Christie's office, the other is a light glowing on the basement level. "I just keep them for…" I suck in another deep breath of stale tobacco smoke, "special occasions."

It's really too cold to have the window open, the ever-present wind on the island gleefully whipping into the room. We're both wearing heavy sweaters, though, and we stay seated on the window bench, smoking.

There's a terrified scream that morphs into agony and then sobbing. Then, another. And another and then one more.

Flicking my butt out the window, I stand up and stretch, and so does Konstantin.

"Goodnight," I grin. It must not look right because Kon, who knows me better than anyone, flinches just a bit when he looks at me.

CHAPTER TWENTY-ONE

In which we learn how cruel life can be to a ten-year-old.

Tatiana...

The Academy does two things well, train future sociopaths and spread gossip, so by the time we walked into breakfast the next morning, half the dining hall falls silent, staring at us.

Two girls from my Interrogation class - who'd never spoken to me - hurried over the minute we sat down.

"Hey hon, how are you doing?" Tansey Marchand is the daughter of a powerful Mob boss in New Orleans, and she adds a little extra sugar to her Southern accent. "It's just so terrible, what happened. You can always talk to me if you need a sympathetic ear. Mateo and his whole slimy group are trash. Just trash."

I stare at them, drinking my coffee. Why do people like to watch the grief of others so much? As if hearing all the ugly details of my pain and terror would keep it from happening to them? It's why I refuse to talk about my parents to anyone but Lucca and Mariya.

"Thank you, Tansey," Mariya said dryly, "you can move on now, your good deed is done for the day."

Tansey stares at Mariya, eyes narrowed. "Well, bless your heart." Tossing her curls over her shoulder, she flounces away, her friend in tow.

"You know she just told you to go fuck yourself, right?" Konstantin said gleefully. "For a Southern girl, that's the worst thing she could ever say to you."

"It definitely seemed like the message based on her expression," she snickers.

"That didn't take long to make the rounds, did it?" I ask, rubbing my eyes.

Lucca kisses the top of my head. "They don't matter. Ignore them."

It was a week before I saw Mateo again.

"What is that fucker still doing on campus!" hissed Camilla. "I'm going to stab him in the throat with my pen!"

Just the sight of him makes my stomach churn violently, and I look down at my white-knuckle grip on my book bag. "I thought he left the school with the other three."

Athena caught up with us. "He should have, the little prick. But apparently, his father insisted he stay and finish the year since he'd already taken his punishment. His dad's a real *bástardos*, too."

Camilla steps closer to me as he approaches us, but she doesn't need to worry. Mateo turns when he spots us and goes the other way. He looks pale, nasty like he hasn't showered. As I glance down at his right hand, I drop my bag.

There isn't one. A hand. Just a bandaged stump.

"I'm going to be sick," I whisper.

"Don't you dare," Athena says, linking her arm with mine for the first time ever. "He got exactly what he deserved."

With Mateo keeping away from me, life at the Academy settled into something that perhaps wasn't perfect, though it was close. There was so much laughter and happiness in the moments spent with our group - the first people ever that I could confidently say were my true friends - and with Lucca.

He was very careful to not touch me in any way that could be considered sexual, though I spent nearly every night with him. This went on for over a week before I straddled him in bed - naked - and told him no one was getting any sleep until he made me come.

"Can I ask you something?"

"Hmmm?" I mumble, lying on top of him and playing with his hair.

"Did you tell your bodyguard about the attack? Your brothers?" Lucca strokes his calloused fingertips down my arm.

"No, I didn't."

"Tell me why," he said, concerned. "Don't you think this is something they need to know? The Costa Mafia isn't one of the most powerful ones in Europe, but they make up for it by being the most evil."

Frowning, I roll off him, sitting up. "I haven't considered the repercussions, damn it. I didn't tell Lev because…" I waved my hands, trying to shape my emotions into words. "Lev's taken care of me for half my life. He came at a very bad time for me, and he helped me cope. I felt safe with him. If he finds out this happened while he's been rotting away in town not ten minutes from here, it would…" Shaking my head, "It would kill him. He's risked his life so many times to protect me. If I tell my brothers, they'll completely lose it. I have no idea what they would do but it would take their attention away from this threat that's trying to destroy our Bratva."

Lucca sits up, pulling me onto his lap, wrapping his arms around me. "What happened back then? What did he help you with?" His fingers slide down my back, lightly touching my thick, ugly scar. "Does it have something to do with this?"

I try to pull away, but he keeps his arms around me and he's warm and I rest my cheek against his lovely, sculpted chest so that I don't have to look at him.

"I was kidnapped when I was ten. My bodyguard was an older soldier who was furious about getting assigned to me. He felt like it was demeaning, I suspect, like he was too old to handle anything that would bring him more attention or praise.

"So, it was easy for the men to take me. Albanians. They were trying to get a foothold in Canada and they thought I was an easy way to make the Aslanov Bratva lose face. 'Look, they can't even keep track of their little girl!'"

He's listening carefully, rubbing his hands on my back. "You must have been terrified. Only ten years old."

"My captors told me that they would start cutting off pieces of me to send to my father," I said, "I was lucky, though. My brothers tracked them down pretty quickly, just a couple of days later. I was chained in a warehouse, in the basement. When the Albanian guarding me realized they'd broken in and killed everyone, he stabbed me in the back. He was aiming up, trying to hit my heart but the blade bounced off a rib. It's an ugly scar."

"It's beautiful," he insists, leaning down to press his lips against it. "It's beautiful because it shows you were strong enough to survive."

"I didn't feel very strong," I said. "My mother wanted to pretend it didn't happen, like it would just… go away if we never talked about it. I couldn't sleep, I'd wake up screaming because I was so scared the men would come back. Roman sent Lev from Moscow to be my new bodyguard. He's the one who taught me to breathe through panic attacks, he started training me in self-defense but my mother put a stop to that. She said it was unladylike, but I suspect she hated seeing me train because it reminded her that I could be kidnapped again."

Lucca cups my face in his hands, kissing my forehead, each cheekbone, and then my lips. "You are strong. Courageous.

Thank you for telling me, *piccolo bacio,* my little kiss."

Lucca...

Late December...

It's been so long since I've been happy - truly happy - that I've forgotten how effortless it is. No paranoia about whether it's real, no anticipation of the one-two punch sure to come for having the audacity to feel this way. The anxiety that it's going to be taken away is absent when it comes to Tatiana.

I don't know if it's because she's been sheltered so much, but she doesn't have the artifice, the cynicism that most women in our world do. When I walk into a room, she lights up, genuinely happy to see me and not afraid to show it.

Tatiana and Mariya are sitting on our couch, laughing over something they're looking at on Tati's illegal laptop.

"What's making you laugh?" I ask, dropping a kiss on her shoulder. "Or do I really not want to know?"

"Oh, Mariya's showing me a hairstyle she wants to wear for the Christmas party." She turns the screen toward me and I try to disguise my laugh as a cough.

"I see. It's very... complicated." It's a horrible mix of braids, the fabric things girls put in their hair - scrunchies? - and fake flowers.

"Kon insisted that we needed to go to the party together to 'keep up appearances,'" Mariya said, making a mocking quote sign with two fingers. "So, I want to look my best."

"Yeah, I can see that," I agree, straight-faced. "Kon's not... uh, smooth when it comes to you. But I promise his heart is in the right place."

"Smooth?" Mariya snarled, "He certainly seems smooth enough

with the fifty percent of the female population he's banged here on campus. Believe me, no one's shy about letting me know they've slept with him."

I winced. "Look, I'm sorry. They're bitches for bragging to you like that."

"That's what I told her!" Tatiana adds.

"I can promise you that since you came here, he hasn't been with anyone," I tell Mariya, watching her mutinous expression. There's the slightest hint of hope there, too.

"Then why is he such a grumpy asshole to her?" Tatiana asks.

"Let's be fair," I said, rubbing the back of my neck and wishing I'd never come in here, "they both look like they want to stab each other whenever they're within a one-meter radius. So, it seems like something she and Konstantin should discuss."

I try to change the subject before the person getting stabbed is me. "So, are you trying out the same look for the Christmas Eve party, baby?"

She raises a haughty brow. "I don't know. No one has asked me to be their date."

Oh, shit.

"My beautiful *piccolo bacio,* I ask you to forgive my thoughtless assumptions and I would like to formally request the honor of your presence at the party as my date?"

"Man, he's smooth," Mariya compliments me, nudging Tati, "you should definitely reinforce that kind of boyfriend behavior."

"Very well," Tatiana examines her fingernails, "since no one else has asked me and I *am* free…"

"Excellent," I kiss her hand, deeply relieved this isn't going to cost me a kidney or something.

"Let's go over to your suite," Mariya says to Tatiana, "we can go through your closet and find something that'll make you look insanely hot."

"It wouldn't matter what she wore, she will always be beautiful," I said, kissing her goodbye.

"Lucca should really give lessons on how to talk to women," Mariya says as they leave.

I just smile, glad they're leaving before I open my mouth and fuck it up somehow.

CHAPTER TWENTY-TWO

In which Lucca wins the title of Best Boyfriend Ever.

Tatiana...

"So, what are the formal dances like in Vancouver?" Mariya asks, applying some eyeliner with a dramatic swoop on my eyelids.

"I don't know," I admit. "This is the first dance I've ever been to."

"You're kidding." Her hand is still up, gripping the eyeliner wand as she stares at me.

"There were a couple of formal affairs that I went to with my parents," I shrugged, "but I never danced with anyone. Don't give me that look, I know I was raised as a professional shut-in. No need to make me feel any more pathetic than I do."

"Sorry," she finishes her magic on my eyes. "I thought no one could be more oppressive than my mother, and even I got to go to a few dances, though never with a date. Being promised in marriage at the age of fourteen will do that."

"Were you angry when Maksim told you about the arrangement with the Turgenevs?" I watch her expression, but she keeps her eyes on the makeup bag.

"Honestly? No. My sister-in-law Ella lost her fucking mind. I heard she trashed Maksim's office when she found out. She made him promise to ask me, instead of telling me. And he did. At the time, I thought Konstantin was cute, can you believe it?" she snorted.

"Well..." I shrug awkwardly.

"Of course, I didn't know what a dick he was at the time," she said sourly. "But it could be worse. Maksim could have promised me to some eighty-year-old."

"I can't see him ever doing that," I said, hiding a smile.

"Probably not," she admits, chuckling a little. "It may not be so bad. Look at Ekaterina! She's really happy with her arranged marriage. As a matter of fact, since my sister is married to Lucca's brother, we could really be family if you two…" she wiggles her eyebrows at me meaningfully.

My smile fades as I think about it. Would Roman let me marry someone of my own choosing? "Lucca's estranged from his family and frankly, they sound like assholes to me," I said, standing up to step into my dark green silk dress.

"Did he ever tell you what the hell happened?"

"Yes," I said, struggling to get at the zipper. "It's not my story to tell, though it's hard to want to be a member of a family that could throw away their own brother like that, especially after losing their parents."

She bats my hands away from the zipper and pulls it up for me. "Lucca's a good man," she agreed, "though falling in love with you has brought it out of him. Hopefully, they'll have a chance to see that."

"Love?" I'm about to scoff and dismiss her comment, but suddenly, I'm not sure what to think. The tender way he treats me - for such an angry man - how he comes to my rescue, over and over. Do I love him?

Watching me, Mariya grins insolently when I stare back at her, wide-eyed. "Oh, shit I love him, don't I?"

"Yes, my simple-minded friend, you do. And he loves you. It is painfully obvious. And nauseatingly adorable, if you want the truth."

Lucca...

"The Ares Academy has to be the only fucking college on the planet that expects you to pack a tux," Aleksandr says sourly, straightening his cuffs.

"Yeah, but you look hot as hell," Konstantin leers, patting him on the shoulder, laughing when he irritably swats his hand off.

We agreed to meet the women at the main hall, where the cavernous granite and wood space has been transformed with multiple glittering Christmas trees. Fabric swags and lights are draped from the oak beams overhead and tables are covered in tartan red and green, with endless platters of food.

Say what you will about our power-saw-loving Dean, the woman knows how to throw a party.

"Here they come," Aleks nudges me.

Fuck, she's incredible.

Tatiana's looking around, and I catch the moment she sees me and gives me that smile, the smile that tells me she's so happy to see me. No pretense, no playing hard to get.

Since men at the Academy outnumber women by nearly two to one, just having a date for the party is a major coup. Having a woman as beautiful as Tatiana? I'm just spiteful enough to enjoy the longing stares the other guys are giving her as I walk up to meet her.

"*Ty samoye prekrasnoye, chto ya kogda-libo videl,*" I whisper, cupping her face to kiss her.

"I'm the most beautiful thing you've ever seen?" Tatiana says, "And in Russian? You're too good at this, *Velikolepnyy.*"

"I'm still gorgeous, eh?" I grin down at her, giving her another kiss.

"In this tux? Oh, yes," she says with a misty look of appreciation.

I laughed. I seem to do that a lot around her.

Aleks is with Camilla tonight, and we're both pulling our girls out onto the dance floor when I spot Mateo. "That *pezzo di merda*, that piece of shit is here?" I murmur, disgusted. "Who's willing to date a rapist?"

He craned his neck, looking over the crowd. "It's the girl from the Marchand syndicate in New Orleans."

"Tansey Marchand," I say with disgust. She's preening in a very low-cut black dress and her left boob is already ready to pop out of the fabric.

"What are you two looking at?" Tatiana asks, standing on tiptoe.

"Nothing," I said, pulling her closer. She laughs as I twirl her out in a spin and back again.

"Impressive," she says, smoothing my lapel, "dance lessons as a kid?"

"All of us had to go through them," I groaned, "my mother insisted. Dario was better about finding a way out of them because he's such a sneaky bastard, but-"

She's watching me closely, and I turn my head. "It's okay to miss them, *Velikolepnyy*. Especially at Christmas."

I give her a cold smile, spinning her out and back again, a little harder this time. "No. Because they are not missing me, I can promise you."

It's a hell of a party. The booze is flowing freely and even the professors look like they're enjoying themselves. I keep an eye on Mateo, making sure he's on the other side of the big hall from wherever we are.

Tatiana's face is flushed and she's giggling a little as I take her outside for some air. "Baby, you're not drunk, are you?"

"No!" she promises, eyes wide.

"Good, because there's so many things I want to do to you." My hand slides down the soft skin of her back. "I'm really appreciating this dress, by the way. It looks like I just need to unzip it and it will…" I kiss the side of her neck and nip at her shoulder. "Just fall right off of you."

She sags against me with a little moan and I grin, sliding my tongue between her lips. Curving my hand around the back of her neck, I leisurely trace her lips and teeth before drawing her tongue into my mouth, sucking on it lightly. She tastes like the cherries and chocolate from the dessert table.

Groaning, I pull back, trying to find my willpower before I rip off that dress and fuck her right here on the terrace.

"Come here, I have something to show you," I said, pulling off my tux jacket and putting it over her shoulders.

"When you mentioned you had something to show me, I kind of thought you'd be taking me back to your rooms and taking off-"

"Hush, woman! I'm trying to be romantic here," I scold her, leading her through the center courtyard and to the side, to the first of the big greenhouses. Laughing, she follows me inside.

"Oh, this is so pretty," she sighs, looking around us.

The college supplies a large amount of the food served in the dining hall from the greenhouses, but the most beautiful one holds all the flowers and the exotic botanicals the faculty uses for everything from poison to teaching first aid remedies in the field. I bribed the gardener to string Christmas lights in the greenhouse and then the same amount of money to give me the key and leave.

"C'mon, let me show you around," I say, taking her hand. The air's warm and moist, fogging the glass of the greenhouse and giving us some privacy. She delicately touches the petals of some white and purple orchids, leaning in to sniff some roses so dark that they seem to be black.

"How do you know your way around so well?" Tatiana asks, touching the silky leaves of a greyish-green plant.

"Maybe don't stroke the leaves on that one," I caution, "the tiny hairs that make the leaves so fuzzy on the Velvety Nightshade also contain the toxin that can kill you." I kiss her as she yanks her hand away. "You'd need more exposure than that, though." I help her step over a gravel-filled drain in the stone floor. "My first year here at the Academy, I was always getting disciplined."

"For what?"

"Starting fights. Finishing them. I ended up here a lot with Professor Poison. Ah, sorry, Professor Palomé. Being in the Assassins major, there was so much to learn here, it's fascinating," I said, holding the huge leaves aside from an Elephant Ear plant to let her through.

"Why Signore Toscano, I'm seeing a whole new side of you," she teases, rounding a table of brilliant red poppies. "Wh- what is this?"

I stand behind her, wrapping my arms around her waist. "It's for you. Merry Christmas."

"Bozhe moy, oh my god, Lucca!" Tatiana darts toward the bed. "How did you do this?"

There's a huge bed, surrounded by pots of flowers and a decorative iron arch covered in wisteria. The bed is piled high with pillows and cashmere blankets.

"This is so soft," she crooned, petting a blanket. "Is it made of puppies? Unicorn skins?"

Pulling the cork on a bottle of champagne on a tray next to the bed, I fill a flute and offer it to her.

"Can I make the toast?" she asks.

"Of course."

Her eyes twinkle, "I would like to thank fate for the day I got the living hell kicked out of me."

"What?" Damn, she always makes me laugh. "Why would you make a toast to the Jankowski Beatdown?"

"Because," she insisted, "it was the best thing. Because of that very, *very* painful afternoon, I met you. And being with you is the best of all things."

Throat tight, I lightly tap my glass to hers. "Cheers, my sweet girl."

Tatiana...

Lucca takes his time, slowly unzipping my dress, kissing each inch of skin revealed and he is right: when the zipper reaches the bottom of its track, the fabric drops off me gracefully. I couldn't wear a bra with the low back of the gown, so I'm there standing a bit awkwardly in my undies and heels, and he is fully dressed, looking unreasonably handsome in his tux.

"Take off your panties," he says, and I do, feeling his hand slide over my ass. "Mmmm. *Bellissima.*"

I always love watching Lucca take off his clothes, his long fingers elegant and agile, stripping away each item with grace and an economy of motion that I envy. But he's not doing any of that right now, and my naked self feels even more... nude, I guess as he circles the bed, hands in his pockets, admiring me from all angles.

Hitching his dress pants, he kneels in front of me, kissing between my breasts and gently pushing me back against the soft sheets. Sliding his hands between my knees, he pulls them apart, making a pleased noise deep in his throat and the sound makes me melt like butter in the microwave.

"This was meant to be my big, romantic move, *piccolo bacio.*" He's looking up at me from between my legs with such a wicked grin. "Looking at you, so pink and sweet... you're already slick, did you know that?" I give a little yelp when he abruptly tugs on the trimmed curls between my legs. The sting is sharp and it sends needles of warmth through my center in a confusing way that shouldn't feel good, but it does. "Part of me wants to worship and the other half wants to just... defile you. So, I'll give you the choice. What do you want from me tonight?"

I'm so drawn to him, like a distant, icy planet, and he is my sun. My orbit around him warms me. He thawed something that's been frozen inside me forever.

"Everything, Lucca," I say. "I want all of you."

His smile is beautiful for a moment, a ray of light shining on me before his amber eyes narrow with pleasure.

"I don't think you know who you're dealing with here, *piccolo bacio*," he drawls in his most delicious, darkest voice. "I think you're underestimating what I can do to this tight, perfect pussy." He tugs on my curls again, grinning at my moan. "I can suck your innocence, your shyness, sweetness right out of you and leave you panting, soaking wet, my kinky, hungry little doll begging me to fuck you until you can't walk without a limp."

I try to say something but only a weak puff of air escapes my slack lips. His dirty talk. Damn Lucca and his deep, gorgeous voice and his filthy imagination!

He slides two fingers onto my center, spreading my lips wide as he makes a deep, pleased-sounding growl. With those wolf eyes glinting up at me, he licks me with the flat of his tongue, from my clitoris to my back passage and up again. He does this glorious move several times, making me half insane with the sheer pleasure of it. My nerve endings feel like they're on fire, my skin too sensitive, but when I try to close my legs for a moment his wide shoulders block them open.

"Don't do that again," he's talking against my clitoris, his lips shaping words over the swollen bud and I swear if I couldn't I could feel the words at the center of me. "Stay just like this, baby." His mouth nibbles very gently against my lips and then his teeth fasten on one, pulling it, and then the other, making me grab my own hair, pulling it and trying to keep my sanity.

The things he can do with his long fingers defy all logic and reason, and when he slides two inside me, stroking along my walls, and finding that spot that my fingers can never reach, he scratches it very lightly, and my back snaps into an arch. "Ah, there you are..." he whispers, pressing hard on me inside, and his big, warm hand pushes on my abdomen and the squeeze between the two sends me into my first orgasm.

"There's one," he says, drawing a number on my thigh in my own slick. The second comes as he keeps his fingers inside me and pinches my clit sharply.

"Bozhe moy!" I gasp, shocked that he could make me come again so quickly.

"Not god," he disagrees, kissing his way up my stomach. "I'm doing this. Say my name when you come."

His shaft is pushing against my leg as he leisurely sucks one nipple while pinching the other, moving back and forth between them. The heat of it, and the slight movement from the blood pulsing through it makes me want it in my mouth. I want to run my tongue along the veins making it swell, taste the heat of him.

Groaning, he kisses me and I can taste my come on his tongue. "I'm not the only one gifted with dirty talk, am I baby?"

"Did I say that out loud?" I cringe, but he captures my face in his hands and makes me look at him.

"Goddamn, that was hot," he growls. "But if you put me in your mouth right now, I'm going to go off like some asshole teenage boy. I need to be inside of you. Turn around."

Rolling to my hands and knees, I shriek when I feel his teeth on my ass.

"Your ass is perfection, I had to take a bite. Sorry," he says insincerely. Then his mouth is back on me from behind and I bury my head in the pillow so I can scream as he gives me my third orgasm, painting the number on my thigh with his fingers, wet from being inside me.

"Please, please Lucca," I groaned, "I need you inside me."

"Where?" he asks, all innocent inquiry and I want to kill him. "Here?" His slick finger circles my ass and I stiffen. He kisses my right cheek and his big, warm hand slides down to cup my pussy. "Maybe you're not ready for my cock inside your ass, but I promise you, that's on the to-do list. When it happens, we'll go slow. Maybe I'll stretch you first with a plug, make you wear it to class to get your ass ready for me."

My face is back in the pillow, trying to smother my needy moaning. When I feel the head of him enter me, the rush of relief is insane, making me dizzy. Arching my back, I try to push more of him inside me, and his hands clamp down on my hips.

"Ah, ah!" Lucca says sternly, "I'll give you what you need, *piccolo bacio,* when I decide you're ready. Your greedy little pussy can wait." After another torturous minute that feels like an hour, his hips push sharply against mine, driving his cock high inside me, his piercing pressing and pushing against all my nerve endings and delicate spots. One thing hasn't changed from the first time with him, the sting and stretch as his shaft fills me to bursting. I think it will always be that way and I'm starting to crave the ache and discomfort as it melts into liquid pleasure.

He slaps my ass, hard. One side and then the other and rubs my skin as he slams into me again, a groan escaping him that's as deep as mine. His sharp hip bones slam into the softness of my ass and I have never felt him so deep. The heat of him driving inside me burns my center, my chest, makes me gasp for breath because it feels like there's no room for anything inside me but

Lucca's cock.

I'm so close, *so* close and then he freezes. "Oh, *merda!* Shit! I forgot a condom," he groaned. He starts to pull out of me and I clench my muscles around him, enjoying his growl.

"It's okay," I'm a little breathless but I get the words out. "One of my presents for you is that I'm on birth control now. We don't need a condom."

If I thought he was greedy before, now he's unhinged.

"I can fuck you raw?" His hands tighten on my hips, fingers flexing. "Baby, that's the best gift you could give me."

His hips pull back and slam into me again and this time I don't even bother to try to bury my shriek in the pillow. He feels impossibly larger and every time he thrusts inside me I feel like he's splitting me apart and I want it. I brace my arms against the mattress and turn my head, trying to find his lips, wanting to scream my pleasure into his mouth. His hand reaches under me and gives my wet, swollen clit a light slap, I'm shocked into coming again and he kisses it from me, wrapping his arms around me to hold me up as I scream his name.

"Wait," he gasps, "I want to see your face when I come inside you for the first time." He flips my shaky body over and slides inside me again. Caging my face with his forearms, he looks into my eyes. It's so painfully intimate that I close them for a moment. "No, open your eyes, sweet girl," he says, kissing me. "I need to see you."

The moment is different now, not as filthy, not as aggressive. Lucca is almost tender, stroking in and out slowly, letting me feel every inch of him inside me as the ring on the tip of his cock rubs against my clenching walls.

"So beautiful," he groans. "Your heart. Your face. God, I want to stay inside you forever." His head drops to my chest for a moment as he takes a deep breath. "I love you, sweet girl, *Ti amo.*"

The last frozen shard in my heart shatters and his heat pours through me as he comes, healing me, making me lighter than air. "I love you too, Lucca. So much. *YA tebya lyublyu.*"

He's kissing my face; my lips, my nose, my cheekbone, my ear. "*YA tebya lyublyu,* Tatiana."

We laugh together, sweaty, and happy and I know I could never be happier than in this moment.

CHAPTER TWENTY-THREE

In which Lucca and Tatiana are happy. For now.

Lucca...

Sleeping that night was impossible, I woke Tatiana up three more times, twice for sex so aggressive that I was worried about hurting her. Both times, she dug her nails into my skin refusing to let go of me. The third was just as the sun was rising, I slid into her from behind, spooning her and caressing her breasts while I whispered in Italian all the things I wasn't ready to tell her yet. How much I loved her. How she was my family now. That I wanted to marry her and give her all the love and sense of belonging she never got before from anyone, aside from her bodyguard.

"*Ti amo,*" I whispered as I came inside her, thinking of a time I could make a baby with her.

"*YA tozhe tebya lyublyu,*" she sighed.

The fact that my girl is having a little trouble walking comfortably shouldn't have made me as pleased as it does, but I hoist her up on my back, carrying her to her room as she giggles.

"*Mio dio,* my god, you're heavy!" I groan theatrically, letting her down in front of her door.

"So much for Lucca, the master of romance," she jeers, kissing me.

"There's a Christmas Market in Kilronan Village," I said, smoothing her hair away from her face. "It's one of the few times we're allowed off the grounds. I want to take you."

"I'd love that," she smiles up at me as if I'm the center of her world. "Let me shower and get changed into something warmer than my walk of shame formal wear."

Athena opens the door as we're laughing, looking at us both sourly. "Are you two done? This is making me nauseous and I'm really looking forward to the Christmas breakfast at the dining hall."

Her holier-than-thou act is spoiled when Christos Gataki appears behind her, offering us a grunt as he leaves her bedroom, still pulling his pants up.

I avoid giving her shit because she's been - moderately - kinder to Tatiana since the attack. "Meet me at noon?" I whisper to Tatiana, giving her a kiss.

"Sounds perfect," she says happily.

The first stop in Kilronan Village is to see her bodyguard at the Pier House Hotel. I know it's necessary, though I'm not thrilled to see that overprotective fucker again.

"Lev!" Tatiana races for the big Russian, who hugs her awkwardly, like he's not certain it is acceptable. She doesn't give him a choice, her arms flying around his neck. His eyes close in relief, and I realize he loves her deeply, the child her parents viewed as replaceable is precious to him.

"Merry Christmas," I offered.

"Ah, our Christmas is on January 7th," he corrects, "but *Buon Natale,* Merry Christmas to you."

My brow rose, Lev speaks Italian? His accent is pretty good. "Thank you. I know Tati wants to give you some gifts and you two should… you should talk." I give her a meaningful stare and she reluctantly nods. Giving her a kiss on her forehead, I smile down at her sweet, anxious face. "It's okay, *piccolo bacio,* I'll sit in the lounge downstairs."

Looking at his stern face, I force myself to nod politely. "I'll be available if you have any questions." Lev's no fool. He knows something must have happened.

Tatiana...

"Your brothers sent you to this *adskaya dyra,* this hellhole to keep you safe!" Lev thunders, circling his little room. "Then this happens? Why didn't you call me?"

The hardest part of telling Lev what happened to me is knowing that he'll blame himself. "Because I knew you would risk your life to charge onto campus and kill them all. Then you would be shot and I can't-" Sucking in a deep breath and the tears trying to break free, I take a second. "It's okay. Lucca and the guard got there in time. The guards are notorious for looking the other way, but Ivan stepped in and testified on my behalf. He was the one to find the phones they were using to..."

"What!" he said sharply.

"To film the attack," I sigh, rubbing my forehead. "They thought they could blackmail me into keeping quiet."

"Where are they now." His teeth are clenched hard enough to crack a molar.

"Dean Christie cut off their dominant hand, all four of them," I said with satisfaction.

"How?"

"With her table saw," I said, "she's a big fan of DIY projects and keeps a lot of power tools around. Everyone's scared to death of her."

Now I see the beginnings of a smile, but it fades quickly. "You need to tell the *Pakhan* about this."

"I know," I sigh, "it didn't hit me until Lucca pointed out the repercussions of possible revenge or any statement Roman would want to make. But not today, all right? I already talked with him and Ilia and they look so tired. I'll tell them tomorrow."

Lev knelt in front of me. "Do you swear it? If you don't, I will be forced to."

Taking his hands in mine, I nodded. "I swear it. Look, let's go for a walk with Lucca and enjoy the Christmas Market, all right? We can all use an afternoon free of complications and imminent death."

His pursed lips tell me he's displeased with my attempt at lighthearted distraction, but he nods. "Very well. Let's go collect your friend."

My soul is writhing in guilt for not telling him what Lucca really means to me, but that is a complicated discussion that I'll save for another day.

For a tiny village, Kilronan puts on one hell of a festival. The three of us wander through the booths, sipping mulled wine and listening to the slightly off-key but loudly enthusiastic band playing Christmas favorites. There's a beautiful little light village and I pause, pulling on Lucca's hand to make him stop. The children are getting chased through the light displays by clearly exhausted elves.

He bursts into laughter when two of the kids tackle an elf, and I look up at his gorgeous face, made incandescent with laughter. Kon was visibly shocked the first time he heard Lucca laugh when we were teasing each other. He told me he'd never heard Lucca laugh before, not just a polite chuckle, but a real, honest-to-god laugh. The thought makes me terribly sad, and it makes each time he lets loose with me even more precious.

Hugging Lev when it's time to head back to the college, I try not to cry. "It's so hard to say goodbye," I whisper. "I know you're ten minutes away, but it feels like lightyears when I'm not allowed to see you."

"You can see my ugly face all you like by Facetiming me on your illegal iPhone," he says dryly. "You're still keeping up your safeguards so the signal can't be tracked?"

"Yes," I said, rolling my eyes. Giving him one more hug, I whisper, "Thank you for saving my sanity all those years ago. Thank you for keeping me safe."

If I didn't know that my bodyguard was a ruthlessly stoic Russian, I might think those were tears in his dark brown eyes. "Go on with you," he says, clearing his throat. To my surprise, he offers his hand to Lucca, who slowly takes it with a smile. "Look after our girl," he said. I know how much that had to cost him to ask.

"With my life," Lucca promises. Lev looks between us and I know he's quite aware already about what Lucca means to me.

"How are you doing, *piccolo bacio?*" Lucca says, kissing the side of my head as we head back through the gates of the Ares Academy.

"I'm good," I promise, smiling up at him. "Thanks to you, this has been the best day I can remember since…" I pause, trying to remember being this happy before. "Thank you."

"Anything for you," he says, kissing my lips this time.

CHAPTER TWENTY-FOUR

In which everything turns to complete crap. Because life is like that at the Ares Academy.

Billie Eilish - What Was I Made For?

Tatiana...

My *Babushka,* my grandmother, embodied the worst of the Aslanov sour, superstitious roots. If the sun was shining outside, she would dourly predict a deadly blizzard, which would usually descend upon us by that evening.

I should have taken her lessons to heart. Maybe what happened next wouldn't have hurt so much.

Early January...

"Miss Aslanova, Dean Christie requests that you join her in her office." I look up from the test I'm trying to finish on surveillance technology to the guard standing by the lecture hall's door. Professor Campbell rises from her desk, exchanging a look with the guard before nodding to me.

"Go ahead, you can finish the test later this afternoon," she said.

My heart's in my throat, following the guard to the main building. A request for a visit to Dean Christie's office is not ever considered a good thing. Aleksandr is also waiting in her antechamber, looking as alarmed as I feel.

"Did you and Lucca do something illegal and they are mistaking me for him?" he hissed quietly.

"It's true that you two are the tallest guys on campus," I scoffed, "but you look nothing alike, and sadly, Lucca and I haven't done anything that could be considered illegal. We've been boring." *And happy,* I thought with a smile.

The Dean's door opens and we hear her most polished, professional tone. "Miss Aslanova, Mr. Rostova, join us please."

There are two men with her, sitting on the expansive couch, not the horribly uncomfortable chairs in front of her desk. The one in the beautifully tailored blue suit rises and I realize it's my brother.

"Roman?" I gasped, "What are you doing here?" I want to rush over and hug him, but the room isn't right. There's a weird tension and formality, so I take his hand and accept the Russian three kisses. "Is it safe for you to be here?" I whispered quickly.

"We're okay," he murmured, giving my hand a squeeze. Turning to the other man, who is still seated, he says, "Leonid, it's been a long time since you've seen my little sister Tatiana. Tati, this is Leonid Rostova."

"Tatiana Aslanova, you have grown up." He's still seated, which is rude in any culture, but at least it means I'm not required to shake his hand. He's in his sixties or seventies, round, florid face and looks a great deal like…

"Father, how are you?" Aleksandr approaches him stiffly, nodding his head respectfully.

"Leonid Rostova, I see the resemblance now," I smile and nod again, as is proper. "Your son is a wonderful student here."

The old man merely grunts, and I notice he doesn't return his son's nod.

"Why don't you all get comfortable?" Dean Christie says pleasantly. "You are welcome to use my office for your meeting."

"Thank you," Roman says, smiling warmly. I notice the Dean preens just slightly before straightening to her full diminutive height and strolling regally from the room.

Aleksandr is still standing stiffly in the center of the room, and the look of dread on his face is instantly transformed into a bland expression when his father glances over at him. "Come here, my boy," Leonid says in a falsely congenial tone, "there is good news to share."

Roman sits next to me on the adjoining couch and Aleks seats himself on the uncomfortable chair the Dean keeps for students.

"Tati, Aleksandr Rostova," Roman begins, "your father and I have spoken and we feel that closer ties between our families is something that would benefit us all. We have agreed to join the two of you in a marriage to cement this alliance."

My ears are ringing. My brother didn't say that. He didn't. My mouth opens, but there's nothing to say so I close it again.

"Our family is very pleased to welcome such a beautiful, healthy young woman. I'm sure she and Aleks will give us many strong children." Aleks' father is looking at me, and I don't miss the way his gaze slithers down to examine my chest. His tongue darts out to moisten his lower lip and the movement makes me instantly nauseous.

Lucca.

I haven't told Roman and Ilia about him yet, I wanted to get past the attack first. They don't know. If I can just explain this to Roman, I can make him understand-

"We have decided that you will finish this year at the Academy. Since Aleks is a Senior, it makes no sense to have Tatiana stay longer. You will be married this summer after he graduates." Leonid is grinning oddly, like this alliance is making him far too happy for reasons I don't understand.

The buzzing intensifies and I can see his rubbery lips move, but I don't understand what he's saying. Aleks and I can't look at each other.

"Tati?" Roman leans closer to me, looking concerned.

I fold my hands together in my lap, squeezing them into fists. "I- I'm honored," I stuttered, "Aleks is a fine person and- and a good friend. I just…" Leonid's falsely genial expression is fading into something ugly.

"Are you just going to sit there, boy? Speak!" he shouts at Aleks, who recovers quickly.

"I am honored as well. Tatiana has been an excellent representative for the Aslanov family here," he says numbly.

"At last, an alliance between two of the Moscow Six!" Leonid gloats, "This is a fine day."

There's a knock on the door and a server comes in with a bottle of rare and expensive vodka and four glasses. "Dean Christie wished for me to offer this, along with her congratulations," he recited politely, clearly ready to leave this funeral atmosphere.

Roman is still watching me, with a wrinkle between his eyebrows, a worry line I've never seen before. In fact, he looks like he's aged five years since I saw him last. If he's doing this, it must be because he has to have this alliance with the Rostova Bratva. He needs it to shore up our defenses.

This is the only thing I have to contribute to protect our family.

"Thank you, Leonid Rostova. I am honored to become a member of your family. I know this alliance between our families will be very… it- it will be very fruitful." Aleks is looking at me with complete despair, and I'm praying I'm successfully hiding the same feeling. I smile and nod firmly at Roman.

"Excellent," he smiles too, and my heart sinks deeper at the relief I see in his gaze. "Let's have a drink to celebrate."

"What the fuck just happened?" Aleksandr said.

He's walking like an automaton next to me. We both numbly drank the toast with his father and Roman and they left almost immediately after.

"That's the first time I've seen my brother in almost a year and I got a full ten minutes of his undivided attention," I said bitterly. "What... did you have any idea that they were planning this? Did your father talk to you about it?"

We're just wandering, not sure what to do. I can't go back to class, and poor Aleks doesn't look like he's doing any better than I am.

"No," he said bleakly, "but I never expected him to. Leonid Rostova simply bellows orders and expects them to be followed before he's even finished the sentence."

"I'm guessing you're not close," I said. It's a silly concept. Most bratva organizations are not comprised of warm family feelings.

"He's a fucking pig," Aleks said, his pale skin reddening. "I know this wasn't what you were expecting."

The enormity of what just happened hits me like a punch to the heart. "Oh, my god. What am I going to tell Lucca?" I sit down on a nearby bench, covering my mouth with my hands, if I can just block the words from coming out, this won't be real. I won't lose him.

"Mne zhal'... I'm sorry," he said hoarsely, sitting next to me and putting a tentative arm around my shoulders.

"And- and you. You have someone you love, too." My face is wet. I didn't know I was crying. "I'm sorry, Aleksandr."

"I can..." he runs his hands through his pale hair, gripping the ends and pulling. "I can talk to my father, I could try-"

"You can't," I shake my head, "you can't. You know that. Roman wouldn't have- he wouldn't do this if it wasn't important. It's um..." I laugh bitterly. "It's the only thing I have to offer our family."

"What do you mean?"

"Things are bad. They're so bad right now. I never talk about it. Not to anyone, but what the hell, you're going to be my husband, right?" My throat closes.

"I know your parents were murdered," he said quietly. "That's part of why you're here, right?"

"The Aslanov Bratva is under attack, there's been so many terrible things. Attempts on my brothers' lives. Someone tried to kidnap me at our family's estate in Vancouver. Shipments intercepted and stolen, warehouses burned down, our soldiers killed… it never stops. Roman must believe this alliance will help us."

"I knew some of this, mostly gossip," he admits, "but I didn't know how bad it was."

"I'm sure my brothers are working overtime to keep it quiet, as much as they can anyway." I'm trying to wipe my wet face and I'm mostly smearing the tears around. "I'll…" my head drops and I take a deep breath. "I'll be a good wife, Aleks. I promise you. I'll be loyal."

"*Trakhni menya,* fuck me," he groans, "of all the women my father could have picked. I've had a front row seat to your romance with Lucca. What are you going to tell him?"

"Tell me what?"

We both jump up from the bench like we'd been caught making out. Lucca is standing in front of us, looking torn between angry and worried. "What's going on? Athena told me you got called into Dean Christie's office. I've been looking for you."

Aleks looks at me sadly. "Are you going to be okay?"

"Yeah," I nodded too hard, like that would make it all make sense. "Thanks."

Lucca watches him walk away with a frown.

"Hey, let's go…" What was I going to say?

"You're crying?" He cups my cheeks tenderly between his lovely, warm hands. "What happened, sweet girl?"

"Can we go…" I rub my forehead. "Can we go to the greenhouse?"

His thumb is stroking my cheekbone. "Are you sure you don't want to go back to my place?"

I can't do that. See his bed, smell his rum, wintergreen, and cedar scent. "The greenhouse. Okay?"

"Of course, come on." He puts his arm around me protectively and I lean into it, soaking up the feeling of safety he gives me.

The flowers are as fragrant as they were on Christmas Eve, those unusual roses still blooming with their lush ebony petals. Lucca sits down, pulling me onto his lap. "Talk to me, *piccolo bacio*. Who made you cry?"

Burying my face in the space between his neck and shoulder, I selfishly breathe in deep, trying to memorize how he smells, the warmth of his skin. "My brother Roman came to see me," I said with a bitter little chuckle. "For a total of ten minutes."

"Is everything okay?" he says, so concerned and kind. "Have there been more attacks?"

"He needs allies," I said, sitting up. "Alek's father Leonid Rostova was there, too. They've…" I start sobbing again, to my shame. I have no right to cry in front of him. It's so selfish. I want to beg him to run away with me. Just disappear. Fuck this world and their arranged marriages. When I look up, I see Lucca's tanned olive skin is turning pale.

"Why were they here?" he asks hoarsely.

"They…" I'm crying too hard to get the words out.

"Why were they here, Tati? Why were you crying with Aleks?" His voice is rising.

My hands drop limply to my lap. "They've arranged a marriage for Aleks and me to cement an alliance between our families. My brother needs this. We're getting married this summer."

"What the *fuck?*" Lucca's on his feet, looking at me incredulously. "You're going to tell him no! I'll- I'll call Giovanni and request he meet with Roman and make an alliance between our families. We're the most powerful Mafia in Italy and the US! We're a much better match! This is-"

"I can't," I interrupt him. "You know we can't. The alliance is made. To go back on an agreement with another Bratva is unforgivable, especially with one of the Moscow Six Families. It could destroy the Aslanov Bratva."

"I don't care!" he shouts, "You can't want this!"

"You know I don't!" I follow him as he backs away, "Of course I don't! I love you; I love you so much and this…" I'm sobbing again, my throat too thick to speak.

"Well, then you can't, Tati! You tell your brother we're together. Tell him I took your virginity and that I want to marry you!" His eyes are wide and the pain there is unbearable. "I'll tell him then; I'll call your brother and-"

"Lucca, stop! You can't." I try to take his hand but he grabs me instead, holding me tightly against him.

"You're not marrying Aleks," he moans, "you're not marrying anyone but me."

It would be so good to just sag into his warmth, his strong arms and just pretend that we could fix this somehow. "If this was your family," I said, running my hand through his thick hair, "if the Toscanos were in terrible danger and you could do something about it-"

"No! Not if it meant losing you!" Lucca kisses me with the desperation of a dying man, pulling me tighter like he could absorb me into him.

"You would, *moya milaya,* my sweetheart. This is all I have to give for my family's safety." I laugh bitterly.

"It's what I was made for."

He abruptly pulls loose from me. "That's it then? You're serious." His features darken, like a cloud over the sun. "You're giving us up so easily."

"It's not easy," I whispered. "You are everything."

"Liar." He walks away, so quickly that he's out the door before I can call after him, beg him to come back. I stand there among all the beautiful, poisonous flowers and cry like my soul's been torn from my body.

CHAPTER TWENTY-FIVE

In which all hope is lost. And toenails.

Blue October - Into the Ocean

Tatiana...

A month later...

The weeks pass in a haze of misery.

Focusing on anything seems impossible. I've been surviving on room service to avoid seeing Lucca in the dining hall after he convinced Professor Zimmerman to allow him to transfer out of our combat class. I get it. He doesn't want to look at me, now that I'm yet another person who has left him. Aleks and I tend to avoid each other, too. It's painful to be reminded of how much the other person is giving up.

"Tati, have you... it's next week... are you... *Tatiana!*"

Yelping, I look up at Camilla, who's glaring at me with her hands on her hips. "*Fille,* have you heard a single thing I've been saying to you?"

"Sorry," I mumble, "what?"

"I said that our Torture and Interrogation test is next week. Have you been studying any of the techniques?"

"Um..." I try to remember what I've read. "Yes."

We're sitting in the ancient library, one of the most beautiful buildings on campus with Gothic-style arches and beautifully carved shelves crammed with priceless books. There are five massive fireplaces scattered through the building and it's always a little chilly, to protect the delicate, ancient reading material. It's always been one of my favorite places here, where I could hide from all the drama and anxiety always raging through the campus.

She shakes her head sadly. "You are a mess. The R TI test is serious, *fille*, you need to be ready. Students flunk out of the Academy for failing to pass this test."

I only have until the end of the school year before any semblance of choice in my life is gone. What does it matter?

"I'll be ready," I promise.

"All right," she says, still watching me with concern. "Let me know if you want to study together."

"Thank you," I force a smile, watching her obvious relief. "I'll be... you know. I'll be fine."

Leaving the library, I head for the shooting range. One of the only things that can mute my internal screams is shooting the sniper rifles. Putting on the headphones silences the outside world and then it's assemble the weapon, determine the length of pull between the butt and the trigger, adjust the scope, load the ammunition, and sight the target.

Taking out moving targets is my new skill. The intensity of the focus required wipes my mind clear of anything else. For a little while, at least, my heart and brain are blissfully blank.

When I finally run out of my ammunition allotment, it's dark outside.

"While I appreciate your dedication to your craft, even a perfectionist needs to take a break sometimes." Professor Suarez steps into my shooting booth, looking at the digital readout for my session. "You still had a ninety percent accuracy score with five mph wind resistance on a moving target? That's very well done, Miss Aslanova." He glanced at me, his keen brown eyes examining me. "You don't look like you've been sleeping well, rest is essential to keeping your focus."

I don't bother telling him that I wake up at 3:36 every morning and usually can't get back to sleep. Or how I creep into the library and sit on one of the couches, staring sightlessly at a book. "I'm fine," I mumble, nodding firmly like that's totally going to sell it.

Folding his arms, he watches me closely. "You know, Dr. Giardo can give sleeping aids if you're really having trouble getting your rest. The Academy is a very demanding school."

The gossip network here is far too thorough for Suarez not to have heard of my sudden engagement, but I appreciate the effort he's making. "Thank you, sir. I'll just clean up here and be on my way."

He's frowning, and it's oddly comforting to see his obvious concern. "You're one of my best students, Miss Aslanova. But it is also very easy to get seriously injured if your focus is off when you're handling firearms. My office door is always open if you feel like you need to discuss…" he hesitates, "anything."

Finding a real smile for him, I say, "Thank you. Truly. I've looked up to you since the first day of class and I appreciate you taking me under your wing when I was essentially useless at… well, everything here. I hope I can make you proud of me."

"I already am," he patted my shoulder. "I hear you'll be leaving at the end of the school year. That's a shame, I think you show great promise."

"That's the nicest thing you could possibly say to me. Thank you, professor, really." I'd like to say something else. Like how I want to stay. How for the first time in my life I believe I have something to offer other than my Bratva Princess position and ability to bear heirs. None of that matters, though. Clearing my throat, I nod. "Goodnight, sir."

"Get the fuck out of bed!"

There's a bright light blinding me as someone yanks me off my mattress, landing with a thump on the floor. I reflexively kick out, hitting something solid and hearing a curse.

"Serves you right asshole," another voice says.

A bag is yanked over my head and I violently head-butt the assailant behind me. Another curse. "Now who's laughing, asshole?"

They zip-tie my hands and ankles with impressive speed, there must be three people holding me down to get it done. I let out a scream that makes my vocal cords rattle, and this time they all laugh. "Scream all you want, no one's coming."

I struggle and writhe against them until they drop me onto the floor, jarring my ribs. "We can roll you down the fucking stairs or you can hold still. Your choice."

If you're outnumbered during an attack, save your strength, Lucca had instructed me once, *try to determine the enemy's numbers and pay attention to your surroundings.*

After nodding reluctantly, I'm thrown over someone's shoulder. I count the number of steps, knowing we're out of my room now, then the suite. There are sixteen steps from the second floor to the first, and then the cold air hits me as we leave the building. I'm in my sleep shorts and a tank top. I don't hear any guards shouting, so we must not be heading for the gates at the main entrance.

The man carrying me breaks into a brisk jog, which slams me painfully up and down on his shoulder and I grit my teeth until I hear another door open and it's warmer again. Then there are more stairs, going down this time and it gets chillier as we descend.

I'm thrown into a chair and the zip ties are cut and my hands are re-tied to the arms of a metal chair within seconds. There's no give, so I'm guessing it's bolted to the floor. The last thing I hear is the door slamming shut and I'm alone, shivering, and bound to this chair.

Of course. The Interrogation Exam, the RT I. There's no way an outside force stormed the Academy, kidnapped me, and stayed on school grounds.

"A little dramatic, isn't it?" I sighed, not expecting an answer.

It's hard to tell how long I've been down here. I managed to doze on and off for a little while, but my hands and feet are numb from the cold, so I'm guessing it's been a few hours at least. Grimly rotating my wrists and wiggling my toes, I wonder what the plan is. I shut down every nightmare scenario that tries to invade my mind. That's what they want.

The captive's mind will handle much of the torture for you, Professor Campbell told us, *leave them alone, uncomfortable, bound, and let them envision every terrible thing that they can imagine.*

I jump a little when the door slams open. "Good morning, princess. Have a nice rest?"

I say nothing.

My head snaps to the right as someone backhands me. It hurts like hell, but there was a certain amount of control behind it, like they knew just how much force to use.

"Tell me your name." The voice is unrecognizable. Do they bring in outside talent for the exam? He's got an American accent.

Don't answer their questions, don't be tempted to be a smart-arse. It's Professor Campbell's voice in my head again. *Everything you say will be twisted to take the interrogation into a new direction you won't expect. It's too easy to blurt out information.*

So, I say nothing.

It's then that I feel his hand on my ankle, and my entire leg seizes with agony. A scream rips from my throat as the burning from my little toe sears up my foot like it's been doused in kerosine and set ablaze.

"Well, damn. You're a bleeder, huh?" He sprinkles something on my toe that sends another bolt of torment through me and I cry out again. "Jeez, princess. It's just QikClot powder. You have to toughen up. I yank off one itty bitty pinkie toe and you scream like I chopped off your foot? Though, that could be next. Wanna tell me your name yet?"

Fuck you fuck you fuck you fuck you I hope you die you evil fuck you fuck you...

Nothing. I'll never say a word.

"I'll come back in a while, give you a chance to think about what you want to say to me." The voice is laced with humor and this does not reassure me. "Are you thirsty?"

Not a shrug, no nodding of my head.

"That's fine. I'll give you a drink of water before I go."

A bucket of cold water splashes on me, drenching the hood on my head and soaking my skimpy clothing. There's laughter before the door closing cuts it off and I'm alone again.

I shift, moaning as the movement disturbs my toe, beating agony in time with my heartbeat. I'm so thirsty... I tried to suck the moisture from the hood covering my face but don't get enough to even wet my lips.

It feels like it's been longer this time, and my thoughts keep drifting back to Lucca, the inexorable gravity that's always pulled me to him. Is he all right? The few times I've seen him in the distance on campus, he always looked so angry. Mariya told me several girls offered to "comfort" him after our breakup, but he ignored them all. Is it wrong that I've been so relieved, hearing this? She says Lucca's sullen and uncommunicative and when she visits Konstantin, he goes into his room or leaves.

Aleks told me that his father sent him an engagement ring for me, some giant, ostentatious piece of crap. He sent me a picture from the purloined iPhone I gave him after programming it to my Skylink account. It gives us a chance to share any bits of information about what's going on with our families, and it does seem like the influx of soldiers from the Rostova Bratva is helping my brothers in the battle to hold our territory.

He texted me the picture of the ring with an assurance that I didn't have to wear the thing until we left the Academy. I don't think I could endure the constant reminder weighing down my arm.

"Rise and shine, princess!"

The door slamming open and bouncing off the wall yanks me out of a fitful sleep. I can't feel my arms and legs anymore, and there's a bone-deep shuddering that I can't seem to stop. On the bright side, I can't feel my toe, either.

"You really should tell me your name. You're blue. I mean, like Smurf blue. I'd hate to see you die of pneumonia before we even get a chance to chat." I hear a scrape of a chair, and he settles himself in front of me. "Your tank top is still wet. You have great tits, princess. Tight little nipples."

I say nothing. There's a dark part of me, a small voice but growing louder that speaks up after his threat of dying from pneumonia. I've had it before, when I was fifteen. I ended up in the hospital when the standard antibiotics couldn't clear it from my lungs. The doctor said I would be more susceptible to getting it again.

Would it really be so bad, the cold little voice suggests, *if you just... let the pneumonia do the work? You don't want to exist as just a breeder for the rest of your life. Longing for Lucca forever and knowing he's in love with someone else? Another woman having his children?*

"...getting hungry yet, princess? You must be..."

You're not really disobeying your family if you die, the voice whispers this time, more intimately, *it wouldn't be your fault. They'd figure out something else if they can't use you.*

Another slap jolts me out of my thoughts. "You're hurting my feelings, princess. I feel like you're not listening to me."

There's a click and a light so bright that it's glowing through the thick material of the hood. He rips it off me and a groan escapes as I squint, trying to turn away from the light searing my corneas.

He starts laughing, it's harsh and mocking. "Aw, princess. You pissed yourself. Did you even know? Yeah, you've been sitting in your own piss. That's fucking pathetic."

Don't underestimate the impact of humiliation. It's Professor Campell's voice again. *Sometimes, the words can cut deeper than a knife. Be prepared for that.*

"If you give me your name, princess, I'll get you out of this chair and you can take off those piss-soaked clothes. Take a nice, hot shower, put on something warm? I'll even slap a band aid on that toe." I still can't see enough through the spotlight to determine anything other than his shape. "What do you say?"

I close my eyes again and he leaves, slamming the door behind him. The light stays on, searing my eyelids.

Professor Campbell's voice is trying to remind me of what to do next, how to prepare for the next round of torture. But the cold little voice is whispering in my ear, and she's drowning out the professor.

It wouldn't be so bad. You'll just go to sleep. It's not like you let Roman down. He sent you here. It's not your fault you got sick...

"What the fuck did you do to her!"

Oh, I didn't even hear the door open this time.

"Stupido bastardo! She's ice cold! Fuck- I can't find a pulse!" I hear the sudden terror in his voice and I realize that it's Lucca. I feel hands tearing at the bonds on my wrists and ankles and I moan as I'm lifted out of the chair. My head lolls against his shoulder and the comforting scent of his cedar, rum, wintergreen, and worn leather fills my senses. He's putting his jacket around me before taking off for the steps leading out of the basement at a run.

"Where the fuck is Dr. Giardo! Why the fuck wasn't he checking on her! He's supposed to monitor all the interrogation subjects!" I hear terror in his voice and I feel sad that he's upset. Even though he's jostling me painfully as he breaks into a run, I don't care. I'm so happy he's holding me. He's so warm…

CHAPTER TWENTY-SIX

In which love is stronger than despair. Also, Aleksandr's dad is such a perv.

Tatiana…

"*Ti amo, dolce ragazza. Per favore svegliati.* I love you, sweet girl. Please wake up…"

There's the whisper of a prayer. It's in Italian but something about the rhythm tells me I'm right.

Lucca… my mouth shapes the word but I don't think I spoke it. A calloused finger strokes over my lips.

"*Piccolo bacio.* Wake up, baby. *Ti amo…*"

Bozhe moy, I feel like a litterbox that hasn't been cleaned in a year.

"Tati?"

It's Lucca, my eyes open and he's blurry. Trying to smile as much as my cracked lips allow me, I whisper, "Hey, *velikolepnyy.*"

He presses his lips to my forehead and pulls away abruptly, yanking open the door. "She's awake!"

"Move over!" It's the cranky voice of Dr. Giardo. "Miss Aslanova, you gave us quite a scare." His thumb pulls open my eyelid, shining his light against my defenseless cornea. "Why didn't you tap out?"

"What?"

Is that my voice? I sound like I'm 800 years old.

"Why didn't you call an end to the exercise when you reached your limit?" Giardo elaborates crossly.

"Oh," I croaked. "I didn't know I could."

He pulls back. "Did you pay attention to any of the instructions? At *all*?"

I'm looking past him to Lucca, who is hovering as close as he can. He looks so beautiful, his amber eyes glowing for me like they used to.

"Well, you passed the exam with flying colors," the doctor grumbles, checking the rest of my vitals. "You'll stay here in the clinic until you've recovered from pneumonia and the additional lung infection. Your classmates can bring your study materials here." He stabs a finger at Lucca. "You have fifteen minutes, then she needs her rest. Don't agitate her."

Extending my hand, I see there's an IV taped to it. There's a breathing tube looped under my nose and a plethora of machines around me. Lucca looks down at my hand for a moment and sighs, taking it and sitting gingerly on the edge of the bed. "Why did you do that? Do you know how close you came to dying?"

"You saved me, right?" I croak, "I remember... your jacket? And you were so warm."

"You lasted the longest of any of the Spy group," he said angrily. "They're supposed to monitor your vitals. I had to get past the guards into the Catacombs to look for you. Fuck, Tati! You were blue and you weren't moving. Those *stupidi bastardi* didn't even notice how bad off you were. The notes praised you for being so *tough*. 'She hasn't spoken once!'"

"I'm sorry," I whispered.

He gently lifted my head, helping me take a sip of water. It felt so good going down my sore throat. "Take a little more," he said. "I've been feeding you ice chips for the last week."

"A week?" I rasped, "I've been here for a *week?*"

"Yes," he nodded.

"I'm sorry." His hand smooths my lank, greasy hair back from my forehead, and I close my eyes. "I must look and smell disgusting," I groan.

"You've smelled better," he's trying to smother a grin.

"Nice bedside manner," I sass weakly.

"Everyone's worried as hell," he said, "the Dean and Professors Suarez and Campell even came by to check on you. Campbell said to tell you that you get a guaranteed passing grade for the rest of the year in her class. In fact, she would really prefer that you not participate in any more practical application exams."

My little chuckle turns into a very unattractive coughing fit. Lucca helps me sit up to catch my breath. Over his shoulder, I see an uncomfortable-looking little metal cot with a blanket. "Have you been sleeping in here? Your back must be killing you."

He snorted, "I… persuaded Dr. Giardo into letting me stay here, but he made it as miserable as possible."

"He really sucks as a doctor," I agreed, resting my head against his shoulder.

"I thought you were dead in that room," he said, the pain in his voice evident. "Why would you do that, baby?"

"I'd like to see my fiancée!"

It's Aleks, and he's practically shouting outside the door. He opens it painfully slowly and I realize he's giving Lucca a chance to back away.

"There's my soon to be daughter-in-law!" Oh, not *him.* It's Leonid Rostova, not quite shoving his son aside to get a look at me. Lucca fades into a dark corner of the room like a sentinel.

Leonid looks me over thoroughly, and apparently even being

disgusting and unwashed is not enough to discourage his leering. *"Bednaya malenkaya tykv*, poor little pumpkin," he croons. His gaze fixes on my left hand. "And where is your engagement ring?"

"Ah, Aleks has been keeping it for me while I'm here in the clinic," I lie. "We didn't want anything to happen to it." I force a smile, pleading with my eyes for Aleks to step closer. "Hello, *moy zhenikh,* my fiancé."

I see Lucca stiffen out of the corner of my eye, and he slips from the room.

"Hello, *moy predpolagayemyy,* my intended," Aleks says, edging past his father, blocking him slightly. "You look much better today."

"It would be hard to look worse," I give a weak little laugh before I get a good look at him. *"Bozhe moy!* What happened to you?" He's sporting a monster of a black eye; a split lip and I can tell he's favoring his left side a little.

"Just a sparring session gone wrong," he says dismissively. Aleks is huge like Lucca, though more of a gentle giant. It's hard to picture who could have messed up his face like that unless they had lots of help.

"That you should lose to anyone is an embarrassment!" Leonid scoffs, "You will meet them back in the ring and beat them half to death. I will expect pictures of their damage."

I take Alek's hand and squeeze it. His father is a complete bastard. "With great respect, Leonid Rostova, your son has done so much damage in the ring that I fear the administration will throw him out if he sends yet another student to the medical clinic."

This definitely seems to cheer up the old pervert. "Well, if you say so. We do want Aleks to graduate at the top of his class."

"He's a true leader, even in the Leader's division," I smile weakly.

"Very well," Leonid approves. "I shall tell your brother that I have seen you for myself and you are recovering nicely, Tatiana Aslanova." His eyes wander down the front of my thin gown again and I wish there were hospital-issued turtlenecks.

"Thank you, Leonid Rostova, you are very kind," I manage to sound pleasant, even though just looking at this man is making me nauseous. "My brothers are well?"

Why didn't they come to see me?

"Ah, well. They are very busy, as you can imagine." He pats my hand heavily with his sweaty one and I force myself not to cringe.

"Come father, I know your time is short." Aleksandr thankfully intervenes and Leonid reluctantly pulls his hand away.

Lucca slips back in as soon as they've left the clinic. "You are *not* continuing with this insane agreement!" he snarls.

"I just woke up about ten minutes ago," I said, rubbing my eyes. "Will you please just sit with me? Please?" I'm embarrassingly close to tears and he seems to understand.

"Here, you need some water," he helps me sit up again, waiting until I've finished half the glass. "Good girl," he whispers, kissing my forehead.

"Maybe you should have gone into medicine," I sighed, letting myself slump against him.

He chuckles as if I've just said the cutest thing. "I'm better at taking bodies apart than putting them back together again, *piccolo bacio.*" Moving me with painstaking care, Lucca sets me on his lap with my cheek against his chest.

I'm about to fall gratefully back to sleep when it hits me. "Did you beat up Aleksandr?"

His entire body turns to granite. "Yes," he admits. "*Quell'inutile figlio di puttana,* that useless son of a bitch was supposed to look after you and keep you safe. He never questioned why you were down in the Catacombs so long? The fucking idiot! He didn't even try to hit me back. He just stood there."

"That's not fair," I mumbled. Oh, his chest was so warm. I didn't think I would ever feel warm again. "How long was I down there?"

"I looked at the notes," he swallows, "they ripped off your toenail the first night and kept you hooded and soaking wet for two and a half days. Then another twelve hours in the spotlight. They never checked your vitals after the first night. No food or water for seventy-two fucking hours."

"They must really have hated me," I sighed.

"I called Lev for you," he continued, "he nearly got shot at the gates, trying to get in. I'm pretty sure Dean Christie realized this was a clusterfuck, because she allowed him to stay with you for the first two days when we weren't sure…"

"I'm sorry," I whispered, stroking his ribs with my finger.

"Stop saying you're sorry," he said, taking my hands and kissing it. "This isn't your fault. That interrogator fucked up."

"Where's Lev now?" I groaned a little, shifting position. "Is he okay?"

"He's fine," Lucca said in an odd tone.

"What does that mean?"

He curled his arms around me, bringing me closer, and whispered in my ear. "He's in Florida. He tracked down that bastard."

"Do you mean…"

"He took his time," he said viciously. "He'll be back tomorrow."

It was too much. Too much death and pain. "Will you stay with me?" I asked, all dignity gone, "Just till I fall asleep?"

I feel his warm lips on my forehead. "Of course. And I will be here when you wake up."

CHAPTER TWENTY-SEVEN

In which Mariya proves how delightfully cunning she can be.

Lucca...

When my phone vibrates in my pocket, I groan quietly. Taking calls in the medical clinic seemed like an obvious way to get caught, but when Lev's name flashed on the screen, I had to answer.

"Hey," I whisper.

"How is Tatiana doing?" Lev sounds exhausted.

"She's good. She regained consciousness today. We talked for a couple of minutes and then that asshole Aleks came bursting in with his father, who is a fucking pervert. He talked to Tatiana's tits the entire time." Just thinking about it is pissing me off again.

"He's a powerful *Pakhan*," Lev sighs, "and yes, he is a lecherous bastard with a fondness for young girls. But our Pakhan must have weighed the risks and benefits and found this to be a sound plan." I hear the light clink of a bottle cap.

"Are you back at the inn, having a cold one?" I ask.

"Don't give me shit, boy. This is the first drink I've had in a week," he said, belching for my benefit.

"No judgment here," I shrug. "I *am* judging the Aslanov brothers for not coming to see their sister when she was in critical condition."

"This war-"

"I understand what's going on. My family's been under fire before," I said, trying to hold onto my temper. "But this is bullshit. If I found out my sister Francesa was deathly ill, nothing would keep me from getting back to her."

If fucking Giovanni would allow me - the invisible brother - to see her, I thought bitterly.

"Never mind," I said, "tell me what happened. I want details. Bloody details." Every time I think of what that twisted fuck did to my girl, I'm furious that *I* didn't go track him down. It would have been worth getting expelled from the Academy to end that piece of shit.

Lev made a good point, though. If I'm thrown out of college, who's here to protect Tatiana? Aleks sure as fuck isn't going to do it. So that's why he went to Florida instead of me.

"He's a former Navy SEAL," Lev said, voice thick with derision. "He looked good on paper, I guess. The school outsources the torture-interrogation testing because several of the professors refuse to do it, and the others-"

"Would enjoy it far too much," I interrupt.

"The interrogator was sloppy," Lev hissed. "Poor oversight. Hates women, especially those who defy him. The fact that Tatiana refused to speak after something as brutal as ripping out her toenail made him spiteful. He was out to teach her a lesson." He chuckles, it sounds low, ugly. "She head-butted him during the capture phase and flattened his nose. He intended to make her break right away."

"I'm sure you got this out of him in the slowest, most painful way?" I grin, bloodlust surging through me. The memory of Tatiana slumped in that chair, with her bloody foot and bruised cheeks will haunt me forever.

"Oh, yes."

There was a world of satisfaction in those two words.

"He was *zhalkiy,* pathetic," Lev sneers, "I only cut off two fingers before he was begging me to stop. Offering me money."

"Tell me you took your time," I said.

"Hours."

"Thank you," I said. I meant it from the bottom of my heart.

Tatiana...

After another twenty-four hours in the clinic, I was scratching at the walls like a demented cat, ready to get out. Mariya came to visit and helped me shower and wash my hair. Lucca has to help me to the bathroom, and that is mortifying enough.

"I heard your fiancé and his dad showed up," she said, brushing my hair carefully. It's thick and gleefully rats up with the slightest provocation, and we're working with a week's worth of bedhead.

"He's horrible," I shudder.

"Aleksandr?"

"No! Of course not. His father. The two times I've met him, I don't think his eyes ever left my chest."

"So disrespectful," she agreed. "I know Maksim has been forced to work with him a couple of times and hates his guts. He's a nightmare."

"Thanks, you're making me feel so much better about my future," I said. I buried my face in my hands, which yanks the brush out of her hand.

"No sudden movements! God, I've trimmed hedges more manageable than your hair."

"Please," I scoff, "like you even know when your gardener's shed is."

The brushing slows. "We have to talk about it," she says gently, "are you really planning to go through with this?"

"With what?" I evade.

Leaving the brush stuck in one of my snarls, Mariya comes around to sit in front of me. "You can't avoid this and you know it. When Lucca came racing across campus, holding you, I had never seen anyone so terrified. Those first couple of days, when we…" she turned her head and I realized she was trying not to cry.

"When we thought you were going to die, he refused to leave you, and you held onto his hand. You wouldn't let go, even unconscious and barely able to breathe. You love each other so much. In one of those sappy 'until the end of time' songs sort of ways. There's no way you can go through with this arrangement."

"Really?" I want to scream, be angry, throw things, but I'm too weak to do anything but shake. "Do you think I want to, Mari? You're like me, you're in an arranged marriage, too. What do you think would happen if you marched up to Maksim and said, 'Hey, I'm madly in love with someone else and gave him my virginity and anyway, I want to break these unbreakable vows between Bratvas and marry him instead.' How do you think *your* Pakhan would take it?"

"Well, you got together with Lucca before the arrangement, so the virginity thing doesn't count," she said. "Do you remember my brother Yuri's arranged marriage to that girl from the Balabonov Bratva? Tania stood in the middle of the cathedral and shouted 'I object!'"

"Oh, I remember *that*, I was there." I said happily, "best not-wedding ever."

"Yuri and the Balabanov Bratva managed to make an agreement that worked for both sides-"

"With a huge loss of face," I interrupt.

"That turned into nothing," she retorted, "Yuri and Tania are proof that true love can triumph over even the bullshit Bratva alliances."

"Your family wasn't under fire, Mari. When my parents were murdered, it was just the beginning. Roman and Ilia are no closer to finding out who's behind trying to destroy our family, or who tried to kidnap me, and-"

"What?" She grabbed my arm. "When? When did this happen?"

"The night they blew up my parent's plane," I whispered, looking at the open door to my room. I don't need anyone overhearing us. "They tried to kill Ilia and Roman at the same time, it was a wide-scale coordinated attack."

"So, it must be more than some rival Bratva, or whoever," she said, eyes narrowed. I can always tell when Mariya's analyzing something because her eyes dart back and forth, like she's watching a tennis match. "Multiple targets, several different enemies, but they're all colluding against the Aslanov Bratva. Look, this is my turn to tell you something that can never be repeated, okay?"

"Of course," I nodded.

"The same thing happened to my family. Maksim needed alliances and that's how I ended up promised to Konstantin. The important thing here is that there were three different syndicates, too. Lucca will know about this. His brother Dante-"

"Yes!" I interrupted, "Lucca told me about it. He said his parents were murdered at a New Year's Eve party. His older brothers were there, too. Dante was trying to kill them all."

"Right," she nodded, "it was also a rival Bratva, the Sokolovs, and even worse was the Irish mob, the O'Connells, *pust' oni gniyut v adu*, may they rot in hell. Maksim's wife, Ella? Her own brother was an O'Connell and he was in on it. So, these syndicates all stood to gain something, and they weren't afraid to murder their own family to get it."

"What a mess," I sighed, "thank god your family figured it out before those scum managed to kill you all."

"There's two things that feel off here," she said, her eyes darting back and forth like a pinball machine. "You getting kidnapped is one. According to everything you told me, they killed - or tried to kill - everyone but you. Someone must have been planning to marry you and take control in that way.

"The second thing that seems so weird to me... I haven't heard anything about your brothers seeking alliances with any of the other Russian families. You're one of the Moscow Six, for god's sake! And they aligned with the sleaziest Bratva in Russia? Have they reached out to anyone else? Any of the Mafia families? The Irish? Hell, the Cosa Nostra? The Scots? Your father did business all over the world!"

"They definitely caught Roman on his back foot," I said, "I'm pretty sure he wasn't planning to become the *Pakhan* for a long time. My father was very 'you'll become *Pakhan* when you pry it from my cold dead fingers,' and- *bozhe moy*, I can't believe I just said something so dreadful." I put my hands against my eyes, trying to force the tears back.

She grabs my wrists, pulling my hands away from my face. "Look. The Toscano Mafia is insanely powerful. They would be a great alliance for your family, and let's not forget the important connection between the Morozov Bratva and the Toscanos. Through Kon and me, the Turgenev Bratva. There are all kinds of complex interconnectedness here that Roman may not be aware of. If we speak to our families, we can offer something much bigger to your family's Bratva. Plus, Roman and Ilia will certainly have a lot more help finding out who's behind this."

"As always, fam, you're a genius. You really are disgustingly brilliant," I said.

"Thank you," she preens.

"Your brother Yuri's situation aside, you *know* how absolute the vows of an arranged marriage between Bratvas are. If we break them, our family has no honor. No other family will have anything to do with us. You know I'm right."

"Well, I don't know what the deal was between Yuri and the Balabanovs. I never got that much information, though you'd be impressed with how much my sisters-in-law tell me. There was some combination of… like… blackmail and mutually assured destruction. As for you, it's almost March, which means we have three months or so before Aleksandr graduates and you're forced to get married."

"Meaning?" I said, so pathetically grateful to see even the slightest glimmer of hope.

Mariya smiles, her eyes tilting up like a fox's. "We have ninety days to find a way for Roman to cut a deal with the Rostova Bratva that does not include you."

CHAPTER TWENTY-EIGHT

In which there are warm baths and many questions.

Moulin Rouge Soundtrack - Come What May

Lucca...

When Dr. Giardo finally released Tatiana two days later, she begged me to help her back to student housing early in the morning, saying she didn't want to be center-ring in the Academy freak show. I got why, stares and false sympathy are irritating as fuck, no matter who they are directed at.

She tries to protest when I carry her, and I ignore it. All I can think of is racing across the lawn to the clinic with her in my arms ten days ago.

When I turn in the direction of the men's side of the building, she stiffens. "I should really go to my room," she said weakly.

"Don't worry," I said, "I don't intend to soil your virtue."

"You already did that," she interrupts.

"I'm taking care of you. And as I recall, you were an enthusiastic participant in the soiling."

"Let's not call it that," she sighs, but she doesn't argue as I carry her up the stairs to my place. "Is Konstantin going to mind that I'm in his space?"

"No. He and Mariya have been really worried about you, so I expect she'll be over a lot, too."

"On the bright side, Athena always wanted to have her own place, she's sort of getting her wish," she said. "Also, she is very loud and I'm happy not to have to hear it."

"What, like her music?" I ask.

"No, her... you know," she said, flushing a little.

Given how pale she's been, the extra color in her skin is a relief. I'll just have to keep embarrassing her. "You mean when she's fucking?"

"Will you stop that?"

Yeah, she definitely looks healthier when she's blushing.

"Go over the six fastest-acting plant-based poisons with me again," Tatiana said, rubbing her forehead.

"We've run through prep for this test three times," Mariya whines, clearly bored out of her mind. "Let's do some plotting instead."

Konstantin looks up from his gaming console. "Plotting?"

Mariya and Tatiana talked us through their conversation from yesterday.

"I've thought about it since my genius friend," Tatiana nods at Mariya, who's attempting to appear modest, "laid this all out for me, and it's raised more questions. Why *did* my brother seek an alliance with the weakest of the Moscow Six? My father had connections everywhere, surely Roman could have reached out to more reputable ones."

"With attacks coming in from all directions, Roman can't know who to trust, especially if your father kept so much of his business from him," I said.

"Yeah, but Roman and Ilia knew one of the biggest threats was to Tati, right?" Kon asked. "I mean, the reason she's here is to keep from being kidnapped. Did he just pick the Rostova Bratva because Leonid has a son of marriageable age?"

"Yeah…" Tatiana rubbed her forehead again, she was exhausted, I could tell. "My father spent a lot of time with Leonid. I know they did business. Maybe Roman and Ilia decided he was the first, safe choice."

"Baby, it's late and if you're going to get better, you've got to sleep," I said, rising from the couch and stretching. Before she could argue, I scooped her up and carried her to my room.

"Night night, Nurse Toscano!" Konstantin called.

"Flip him off for me, would you? My hands are full." I said to Tatiana, laughing when she used both hands.

Carrying her into the bathroom, I sat her on the counter and started the water in the tub. "How about a hot bath?"

"Oh, that would be so nice," she sighed. "That horrible little shower in the clinic was not enough."

Leaning closer, I took a long, pointed sniff. "Well, I wasn't going to say anything…"

"You are a very bad boyfriend," she said severely.

"Is that what I am?" I grinned, lifting her into the water.

"Only if you get in with me," she said, wiggling her fingers at me. I have my clothes off and I'm sliding in behind her in seconds. "Thank you," she sighed, turning to her side so she could curl against me like a cat, resting her cheek on my chest.

"It's just a bath," I chuckled.

"No, it's not," she said, "you saved my life. Again. You looked out for me even after I was promised to someone else."

My arms tightened around her, thinking of her tied to that chair, unconscious. *"Piccolo bacio,"* I sighed, "I will always come for you. There is no one else for me. There will never be anyone else but you."

"I remember sitting there with that hood on, so cold… I couldn't stop shaking, it was bone deep, and I just…" She laced her fingers with mine, "I thought about you, how you would fall in love with someone else, have a family with them. And I would be nothing more than a breeder and an ornamental wife for the rest of my life and I…" her voice choked on a sob.

"I think I was already sick, but this little voice kept whispering to me, that if I just let it happen, if I just drifted away… it would be all right if I was gone. Roman would think of something else. I couldn't picture my life without you. Not one with any meaning, anyway."

I can't move, listening to her voice growing sadder, and quieter and I can't take it anymore. "Listen to me," I said urgently, "don't you ever think that way again, ever! We will find a way out of this."

The same cold terror I felt in the Catacombs when I found her gripped me again. She would rather die, torn between disappointing her brother or losing me. "There is always a way, my sweet girl, I promise you. We'll find it. But you can never let yourself lose hope like that again. Swear it."

Tatiana looks up at me, her wet eyes are forest green, glowing with little flecks of gold. "I vow to you that I won't let myself think that way again. Thank you for not giving up on me."

Lifting her by her hips, I turned her to straddle me so that I could hold her to me, squeezing her as tightly as I dared.

"You're so nice and warm," she sighed. "I love you."

Why is my chest so tight? Like a fist, twisting my heart. "I love you, too. Always."

Her hand slides between us, gently holding my cock, which is already growing hard. "No, baby you have to take your hand off me," I groan.

"I don't want to," she whispered, kissing my neck, my jaw. "Will you put it inside me?"

"You're not well, you just got out of the clinic–"

"This will make me feel better, I promise," she insists, moving her hips, pressing against me.

Damn her, she's irresistible even though I'm cursing myself for giving in to her. "You let me do the work, then."

The warm water around us slicks along her pale skin, making it glow in the dim light of the room as I slide my hands along her ass, squeezing as I lift her, bringing her breasts to my mouth as I suck on her pretty, rosy nipples.

Tatiana wraps her arms around my neck, "I've missed this so much," she sighs, pressing harder against me. Moving my fingers to check her, I feel her slick, thicker than the water and making it so easy to slide the head of my cock into her. My piercing pushes against her silky walls and she moans. I want to remember every second of this, I want to go slow, moving an inch at a time, even when her hips move invitingly, trying to draw me in. "Don't try to rush," I said, kissing her wet skin, "it will be so much better if you can hang on."

Dio, she's even tighter, more snug than I remember, squeezing my dick, holding it inside her. It takes forever to get all the way inside her, my balls pressing up against her, and every second is better than the last. The thought that I almost lost this feeling, that I almost lost her makes me groan, wrapping my arms around her.

"*Moya dorogaya, moya lyubov'*, my sweetheart, my love," she moans, "please move, I need you to."

Angling my hips up, I can tell when my piercing rubs against her G spot as she gasps and moans louder, pushing down against me. "I'm not going to move, you're going to come just like this," I promise her, kissing her and slipping my tongue inside her mouth to play with hers. "Squeeze against me." She does, and my head drops to her shoulder with a groan, trying not to come.

"Again," I order moving my hand off her ass and between us, circling her clit with my thumb.

"Your piercing is... *Bozhe moy*, it feels so good," she moans.

I hold her hips steady, keeping the head of my cock inside her right where it is. "Good girl, you're doing so well for me," I tell her, "just like that. Make yourself come."

Everything narrows down to this moment, being inside her again, the warmth of the water, the incredible heat of her pussy, and her moans and gasps in my ear. She's happy here. She belongs here, with me.

"There you are," I whisper, gently biting her neck, "I can feel you ripple against me. You're ready to come, aren't you baby? Squeeze one last time and you'll come harder than you ever have." My thumb rotates over her clit very slowly, and then I press down firmly as she comes, crying out, shaking, holding me tightly like she might fly away, and I feel my come squeezed out of me and my heart skips a beat, it's so intense.

We stay like this, holding each other and shaking a bit, and then I let out the cooling water to fill the tub with hot water again, carefully washing her. I keep my cock still inside her until I reluctantly, carefully lift her off me and wash between her legs. She's so relaxed, and I laugh as I help her out of the tub and carry her to bed, helping her put on one of my t-shirts and some underwear.

"Here, you need to take your meds, and then you can sleep," I hold the glass of water for her, watching her drink before sliding in behind her, pulling up the blankets.

"You take such good care of me," she mumbles drowsily, "I love you."

"I love you," I kiss the top of her head, "and I'll always take care of you."

Listening to her soft breathing, I think about how strange it is.

I've never taken care of anyone but myself. I want to take care of Tatiana for the rest of my life.

Tatiana...

When I open my eyes, the gray light of dawn is peeking between the dark blue curtains in Lucca's bedroom. His long body is pressed against my back, my butt cradled firmly against his pelvis and his cock lies between us, still thick and heavy.

Aleksandr.

I groan silently. This goes against every rule, every standard I was raised by. But I know he doesn't want this any more than I do.

Sliding carefully out of bed, I freeze for a moment as his fingers flex against my hip.

"Where are you going?" he mumbles.

"Bathroom," I whisper, "go back to sleep."

I know he's exhausted too, he's been caring for me non-stop while keeping up with his classes.

Taking my phone into the bathroom, I lean against the counter and text Aleks.

Hey, I'm out of the clinic. Can we talk today? It's important.

He replies immediately. *Yes. I'm out running. Are you well enough to meet me?*

The bench by the greenhouse, I text back. *Give me fifteen minutes.*

CHAPTER TWENTY-NINE

In which it is time to face the music.

Tatiana...

Aleks is pacing by the bench by the time I manage to dress and sneak out of Lucca's room. I hate how slow I am, how long it takes to do anything, and I must look terrible because he looks alarmed when he sees me.

"Der'mo! Shit, look at you." He pulls off his grey sweatshirt and puts it on the stone bench before helping me sit on it.

"I'm not an invalid," I grumble.

"You look like one."

"Thank you for your refreshing honesty, Aleks," I sigh.

"Sorry." He sits next to me, giving me plenty of room. "Seriously, how do you feel?"

"Better, thanks. I'm being treated like I'm breakable, Lucca won't let me-" I shut up, pressing my lips together.

"It's okay," he says gently. "He saved your life. I don't deserve to be your fiancé."

"You didn't know," I said, patting his arm. "None of this is your fault. We need to talk about it, though."

"I know," he said, leaning back with a groan. "This is fucked up. My father's marriage to my mother was arranged, and he was the one to broker the alliance. He's never shown any interest in doing this to me, and suddenly we're engaged and he's looking at you like he wants to-" He was kind enough to stop before I gagged.

"Yeah, I noticed that," I said. "Your father is a creep. No offense."

"None taken," he sighed. "My father *is* a pig. He's vicious, and a bully. There's something here that I'm missing. He hates your family."

A ball of ice forms in my gut. "He does?"

"He always used to rant about your father, how he didn't deserve his success. Getting an alliance with the Aslanov Bratva is good, but…" Aleks shakes his head. "The way he looked at you in the clinic, as if he was making sure his asset was intact."

"I've been brainstorming with Mariya, trying to think of something that your father would accept to maintain the alliance without the two of us having to go through with this," I said.

He shakes his head glumly. "I suspect he would enjoy ruining your family over the broken engagement even more than having access through our union."

"Aleks…" I said slowly, "Do you think your father is part of this attack against my family?"

He looked out over the ocean. The water's gray today and the waves are thrashing against the rocks. He's very handsome in his way, but the grief twisting his features makes him look ten years older.

"Yes. I do."

We sit for a moment, watching the turmoil of the ocean. Finally, he stands up. "There are people in his organization that are sympathetic to me. I think I can get some answers with promises for more power for them in the future and some cash."

"I can help with the money," I offer.

He shook his head. "I've got it. Call your brothers. See if they'll talk to you."

"Okay." He nods and turns to walk away. "Aleks?"

"Hmm?"

"Thank you. For what it's worth, you will make an amazing husband one day," I said.

A strange smile crosses over his lips. "I hope so."

Sitting for a while longer, I try to organize my thoughts, wondering if I could approach Ilia first. Finally, too cold to stay longer, I stand up and realize I still have Aleksandr's sweatshirt. As I pick it up, his phone falls out of the pocket.

"Crap!" I stuff it in my coat, looking around to make sure no one's watching.

It's not until I'm almost back to Lucca's room when his phone cheerfully 'pings!' and I curse, pulling it out to silence it. It's a text with an image. A picture of a man, handsome. Dark, curly hair and olive skin, probably Mediterranean. And naked, with his dick in his hand and a smile.

I miss you, baby. June can't come soon enough.

"Where were you!?" Lucca comes striding out of his room in his boxer briefs, looking outraged and I try not to laugh.

"I'm sorry, I went out to talk to Aleks." He's already pulling off my coat, patting my arms and back like he's expecting bullet holes, or something.

"You're freezing," he says accusingly, pulling me over to the couch.

"No, I'm fine, I promise," I said, watching him build up the fire. He's so beautiful, the colorful tattoo of a sea serpent that coils over his back moves as his muscles do, biceps bulging as he adds wood to the fireplace.

"What did he say?" he asks, coming back to sit with me.

Eyeing his gorgeous expanse of bare skin, I ask, "Do you want to put some clothes on first?"

The conceited bastard. He grins knowingly. "Am I distracting you, baby?"

"No!" I scoffed. "A little. Stop gloating!" I call after him as he goes to get dressed.

"What did Aleks say?"

Lucca made me some good, strong coffee and I sipped at it gratefully. "He agrees with us," I said, enjoying the warmth of the mug in my hands, "he thinks his father is part of whoever's trying to destroy my family." Shuddering, I said, "I wonder if his father was the one who tried to kidnap me that night. Would Leonid have forced me to marry *him?*"

"Maybe that was the original plan," Lucca says, jaw tight.

"Aleks says he has people he trusts in his family's Bratva. He's going to try to get someone to talk and see what they know. He suggested I call my brothers."

I won't mention what I discovered on Aleksandr's phone. That's no one's business but his. While some syndicates have shed their irrational hatred of gay members, the Russian Bratvas have not. His father is very likely to kill him - in some horrible way - as a lesson to his people if Aleks is found out. I'll give him his phone back today with his sweatshirt and a vow to take his secret to the grave.

"This is good," Lucca says, running his fingers through his hair. "At least he's on our side. He doesn't want this union either, then?"

"No, he does not," I said, maybe a little too emphatically. He looks at me oddly, but doesn't question me.

"Why don't I bring breakfast up to you, *piccolo bacio?*" he offers, kissing my hand.

"You're spoiling me!" I protest, laughing. "I have to go back to class today."

"All the more reason to save your strength and have breakfast here," he counters, and I relax against him gratefully.

Lucca...

After walking Tatiana to her first class, I spot Mateo glaring at me from across the grass commons. He's looked like shit ever since the Dean's "disciplinary action." I'm still not ruling out killing him this summer once I'm off the Academy grounds. The 'eye for an eye' law here is too solid and I'm not going to risk getting killed in retaliation and leaving Tatiana alone.

"You have a problem, *pezzo di merda*, you piece of shit?"

He sneers, turning away and heading into the gym.

He's been lurking around more, and it's concerning. Since having his hand cut off, he'd done everything he could to stay on the opposite side of the campus from us. He's a problem that I'm going to take care of, sooner than later.

Two weeks later...

Mateo's bizarre behavior starts making sense with a text to Aleksandr's phone.

I know about you, you sick fuck. I'm going to tell everybody.

Aleks burst into the suite, face pale.

"What is it? Are you okay?" Tatiana hurried over to him, putting a hand on his arm.

Don't be an asshole, I thought, wanting to punch him, *she's already chosen you.*

Wordlessly, he showed her the text. "Oh, no." She shook her head, "No, no no no no! Not him! How could he have possibly found out?"

"I don't know," he said, voice tight with dread, "but I have to stop him."

"We'll help," I said instantly. I still don't like their friendship, but he's accepted my relationship with Tati and I owe him. "What does he think he knows?"

They exchange a long look. "You can tell him. Lucca is trustworthy."

Aleks pushes his hair back with a shaking hand. "I'm gay. I don't know how he could have found out, I've been so careful, I- *Fuck!*" he shouted.

"Okay?" I shrug until I realize who I'm talking to. The next in line for the throne as *Pakhan* cannot be gay. "That fucker. We'll figure this out. Let me get you a drink. You need it."

Tatiana's already pulling out her laptop. "He obviously has a way to communicate illegally with somebody."

"Don't be judgmental," I said, "so do we."

Ignoring me, she does something complicated that involves moving in and out of multiple tabs on her computer. "I miss my triple monitors…" she murmured. "Given the likelihood that he bought the phone off Mark Tanner," she says, "I'm going to track backward from his WIFI splitter and see…"

Watching her work is fascinating, her slender fingers flying over the keyboard, following strings of code. Heaving a sigh, she looks up at us. "It's going to take a while. It would be faster if you text him, telling him you'll pay him. Do not specify about what! We don't need any admissions, all right?"

"I'm just going to fucking kill him," Aleks said.

"Not at school," I said automatically. "If you get caught, they'll execute you. Let's find out exactly what he knows first."

He laced his fingers over his head, walking to the window. "I don't fucking believe this." I hand him a bottle of beer and he drains half of it in a gulp.

"Looks like we're going to need something stronger," I said, heading back to my bar cart.

Aleks sends the message to Mateo, and we pace, waiting for an answer while Tati continues to untangle all the cell signals. "We just need a ping..." she murmurs, "Once I have the signal I can de-encrypt it."

It takes an hour before that asshole texts back. "You know he's been staring at the text, gloating," Aleks mutters bitterly, showing us the text.

You perverted fuck. What makes you think you have enough money? Sending the pictures to daddy will be worth so much more.

"I'm going to kill him," Aleks says, striding toward the door.

"Hey, hey, hold up!" I step in front of him. "He's not telling anyone right now; he's having too much fun torturing you. Let Tati work."

"Um... the picture I saw," she ventures, "your boyfriend looks Mediterranean?"

"Yes," he finished his glass of vodka and I silently refill it.

"Where does he live?"

Aleks groans. "In London, but Augustu's family is in Sardinia. The island next to Sicily."

"The odds are insane," I agree, "but if his asshole buddies - who got sent back home to Sicily - have any connection in any possible way... You've exchanged pictures?"

He nods.

"First thing," Tatiana interrupts. "Have Augustu delete every picture of you, including anything of you two together, even if it looks innocent, okay? Let me double-check your phone first and make sure your texting didn't download any spyware."

"Damn, look at my genius," I murmur, kissing her.

"Thank you for being here for him," she whispers, kissing me back.

Aleksandr's phone dings cheerfully again.

You're about to have so much more to worry about than your little boytoy, you bitch.

"What the fuck does that mean?" I said, unease spreading through me. It has something to do with Tatiana, I know it.

"Let's focus on this," she says, looking worried. "He's got at least a dozen pictures on his phone, Aleks. This is bad."

"What can we do?" His grip is so tight on the glass that I'm surprised it hasn't shattered.

"Okay, okay, um…" Tatiana checks something else on her laptop. "Now that I have him, I can erase the data, it's from one of those little assholes in his entourage. But they would still have it. If we get a hold of it, I can send a virus back via text that'll wipe the scumbag's phone."

"You can't set up a meeting," I said, "he'll be prepared for an ambush. We have to catch him somewhere."

"We can track his phone signal now," Tatiana says. "Which means we have to follow him until we can get him out of view of one of the surveillance cameras."

"Wait until tonight," I said. "We'll have better luck. Can you disable any of the cameras?"

She shakes her head, miserable. "I can't even figure out their system, much less how to hack into it. Not by tonight, anyway."

"Then tonight," Aleks says, cold and composed. "I'll handle it tonight."

"*We'll* handle it," I told him. "You can't do this alone."

CHAPTER THIRTY

In which blackmail and murder are no match for a nice, sharp lock-blade.

Mold - Long Shiny Knives

Tatiana...

"You know the easiest way to do this is to use me as bait." I said flatly.

"That's not going to fucking happen," Lucca cut me off.

"Absolutely not!" Aleks said, looking furious at the thought.

"Look. We don't have a lot of time," I said, "Mateo is unstable and impulsive. He may have a way to contact your father already. We must get the pictures off his phone. After that, he's just an asshole with no proof."

"That's not happening," Lucca shook his head.

"We don't have time to get all tricky here." I sighed. "You'll both be following me. Let's go to dinner. Make sure he sees me leaving - alone - and one of you follow me, and one of you follow him. We have to get him. It must be *now*. I just... I feel it. It must be tonight."

They're both frowning at me, and I shake my head. "We're going down to eat, do you hear me?"

Dinner would have been delicious - lamb and wild greens - but all I could think about was not looking at Mateo, gloating in the corner and ignoring Tansey who was trying to chat him up between gulps of merlot.

When I stand up, Lucca and Aleks do as well. "Such nice manners," I said teasingly. "I've got to grab something from the library, I'll see you later."

There is an audible grinding of teeth that I would find amusing if it wasn't for the fact that I am hoping that Mateo - that evil prick - is going to follow me. He wouldn't go after Aleks, he's a coward with only one hand. But he'll probably assume terrifying me with the news is the next best thing.

The island comes alive at night. The wind is even more vicious as it whips around the buildings and lashes the unwary walker with the frigid air. The crows that gather on the cliffs are vociferous talkers when it's as dark as their glossy feathers. And my steps on the limestone path echo, like an extra set of footsteps keeping time with mine.

I'm almost to the library and nearing a small grouping of trees and thick underbrush where I hope the little troll is hiding.

"I keep wondering which one of you Leonid Rostova will kill first. You, for being a whore, or his son for fucking men?"

At least he's predictable...

"Why are you talking to me?" I snap, "Are you looking for another trip to the Dean's office for a date with her table saw?"

Mateo's eyes are glittering, he looks feverish and excited. "Maybe if you suck my dick, I'll think about not telling the *Pakhan* of the Rostova Bratva that you're a whore. Because that's something your asshole brothers could never cover up. But your piece of shit fiancé? No fucking mercy."

"What are you talking about?" I ask.

"You don't know about his little boyfriend? Of course, he looks cozy with Toscano, maybe they're fucking, too." Mateo laughs, it's high and he sounds wildly excited.

"You're lying," I scoff, "that's disgusting."

"*Stupida puttana*, you stupid whore!" Mateo takes a sudden step toward me and I back away, keeping track of where we are in the shadows. When he thrusts his arm at me, I have to stifle a shriek. He loves this, of course. Grinning, he turns his phone to show me the screen with Aleks and his lover, arms around each other.

"Leonid Rostova will skin his precious son alive for fucking guys," he says happily, "and I am going to be the one to-"

There's a glint of silver behind him as a shadow materializes from the darkness. Mateo staggers and his eyes bulge horribly. His mouth opens, a long trail of spit nearly reaching his shirt before he's yanked backward into the trees, their spindly arms reaching down in the wind to embrace him.

Lucca...

I come from a family of assassins. It's how our *famiglia* have made our fortunes in Italy as far back as the 15th century. We have always been obsessed with knives of every kind. Both of my brothers have a huge collection.

As for me? I've found that a simple lock blade works just fine. It takes less than three seconds to step up behind Mateo, stab him in the left kidney, twist as I pull it out, then drive the blade into his right one, another twist and he's dead.

It takes the victim a couple of seconds to realize what happened, and then the agony slams down on them like a hammer, and the few minutes left in their life are spent in excruciating pain. My only regret - as I drag Mateo into the trees - is that I can't make him suffer longer.

Aleks recovers more quickly than Tatiana, who is gaping at me in shock. He scoops up Mateo's phone off the ground where he dropped it as I stabbed him and hands it to her.

"Come on," I whisper, "we have ten minutes to get him to the blind spot by the cliffs before the guards walk the route." I wrap a sweatshirt from the lost and found at the gym around Mateo's waist to keep him from leaving a blood trail. He's still alive, his eyes reflecting his agony, his legs and arms already useless. Throwing him over my shoulder in a fireman's hold, I nod to Tatiana to lead the way, while Aleks follows behind us to make sure we're not seen.

"Stop!" he whispers. We all freeze as two students walk into the library, laughing about one of the professors. "Go on," he hisses when it's clear.

Tatiana walks lightly, stepping into the shadows as gracefully as a dancer, moving from one pool of darkness to the next, keeping us out of sight of the surveillance cameras. When we make it to the edge of the path that crumbles to the edge of the cliff, Aleks grabs Mateo's legs and we swing him between us, as far out as we can hurl him.

His limp body disappears into the darkness, falling to be torn to pieces by the rocks and the ocean.

"Come back over here," Tati whispers, "the guards could be by any minute." Once we're past the library, I take her hand, my finger stroking her rabbiting pulse in her wrist.

"We're going to meet up with Konstantin and Mariya in front of the fireplace downstairs by the entryway," I said quietly. "We're going to make sure we're visible for the next hour. Do you both understand?"

Aleks shrugs, he's much more at ease than I expected him to be. Tati's eyes are huge, but she nods firmly.

When we step into the warmth of the student housing building, Konstantin and Mariya are lounging in front of the fire, sipping wine, and singing some Russian song that I'm fairly certain - knowing Kon - is filthy.

"There you are!" Mariya calls, "Come over and have some wine before this disreputable drunk finishes all three bottles."

We get comfortable, and Tatiana translates the lyrics to the song for me. Which are impressively filthy, just as I expected. The wind outside rises to a howl.

Camilla, who's just joined us, cocks her head, listening as it rips around the building. "That sounds like one hell of a storm brewing," she says.

"Winter storms on the island are vicious," I shrug, "the waves cover everything in a coat of ice."

She shivers, rubbing her arms. "One of you big, strong men go throw a couple of those logs on the fire, *s'il vous plaît*."

We sit around the fire till midnight, drinking and swapping stories with the others, and then I pull Tatiana to her feet. "Goodnight all," I say, sweeping her up in my arms. She rolls her eyes elaborately, waving goodnight to the rest over my shoulder.

Safely inside my room, she turns on me, eyes blazing. "You killed him! I thought we were just stealing his phone," she hissed.

"Mateo was never going to stop," I said. "It doesn't matter whether Aleks' father believed him or not, there would always be something. He had to die. Are you forgetting his threats to you tonight?"

She shook her head.

"Are you afraid of me?" I ask slowly.

"How could I be? You did what you did to protect Aleks and me," she said. "How can… that was seconds, a blink of my eyes. How do you learn…?"

"Are you forgetting who I come from?" I said, walking toward her, backing her into the bed. She gives a little yelp when her knees hit the mattress and she sits down abruptly. "The Toscanos are assassins. We can pretend we own real estate, clubs, restaurants. But we're killers. No amount of legitimate business will ever wipe our hands clean."

"You killed for me," she said sadly.

Kneeling in front of her, I stroke her legs. "That's not the first life I've taken. It won't be the last."

Resting her hands on my cheeks, Tatiana kisses me. "I hope that's the last one you ever have to take to protect me."

Pulling off my sweater, I lean over her, pressing her back against the bed as I unbutton her shirt.

I don't know why I woke up, only that a quick glance at my watch tells me it's 3:48 a.m. and the space next to me is empty.

"Tati, are you okay?" I rub my face, rising and heading to the bathroom. She's not there. Ripping open the door, I search the main room. "Baby?"

Tatiana is gone.

CHAPTER THIRTY-ONE

In which Dean Christie really has had enough.

The Interrupters - She's Kerosene

Tatiana...

Waking with a jolt, I look at my phone, already knowing the time will be 3:36 a.m.

Lucca's lying next to me, his blankets kicked off, as usual. His body gleams in the moonlight, outlining his amazing musculature and those wicked tattoos. How does he sleep so soundly after having killed a man tonight?

His casual lethality was shocking at first, but I shouldn't be surprised. Lucca is the most lethal man on campus, and there's been a barely controlled savagery roiling under his harsh expression since the day I met him. He's used that strength to protect me, time and time again. He asked if I was afraid of him tonight. How could I possibly be, after everything he's done for me?

Slipping out of bed, I stretched, smiling at the ache between my thighs. Thinking about the day ahead, I realize that my meager stash of clothes here at Lucca's are all filthy. Pulling on my jeans and one of his sweaters, I quietly leave his suite. I'll just head over to my place and grab some clean clothes; I'll be back before he wakes up.

I'm just descending the stairs to the main entrance when Camilla races across the floor. "Oh, *dieu merci,* thank god, there you are! There's something wrong with Mariya, I think she is very ill, help me!"

"Where is she?" I gasped, following her outside.

"At the doctor's, hurry!" Her grip on my hand is surprisingly strong.

A man's arm wraps around my waist from behind and his hand over my mouth. Instinctively, I throw my head back, trying to break his nose. It might have worked on that interrogator, but this guy is prepared, moving his head out of the way. I see the cloth, sickly-smelling, slam down over my mouth. I fight against it, bucking and kicking violently, but the lethargy spreads through me, feeling too heavy to fight. Before my eyes droop shut, I realize Camilla's the one holding it.

Lucca...

"Kon, wake up! Tatiana's gone."

He bolts upright in bed, instantly awake. "What do you mean? She's been with you." He's already yanking on his clothes and I feel a surge of gratitude. "How long has she been missing?"

"I woke up three minutes ago, she wasn't here," I said. "I'm going to check her room, wake up Aleks and Mariya, and start looking outside."

Racing out the door, I take the stairs down two at a time, calling her number. When it picks up, my heart leaps, but it's Konstantin's voice. "Her phone is still here in your room."

"Fuck!" I shove my phone in my pocket and race up the stairs to the women's side of the building. Athena answers as I'm pounding on the door.

"What the hell?" she snaps, "Do you know what time it is?"

I push past her, "Is Tatiana here?"

"No..." she watches me search Tatiana's bedroom. "She hasn't been here since you brought her back from the clinic."

"She was in bed with me, I just woke up and she's gone," I said.

"I'll help you look," she said, pulling on her trainers. "What direction?"

"I'm going to head for the front gate," I said, running my hands through my hair and heading for the door. "Will you check the medical clinic?"

"On it," Athena says, racing down the stairs behind me.

There are lights blazing in the main building as I run past it, and one of the guards steps out to block me as I near the gate. "Dean Christie would like to speak with you."

"Not now," I said, "I'm looking-"

"She knows that Miss Aslanova is missing," he interrupts me. "Come with me."

Grinding my teeth, I follow him.

Dean Christie is unapologetically wearing cow-print pajamas with a matching robe, sitting behind her massive desk. "Mr. Toscano, do come in. We're just rounding up Mr. Turgenev and Mr. Rostov now. I have sent Miss Dukakis back to her room."

There's a cold pit forming in my gut and I'm beginning to realize the Dean knows so much more than she should.

"Come, Mr. Toscano, don't look so surprised. I run a school for the offspring of crime families, producing geniuses, sociopaths, and the occasional madman. You don't think I would take notice of what is happening at my school?"

"Where's Tatiana?" I said.

"She's on her way back to the campus, pursued, I believe, by her bodyguard," she said, straightening her notepad on the desktop.

There's a knock on the door, and it opens, two guards escort Kon, Aleks, and Mariya inside.

"Ah, and we add Miss Morozova to the list, of course. Come in," the Dean says genially, "Mr. Toscano is on the hot seat, so you may all be comfortable on the couches."

One of the guards whispers in her ear, and she nods. "Fetch Dr. Giardo and some clean clothes and bring her here."

"Are you talking about Tatiana?" I stood up, nearly knocking the chair over, "Is she hurt? What happened?"

"Be seated, Mr. Toscano," the Dean says, each word encased in ice. "Miss Aslanova is fine. Dr. Giardo is only here as a precaution."

The door to the antechamber opens, and I can faintly hear Tati speaking to Dr. Giardo and the loud, strident tones of Camilla. Looking over at Mariya, I raise my eyebrows.

"She wasn't helping us look," she whispers.

Camilla's voice is cut off abruptly, like someone gagged her. The Dean smiles pleasantly. "Miss Aslanova is in some *dishabille*, Miss Morozova, you may be excused to help her change. And no, Mr. Toscano, she is uninjured and you will not rise from that chair."

Mariya heads out the door, and we all wait in painful silence for another five minutes. When a guard escorts Tatiana in, I ignore the Dean's order and hurry over to help her sit down in an armchair by the fire. She's wearing large, shapeless sweatpants and a t-shirt, and her face is wet.

"Baby, what happened?" I whisper, cupping her cheek.

She leans into my hand. "I'm all right."

I kneel next to her and Lev enters the room, standing behind her.

"Well then, we're all here," the Dean says pleasantly. "As I was saying to Mr. Toscano, I'm disappointed in you all, assuming that I would not be keeping track of unusual activity on campus. Miss Aslanova was abducted by Miss Boucher and two other students who belong to her father's organization. She was drugged with chloroform, but vomited rather violently and regained consciousness before they arrived at the airstrip on the island. She was able to alert Mr. Khorkina, who dispatched most of the group before my guards intercepted the rest and brought them here."

She looked at Lev. "Impressive, really. There will always be a position here for you if you ever wish to change your employ." He smiled graciously.

"Well then," she says, folding her hands on the desk, "now that we have caught up on recent events, let's address why we are here. You three murdered Mateo Costa tonight and threw him over the cliffs."

"I did it," I interrupt her. "They knew nothing about it, I take complete responsibility."

"Hush, Mr. Toscano, I did not ask for your input," she said. "Here at the Ares Academy, I have a very strict two-strike system. Not for silly little things like fights, of course, but attempted rape and attempted blackmail and murder? That falls under my guidelines for termination of a student. Not expulsion. Termination."

The room is completely silent when she finishes speaking, so the gunshot in the antechamber is painfully loud. Mariya jumps and lets out a little shriek.

"Miss Boucher also falls under this category with attempted kidnapping and intent to cause severe bodily harm," the Dean continues casually. "Now then, I believe Mr. Khorkina has the floor?"

He looks a little surprised, but nods to her. "Thank you. Tatiana, I was already awake when your emergency alert went off, that's how I found you so quickly. Well done for keeping your head, even drugged. Your brothers have been kidnapped."

"What?" she gasped.

"I'm sorry." Lev said, "An hour ago, I received this from the

Bratva's *Derzhatel Obshchaka-*"

"Viktor?" she interrupts, trying to focus.

"Yes. He sent me this video." He holds up the phone for her, and Kon, Mariya, and Aleks risk the Dean's wrath to crowd in behind her.

It's a video of Tati's brothers, stripped to the waist and tied with their hands attached to hooks set in a concrete ceiling. They're both looking beat up and bloody, but conscious.

"The kidnappers are demanding possession of you, and one hundred million dollars within twenty-four hours or they will kill Ilia slowly and very painfully. If the demands are not met within the following twelve hours, they will torture and kill Roman," he said, mouth tight and furious.

"Where do I need to go?" Tatiana whispers.

"You're not going anywhere, that is not happening!" I snarl.

"No need," Aleks says. "I know where this is."

"What do you mean?" Tatiana gasps, "How would you know? It's a concrete box."

He laughs mirthlessly. "Lev, enlarge the image, bottom left-hand corner."

We're all crowding in, bumping heads, and trying to see the image as the Dean hums, sorting the pens in her desk drawer.

There's a brown stain on the wall. "See that splatter of blood?" Aleks said coldly. "I watched when it was made. I was sixteen. My father dragged me down to the sub-basement to watch him torture someone. The man didn't have any information to give, he just enjoyed inflicting that kind of agony. When he cut his throat and dropped him to the floor, the blood spray hit the wall. I remember thinking the shape of it looked like a rabbit, and what a stupid thing that was. Leonid never allows these rooms to be cleaned. He enjoys watching the blood stains grow over the years."

"*Gesù Cristo*, I'm sorry, Aleks," I murmured.

He looks at Tatiana and Lev. "This is at my father's ski chalet in Switzerland, I'm sure of it."

"Then let's go," Tatiana said. "Lev, who do we trust implicitly of the Bratva's soldiers?"

"I'll call my father," Kon said, "I know he'll want to be a part of this."

"And Maksim as well," Mariya added.

I only wish I could say the same for my brothers.

"Students of the Ares Academy may not leave the grounds for any reason during the academic year," Dean Christie interrupted.

"You must be joking," Tatiana snapped. "Then I withdraw from the academy."

"That will not be possible," the Dean said, "only a parent or legal guardian may remove a student from enrollment, no matter the student's age."

Tatiana shoots to her feet. "My *legal guardian* is about to be tortured and murdered! I am *leaving!*"

"However," Dean Christie cuts in, "I may, at my discretion, suspend or expel students for violation of the school code. I do believe that the three of you murdering a student and attempting to dispose of the evidence - even in self-defense - does fall under that category."

"I also participated in the murder and attempted coverup," Kon lies, standing up.

"I did as well," Mariya rises next to him.

"No, you didn't!" Tatiana snaps. Turning to the Dean, she pleads, "They didn't! They don't deserve any disciplinary action."

Mariya takes her hand. "You can't stop us, *sestra*. We're coming with you."

Dean Christie stands, surveying us. Even in those ridiculous cow pajamas, she has a certain gravitas going for her. "Very well. You are all suspended from the Ares Academy. Should you wish to continue here after your fourteen-day suspension, you should expect disciplinary action."

She must see the blood drain from my face. "None of it will involve my power tools." Waving her hands impatiently, she says. "Go! You have sixty minutes to leave the school grounds."

There's no way I'm letting Tatiana out of my sight, so I ask Konstantin to pack for me and I take Mariya and her back to their rooms. When Athena opens the door, Meiying and Jun Chen are there.

"Did you really think we were going to let you be suspended without us?" Meiying demanded.

"This isn't your fight," Tatiana said, hugging her fiercely. "We can't ask you to endanger your positions here to-"

"In our family, loyalty is above all things," Jin interrupts her. "You are family. We are here."

Tatiana hurries to her room to gather her things. "How did you know?" I asked.

Meiying tilts her head to Athena. "She came barreling down the hall, pounding on my door. We got most of the information from one of the guards who's... friendly."

"Is that what we call fucking the help now?" Jun smirks. He groans as his sister punches him in the back.

"It's called intelligence gathering, asshole!" Meiying snarls.

"Thank you," I said, gripping his forearm. "Pack and meet us by the front gate within fifteen minutes."

"We'll be there," he says, and they're out the door.

Racing back out of her room with a bulging backpack, Tatiana hugs Athena. "Thank you. So much. I don't know how to-"

"What's the matter?" Athena snaps. "You sound emotional. Are you getting emotional? I don't do that."

"Oh, sorry," Tatiana backs off. "But thank you."

"Eh," Athena shrugs, *"I'm not coming with you."* She adds grudgingly, "But good luck." I wink at her as we leave and she rolls her eyes.

Lev's been busy; two SUVs are waiting for us, engines idling as we all pile in. The iron gates close behind us and I look back, watching the Academy fade into the fog.

"Where are we going?" Tati asks Lev.

"I have a jet waiting, we're flying to Geneva, Konstantin's father Alexi will meet us there. The Rostova chalet is in Zermatt. I don't dare to notify any of our people, I can't take the chance of alerting one of Rostova's spies on the inside. He must have one or two people high up in the Aslanov Bratva, there's no way they could have kidnapped both the *Pakhan* and the *Sovietnik* without accurate intelligence."

"What about the Morozovs?" I ask.

"Maksim says they will intercept anyone from the Boucher *Le Milieu* and control activity there. He's also assembling some soldiers to join us."

"What happened to you, baby?" I put my arm around her, the relief of having her back is overwhelming.

"They tried to knock me out with chloroform," she said, "the people who kidnapped me when I was ten made the same mistake. It makes me violently nauseous. I vomited everywhere - including on Camilla - and I was with it enough to press my emergency button for Lev." She pats her silver medallion and smiles at him.

Ordinarily, I would be jealous to see her smile at anyone else like that. But Lev's smile for her is filled with the love of a father. I'm glad she still has him.

Once we're in the air, Tatiana opens her laptop and lays out some notepads. She pulls up the floor plan of the Rostova chalet and a topographical scan of the surrounding area. "Aleks, there's obviously no information here on what's below the first floor. Can you sketch it out?"

I lean closer to the others. "Let's make a plan."

CHAPTER THIRTY-TWO

In which there is a plan.

Lucca...

"How many soldiers are we expecting?"

Alexi, Konstantin's father is known in our circles as the Angel of Death. He has pale blue eyes and the blonde curls of Archangel Michael but the power and viciousness of Lucifer. I couldn't go home for my summer breaks at the Academy, so I served under him during that time. I have more than a healthy respect for him.

"The drone's thermal imaging showed over sixty men, sir. But Tatiana intercepted communication from the Boucher faction on Camilla's phone, it looks like they are sending reinforcements. She said the phrasing of the message sounded like Camilla's father doesn't trust Leonid to follow through with the alliance once he gains control of the Aslanov Bratva."

"Very well," Alexi says. His fingers tap on the table between us as he thinks. Konstantin is sitting next to him and it's the first time I've seen him go more than five minutes without spouting off with some smartass remark. He has the same healthy respect for his father. Lev is on my left, and Aleks is sitting to my right, trying to look composed, but his eyes are wide. Alexi has that effect on everyone.

"For this to work seamlessly, we must strike at the Bouchers and the Costas at the same time." Alexi's pale blue gaze moves to me. "Maksim Morozov is in discussions with your brother Giovanni. He already has someone planted in the Costa ranks. That insight will be valuable."

My jaw tightened. "With all due respect, sir, I wouldn't count on my family to become involved in this."

His brow arched as he watched me. "We shall see." Tapping the table with his knuckles, he stood, and we all leaped to our feet as well. "This is a good plan, you've all done well," he said. Konstantin's chest puffs out, and I suspect mine is, too. "We leave for the jet in thirty minutes. Lucca, have Tatiana keep monitoring any movements by the chalet. Aleks, gather everyone together."

Tatiana...

I've been so obsessively focused on the schematics of the Rostova chalet that until Lucca dropped a kiss on my shoulder, I didn't even know he'd entered the room. Alexi has us all stashed in his home in Geneva while we prepare the rescue of my brothers.

"You scared the hell out of me!" I wheeze, trying to catch my breath. "What is it with you always sneaking up on me like a creeper? Does it turn you on, or something?"

He laughs, and as always, I treasure it. Moments of laughter with Lucca are still few and far between.

"It's not my fault you're not paying attention," he pauses, "actually, it probably is my fault, since I've been training you."

"How did it go with Alexi?"

"Good," I can tell he's proud and trying to downplay it. "He went over the plan we put together and he thinks it's a good one."

"You mean, the plan you put together and that we all agreed that it was genius," I corrected him.

His amber eyes are warm as he kisses me. "Everyone's strengths played into this plan."

"Spoken like a true leader," I said. "My only complaint is the order of attack. Why can't we use drones for the first round? Why does your team have to be in the lead?" I said, stroking his stubbled cheeks. "This isn't even your family. Why do you have to take on the greatest risk?"

"Because *you* are my family," Lucca said. "I must get into your brother's favor immediately, and you have to agree, this is the best way to do it."

"Please don't joke," I moaned, "there are other heads of family here, they should-"

"No, baby. It should be me," he interrupts, "this is my plan. They all agreed to it. Do you trust my judgment?"

"Of course," I agree without hesitation. "You are my family too, *moy lyubimyy,* my beloved. You are first in my heart now. Even if we save my brothers… if I lose you, I can't…" I drop my head against his chest.

"We were always meant to be together, even when I fought against it, even when *you* did," he whispers, kissing the top of my head. "Do you really think I'm letting you go now?"

Rising on tiptoe, I kiss his mouth, his wonderful full lips, his jaw, his cheekbone. "How long do we have?" I ask, pulling at his shirt.

"Uh, thirty minutes," he groans, helping me with his shirt as our mouths fuse together. I try to pour in all the love I feel for him into that kiss, my belief in him, and the fragile hope that maybe this time, my dour, Russian fears are unfounded.

He rips off my shirt unceremoniously, his arm getting tangled in my bra strap and making me giggle until he wraps it around my wrists, binding them together. "Put your arms over my head," he says hoarsely, and I do, kissing and biting my way down the strong column of his throat. My jeans and undies are dangling off one ankle as he hauls me up with his hands on the back of my thighs, pressing me against the wall for balance as he fumbles with his belt, yanking open his jeans enough to pull out his shaft.

"You're not ready, baby," he groans, stroking two fingers against my center, and I angle my hips up invitingly.

"I will be," I pant, "please don't stop."

He's huge, and I'm grateful that even as turned on as Lucca is, he remembers how big his cock is, that it could do some damage if he isn't careful. But I'm reckless and desperate and I can't wait.

Pressing two fingers into my mouth, he says, "Lick them. Get them wet." Swirling my tongue over the roughened tips of his fingers, I clench my legs around his waist, desperate to have him inside me.

When he pulls them out, I suck in a deep breath as he thrusts them inside me for a moment before I feel the broad head of his shaft press into me slowly.

"*Ragazza bellissima e perfetta,* beautiful, perfect girl," he groaned. "I'm trying to be careful- *fuck!* You're so hot inside." Looking down, I see that he's only halfway in, his thick cock splitting me in half and I bear down, ignoring the sting because it will always burn a little and I need this. I need him as far inside as he can reach because everything disappears when we're together like this.

By his first thrust, I'm already wet and eagerly helping him using the strength in my thighs and gravity to move up and down. He's gripping my ass with one hand to hold me steady and the other cups my breast, his thumb moving over my nipple, pressing down, circling it, and then pinching, sending a bolt of electricity straight down to my clitoris. The air leaves my lungs and I whimper gratefully. I need this, this confusing collision of cruelty and kindness, the pain and pleasure blurring together.

"I can feel you struggle to take in every inch," he whispers diabolically, "and it is the hottest fucking thing. God, it's good. You're being so good for me, *piccolo bacio.* You taking my cock like this."

Groaning, I bite his full lower lip, tugging on it with my teeth, wanting to make a mark on him like he is on me, like the bruises on my thighs and ass. His hand slides up to my neck, holding it firmly but not squeezing yet. "Are you mine?"

"*O, bozhe moy, da,* yes," I wheeze, "always."

"Do you trust me?" His fingers tighten slightly and I feel deliciously light-headed, not capable of comprehending anything but the feel of him inside me. "Do you?"

Sexy Lucca is almost too much. Chokehold Lucca is definitely next-level.

"*Da*, yes, of course I do," I moan, "I love you. I always will. I believe in you, *moy lyubimyy.*"

"Then come for me," he groans, and as I feel a powerful surge of heat from him spread through me, I bury my scream in his neck and join him.

His harsh panting in my ear brings me back to the moment, and I laugh weakly. "I feel so much better." His shoulders are shaking and I squeeze my thighs around his hips. "Are you laughing at me?"

It takes him a minute to answer me, his voice muffled as he kisses my neck. "No."

"Liar," I sigh, "but I don't care." We're so wet that I can feel our finish slicking along my thighs.

"Are you all right?" he asks, adjusting his grip on my ass.

"Yes."

"Good."

"Lucca?"

"Hmm?"

"Are you getting hard again already?"

"No. Maybe a little."

"What is *wrong* with you?" I gasp, wanting to laugh but not able to work up the energy.

He lifts his head, giving me the most wicked grin. "Nothing that another round with you can't cure." He spins us around, landing on top of me on the bed and I give a little shriek, tightening my legs around him.

Like I'm going to say no.

Lucca...

Our transport to a private landing strip near Zermatt is not on the Turgenev private jet. With forty soldiers and me, Tati, Mariya, Meiying, Lev, Jun, Aleks, Konstantin, and an insane amount of heavy equipment, Alexi commissioned an old Russian military transport aircraft. The ride on the Ilyushin Il-112 is extremely rough, and we learn quickly to stay strapped in.

Tatiana is mechanically assembling and disassembling her sniper rifle, and by the fourth round, I put my hand on her arm. "You should try to rest, *amore mio,* you're still recovering from pneumonia."

"I'm fine," she said, picking up the rifle stock to begin again.

"Really, I think-" I look up and Alexi is looking over at me. He shakes his head slightly, and I pull my hand away, watching her begin the process again.

He rises to stand next to us, balancing perfectly against the buffeting of the plane. "Lucca, switch seats with me."

I'm unstrapped and out of my seat before he finishes the

sentence and I see Konstantin smother a smile. I'm going to nut-punch him for that. Later.

Alexi and Tatiana's heads are close together, he's talking to her quietly. Her hands slow on her assembly but don't stop as she speaks with him. Whatever he's asking, she's agreeing to, her beautiful face set and determined.

Finally, he nods and pats her arm gently, letting her get back to her work.

CHAPTER THIRTY-THREE
In which shit gets blown up.

Subtronics - Blow Stuff Up

Tatiana...

Pulling the Barrett M82 out of the case, I put it together quickly, keeping an eye on the compound. I practiced assembling and disassembling it until I was confident I could do it under any conditions. The hardest part is dragging the ammunition up with me. The .50 BMG cartridges are powerful enough to blast through a brick or concrete wall, but they are heavy as hell to drag around. Even Lev is puffing out white clouds of breath into the chilly air by the time we get to the rock outcropping.

The ski lodge in front of me is more like a winter palace, and with some amusement, I see several of the architectural stylings from the hunting lodge of Czar Nicholas, which look incongruous in the snowy mountains of Switzerland.

The enormous stone and concrete wall that surrounds the lodge, however, looks more like something you'd see at a high-security prison, including two guard towers and massive, black iron gates at the entryway. Leonid has cut down most of the majestic, centuries-old trees lining the road leading up to the lodge for a clear line of sight for a potential attack, which is why getting the gates open first is so important to our plan.

While Lev patrols the perimeter around us, I focus on my equipment again. After fitting on the night vision scope, I double-check the thermal filter. It's working perfectly. The Rostova guards are walking the wall in pairs as Aleks predicted.

We are the second part of Lucca's plan. The armored drone will deliver the explosion to the back wall, which should send most of the soldiers in that direction. I'll take out the guards at the front gate and use the explosive rounds to tear open the gate, and then Lucca and Alexi will charge in through the rubble that's left. While the compound is very well guarded, it's obvious that Leonid is confident that no one has discovered his location.

Now that I have everything assembled, there's too much time to think. Lev is silent, eyes narrowed as he roams the rock outcropping. Is Leonid torturing Roman and Ilia? In the video, they had obviously been worked over, but some of the Bratva's cruelest tricks - taking out eyes or cutting off ears - hadn't been employed. That video was from nearly twenty hours ago. What's happened since?

I'd authorized Viktor to release the first series of funds. Fifty million dollars was a blow, but we'd recover. My biggest fear was that Leonid would kill one of my brothers, deciding he didn't need two hostages.

Sighing, I refocus on my position. There are two blind spots where I'll have to use the thermal imaging scope to track the guards and I check them again.

Ten minutes until all hell breaks loose.

When we'd landed, Lucca had helped me organize my gear and the ammunition when we transferred from the plane to the trucks. "What did you and Alexi talk about?"

"He wanted to know if I'd ever killed anyone before," I focused on packing my rifle scopes in the duffel bag.

"What did you tell him?" Lucca asked, putting his hand on my chin, urging me to look at him.

"I told him the truth. That I watched you kill someone and helped dispose of the body," I forced myself to sound unemotional.

He sucked in a deep breath.

"He asked me if I could really pull the trigger, knowing that the person in my sights would die," I continued, zipping up the bag and putting it in the backseat.

"And your answer?" Lucca gently cups my cheek, and I lean into his warm hand, closing my eyes for a moment.

"I told him, absolutely," I said coldly. "There's no sitting on the sidelines. I am all in."

Five minutes, now.

Lucca...

There's no sign of Giovanni and Dario, and I'm angrier with myself for stupidly hoping to see them. Mariya's brother Maksim had called in during the meeting and tried to assure me that they'd be here, some explanation of logistics that I tuned out after a minute or so. I didn't expect anything from them, though I'm a little surprised they didn't jump in on behalf of the Morozovs, given their alliance. Do they despise me that much?

It doesn't matter. Everything comes back to protecting Tatiana. Until Leonid Rostova is dead, her family isn't safe. The satisfaction of wiping out the Costa *famiglia* and Camilla's shitty family of butchers is just a bonus.

A heavy hand lands on my shoulder as Alexi moves next to me. "Are you ready?"

"Yes, sir," I said. Kon and Aleksandr are with us, his guidance is crucial in case something has changed in the chalet.

"Checking in," Meiying's voice comes in through my headset. "All set here. Your drone operator is a weirdo, but both ammo drones are ready to go."

"Two minutes," Alexi's voice breaks in. "In position."

I look over my shoulder one last time at Tatiana's location behind the rock outcropping.

Keep her safe, Lev.

"On my mark," Alexi speaks again. "Three. Two. One."

The drones perform perfectly, the first one drops its payload on the south wall, exploding into a million pieces of rocks and concrete, and the second explodes on top of the huge garage and barracks used for the Rostova guards.

The first guard at the gate drops to his knees, and then face-down, and within seconds, two more guards are staring sightlessly at the sky with bullet holes in their foreheads.

"Good girl," Alexi mutters, looking through his binoculars. "Ah. Look at the east wall."

I check, squinting through mine and another fifteen men are rushing toward the gate.

"They're supposed to be halfway to the back by now," Aleks says, frowning.

Kon's listening to the chatter through his con. "They're taking heavier fire than expected. I think the Boucher troops got here before we did."

There's a steady, metronomic round of fire from behind the rocky outcropping, and another two soldiers drop, even while running and trying to dodge the bullets. I see three fist-sized holes appear in the concrete wall.

"She's using her thermal imaging sight now," Alexi says casually. "Sixty seconds. She needs to clear out the last three guarding the gate and we'll blow the charge."

Kon grabs his father's arm, painting out where two guards are loading the wide barrel with an alarmingly large rocket. "Whoa, nope, nope nope! Blow it *now*, sir! They're setting up a rocket launcher on the catwalk!"

"Shit! Lev, get Tati out of there, they have your position and they're arming a fucking rocket launcher! Go!" I hiss into the headset.

"Copy that," Lev says tersely. I hear Tatiana's voice in the background, coldly insisting "The last one."

"They are ready to fire!" I shouted, forgetting to keep my voice down. "Go *now!*"

The rock outcropping tears apart in the explosion and only Alexi's grip keeps me from breaking loose and running for her.

"We're out," Lev's voice comes over the con, "no thanks to your sniper. But the last man is down, blow the charge."

"It's our turn," Alexi smiles. It is a smile that I hope is never directed at me.

I've been in a firefight before. I remembered most of it as a blur of color and sound. It's not the Toscano way, we prefer more subtle methods but we were getting our people out of South America where they'd been targeted by a local drug lord.

Time seems to slow down, then speed up when we're inside. "This way!" Aleksandr shouts, and Alexi moves past him, firing short, controlled bursts from his AR-15. There are still more soldiers than we expected, and when I glance at the staircase, I see ten surrounding someone hurrying up to the second floor.

"That has to be Leonid!" I call to Alexi. He nods and gestures to a group of his men to peel off and join me. I pull a flash-bang grenade - holding it up to warn my group - and launch it right behind the clot of soldiers taking that old bastard up to either a safe room or another way out of here.

Eight of the Rostova guards are mowed down in seconds, and we charge up the stairs going after the last of them. But there's more on the second floor, soldiers step out from different rooms down the hall, firing as their fearless leader runs as fast as his legs can carry him. Something that feels like a fist smashes into my left thigh and I grit my teeth.

My first gunshot wound.

Ahead of me, I see Jun and Meiying appear at the top of the steps from the back of the house, and their sudden appearance with their group sends Leonid and his bodyguards in a different direction, turning to their right and down another hall. Meiying waves her arm in a circular motion over her head, and I know she remembers our signals from a Leader's challenge last year.

"Drop!" I shout to my men, "They're going to lay down cover fire. We'll go low."

They keep the new guards pinned down as my group gets past them, racing down the new hallway. There's a huge set of double doors that the bodyguards are trying to close in time, but we ram through them, shooting his last two men.

"Get your fucking hands up!" I shout, looking at Leonid's red, furious face. He's breathing heavily and it's clear this is more exertion than he's had for some time. He raises them slowly, grinning at me.

"I had heard you were fucking the Aslanova girl. Is all this fuss really over keeping her? I don't mind sharing." He screams as I shoot him in the knee, dropping like a bag of dirt.

"We're just waiting for word that your captives are freed," I said, "and then I'm going to take a little target practice with all your joints and finally, that tiny pecker of yours."

"Me first."

Aleks steps up behind me and it takes my attention off his father just long enough for Leonid to pull a gun from his jacket. The searing punch of the bullet's impact knocks me off my feet.

"Son, help me!" Leonid's writhing on the ground, still clutching his pistol. "My boy…"

There's a haze of agony that's making it hard for me to concentrate. Aleks raises his gun and shoots his father in the shoulder, making him drop his gun.

"Go get it," he tells Meiying. She's staring at him, shocked, but she's over by Leonid and grabbing his weapon in moments.

"You taught me *otets,* father, that there is only one way to rule over a Bratva. With fear. I intend to follow your example by being the most ruthless *Pakhan* our family has seen." Aleks shoots his father again. And again, each time inflicting the maximum amount of pain as the old man screams and writhes. When the floor is covered in his father's blood, he stands over him, smiling. "And this one is for *moya mat',* my mother."

The Glock Aleks is using packs a powerful punch, and there's not much left of Leonid's head. Jun looks a little green, but Meiying is looking at Aleks with appreciation.

"Gentle giant my ass, I knew you had it in you."

Aleks looks over at me. "Oh, fuck!" He scrambles over, ripping a throw blanket off the couch and pressing it to my neck and shoulder. "Fuck!" he roars. "Get the medic! *Hurry!*"

I see Meiying's frantic face; her hands are pushing on me and I close my eyes. Just for a minute.

CHAPTER THIRTY-FOUR

In which Tatiana will not let go.

James Arthur - Say You Won't Let Go

Tatiana...

Lev has to almost physically hold me down to keep me from racing into the compound when the shooting dies down.

"We can go in, damn it! I need to see Lucca! What about my brothers? What is Alexi saying?" Lev is holding me back against my seat in the jeep, listening to the chatter in the lodge.

"*Bud' spokoyen*, be quiet!" Lev snaps, "I'm trying to hear him!"

Grinding my teeth, I sit in silence, staring at the twisted wreckage of the gates. Fortunately for us, Leonid doesn't want any close-by neighbors who might witness his dirty dealings, so it's quiet around us.

"Your brothers are safe," Lev announced.

"Oh, thank god," I gasped. I want to scream. Or cry. Or both. The huge weight I've carried since that night when Lev shook me awake has disappeared. "What about Lucca? And our friends? Is everyone okay?"

He's relaying the question to Alexi and his expression changes. "We need to go." He starts the jeep - finally! - and races down from the group of trees where we'd been hiding since they blew up my vantage point.

"What's the matter?" He won't look at me. "Talk to me! Is someone hurt? Who?" Lev focuses on the road, weaving around some damage from the explosion as he races through the shattered gates. I hang onto my seatbelt strap, and terror grips my throat, making me breathless. "Is it Lucca? Lev? *Is it Lucca?*"

The second he hits the brakes, I'm out of the jeep, running for the front door. "Tati! Damn it, wait for me!" His voice is fading like radio static and I don't pay any attention.

"Lucca!" I'm shouting as I run and men, some cradling bloody limbs look up as I pass. Turning a circle in Leonid's ridiculous, ostentatious hall I scream it again. *"Lucca!"*

Mariya hurries down the stairs. "With me," she says, seizing my hand and racing back up. I faintly hear someone calling my name behind me but it doesn't matter, none of it matters. Where is he? She pulls me down one hall and makes a right. My lips keep forming "Lucca…" but I don't think I'm making any sound.

Blood. There's so much. Pooling on the marble floor, splashed on the furniture and what's left of Aleksandr's father is lying next to the desk.

Lucca is on the couch, his blood is a shocking, vivid red against the pale-yellow silk upholstery. Aleks is pressing a wad of cloth against his shoulder and neck. I grab Lucca's hand.

"…through his shoulder… nicked a… doctor…" Mariya is trying to tell me something, her voice low and earnest.

"Moy lyubimyy, my beloved," I said, kissing his pale face. "Hold my hand. Hold it tight. I won't let go of you, you won't go, I won't let you, just hold my hand. Keep holding it tight, I've got you."

There's another presence in the room, feminine, I can smell lavender and a soft voice speaks over my monologue. "I'm a doctor, Tatiana. I'll take care of him. Just keep holding his hand."

"Don't let go of my hand, Lucca. I love you. I won't let you go, hold on. Hold tighter…"

"He's stable."

Those are the first words I've understood. Everyone keeps trying to talk to me, hands trying to pull me away and I scream and hit at them until they leave me alone.

"Tatiana?" It's the woman's voice again. "He's stable, he'll be okay. Do you understand me?"

Pulling my gaze away from Lucca, I blink and try to focus. The woman looks so kind. She has a stethoscope around her neck and she doesn't seem too upset by having Lucca's blood on her.

"I'm Dr. Ella Morozova," she said kindly, "I'm Maksim's wife, he's downstairs with Alexi. Lucca took a bullet to the shoulder; it clipped the subclavian artery. I've stopped the bleeding and stabilized his blood pressure. He didn't go into shock, which is good. He has another wound in his left thigh, but that bullet went through." She cocked her head. "Are you with me so far?"

I nodded. Probably too much because I'm a little dizzy but I want her to know I get it. Lucca's going to be okay. "Why is he still unconscious?"

"From the blood loss," she said, "but that's not a bad thing, since I had to do a little emergency surgery, extracting the bullet, and cauterizing the artery. It's probably better that he wasn't awake for that." Ella smiled at me, patting my arm. I like her.

"Okay, that's good," I said, still gripping his hand. "We can work with that. I have the same blood type. We're both B-negative. You can do a transfusion."

Her brow rose. "I was planning to wait until we could get him to a clinic, but it would be much easier on him if we gave him a couple of pints here before transporting him. I'll get the equipment."

"How did you know his blood type?" It was Mariya, crouching next to me with a warm smile.

"We talked about it once," I said, still staring at his face.

"Who knew Lucca was capable of having a conversation instead of fucking all the-" Kon was cut off by Lev.

"Your brothers are here," Lev murmured, "They've been trying to speak with you, but…"

"Thank you," I whisper, "screaming and hitting them would be a terrible reunion moment."

"Oh, you did hit me," said Ilia, resting his arms on the back of the couch. "I forgive you."

"*Bozhe moy*, oh, my god! I'm sorry," I said, hugging him with one arm. It's awkward, but I'm not letting go of Lucca's hand.

"Tati…" Roman is next, kissing me on the cheek. "You were the *sniper?*" His tone is disbelieving.

"She was," came a weak voice. "She took down eight guards, three through a solid stone wall before they found her position. They set up a rocket launcher and she still wouldn't leave until she took down the last guard so we could get through the gates. She barely escaped being blown to hell."

Lucca's eyes are open, and he's smiling for me. "Oh, I was so scared," I whispered, kissing him frantically, "you were so pale."

"I heard you," he said. "Keep holding my hand."

I'm crying, Mariya's crying, Kon looks a little misty and Meiying looks disgusted with all of us.

"*Moya sestra*, my sister, you are a warrior!" Ilia says, hugging me again.

"We have much to talk about," Roman says, looking between me and Lucca. "But it can wait."

"What the fuck! Did I miss all the fun?"

I look up to see a man who looks strikingly similar to Lucca. He's leaning against the door of our room in an impressively well-equipped, private hospital near Geneva.

"Shh!" I whisper, hurrying over to him, "He's sleeping."

He raises a haughty brow. "And you are?"

"Tatiana Aslanova," I said, narrowing my eyes. "Are you Dario or Giovanni? I'm guessing Dario."

"You would be correct," he acknowledged. "Your brothers were the reason for that rather impressive rescue mission?"

"It was a three-pronged assault to take down the syndicates that wanted to destroy the Aslanov Bratva," I clarified. I know I sound snotty as hell, but I'm so *angry* at Lucca's brothers.

"Oh, I know," he agreed pleasantly, "we were busy removing the Don of the Costa Mafia as part of your 'three-pronged assault.' Were you the one who executed his heir at the college?"

"Your brother handled that. And rather impressively, I might add. His knife-work is amazing," I agreed. "He also planned the attack against the Rostova compound and took two bullets bringing down the *Pakhan*."

"Wait- Lucca planned it?" Dario frowns, "I thought Alexi Turgenev handled this mission."

"You would be incorrect." It's Roman, who puts an arm around me. "Alexi and Maksim Morozov have done nothing but sing your brother's praises. He put together the plan during the flight over from Ireland. I am Roman Aslanov," he said, putting his hand out. "I see you've met my sister Tatiana already?"

"Dario Toscano, and yes. She's been very protective of my brother," he said, giving me a sassy grin.

"Lucca nearly died to save us," Roman said gravely, "we owe him a great debt."

"This is... amazing," Dario said, shaking his head. "Wonderful news. My brother has spectacularly redeemed himself."

"Speaking of that..." I took out my phone. "May I have your number?"

"Sure?" he said, typing it into my contacts.

"I'm sending you a file," I said coldly, pulling up the app. "Lucca will not appreciate the fact that I gave this to you. But I think it's important that you know who your brother truly is. After looking through my research, you might wonder why your Consigliere was so eager to throw Lucca under the bus." Dario's so carefree, even now, like disowning his brother wasn't an issue. I hope the records I put together from Dante's - that thieving prick - records shame him and Giovanni the way they deserve to be.

He looked down at his phone with a frown. "Are you talking about-"

"Not here," I cut in, aware that my brother is watching this exchange, mystified, "take some time later when you can go over the information. I think Lucca deserves some groveling from both of you."

"I see..." Dario said slowly. "Well, if you'll excuse me, I'm going to check to see if my brother's awake yet."

"Of course," Roman and I said together. Dario looked at us, chuckling before he headed back to Lucca's room.

"I can see, *moya dorogaya, opasnaya sestra,* my dear, dangerous sister, that you and I need to sit down for a very long discussion," Roman said, smiling at me.

"You and Ilia were right, you know," I said. "I *was* quite capable of thriving at the Ares Academy."

He burst into laughter, linking his arm with mine. "I know you don't want to leave Lucca, but give him a moment alone with his brother. I'll find you a very mediocre sandwich and some coffee."

"Fair enough," I agree, squeezing his arm.

CHAPTER THIRTY-FIVE

In which there is disciplinary action. Because Dean Christie never forgets a punishment.

Lucca...

Two weeks later...

"It feels so strange to be going back to school," Tatiana says, looking out the window as the Aran Islands loom up in front of us while the jet heads for the runway on Inishmore.

"Yeah, like nothing happened and we just spent two weeks living on bread and water, locked in our bedrooms," Kon said.

"Do you think we could get extra credit for this?" Jun asks, "Like as an extremely detailed practical application test?"

"I'm fairly sure we're very fortunate that Dean Christie didn't expel us," Meiying said, filing her nails, "let's not push it."

"What do you think our discipline for suspension will be?" Mariya asked uneasily, "I know she promised none of her power tools would be involved, but with her terrifying imagination, anything is possible."

The next day...

"Good morning, students!" Dean Christie says cheerfully.

"Good morning, Dean Christie," we all reply dutifully.

"Ah, you've all dressed comfortably, very good, very good," she notes approvingly.

We're all wearing sweats and thick socks with our trainers,

standing out in the chilly commons area in front of the main building. My hopes for a simple punishment are dwindling by the second as I look at the genuine happiness on the Dean's face. There are close to a hundred students gathered around us, looking forward to the potential for some macabre entertainment.

"You were all suspended from the Ares Academy for fourteen days for behavior against school policy. This is a serious matter." She's still smiling happily. "Of course, simple suspension is not enough. The high standards of the college need to be maintained with appropriate punishment for misbehavior."

Two of the groundskeepers step up, and with the help of a huge metal hook and a lot of grunting, pull up a steel hatch in the ground, about a meter across. It's pitch black down there, the dim light from the sun illuminating a set of metal rungs like a ladder set into the concrete wall.

"I feel that it's important to reflect upon the seriousness of your actions," she continues. "Often, this is not easy with various distractions available to keep you from addressing this behavior. You will spend seven days in this underground chamber, reflecting upon your conduct. In the dark. There is a liter of water and two nutrient bars a day for each of you. You will, of course, have to work together to find the items and then make sure the food and water are shared equitably."

"Dean, Tatiana is just getting over a bout of pneumonia that nearly killed her!" I step closer to her, stopping when the guards flanking her put their hands on their sidearms. "Please allow me to serve two weeks' punishment instead of risking her life."

"Or I will!" Mariya chimes in.

"I won't," Jun says.

"No, I should be taking Lucca's punishment!" Tati protested.

"Enough!" The Dean's voice whiplashes around the commons

and the other students flinch back. "You will all climb down into the pit. You will stay there for a week. You agreed to accept disciplinary action for your behavior. Now take your sentence with dignity and climb down into the pit."

I go first, swinging down to the first handhold, and testing the stability before descending. "There's fifteen rungs on the ladder," I shouted up to the others. "The metal is a little slippery from the condensation, take your time."

Tatiana is next, carefully making her way down. "I've got you, baby," I said, my arms up in case she slipped.

"Please. After your gunshot wounds and nearly bleeding out, I should be taking *your* punishment," she grumbles angrily.

Once we are all in the pit, the chill spreads up our backs from the damp concrete. The Dean's face appears at the opening. "We'll be back to open the hatch in a week," she said cheerfully. "I am certain this will be a productive time for self-reflection." The steel hatch slides closed and Meiying yelps at the instant, complete lack of light.

"Everyone put your hands out," Mariya said. "Let's find each other and then we can map out the area through touch and find the food and water."

"I'm glad I had a huge breakfast this morning," Kon grumbles. "Mariya? Where are you? Follow the sound of my voice."

"You follow the sound of *my* voice," she snaps.

"Both of you, stop it!" I said. "No fighting for a week, you know that's just going to make this worse."

"Yeah, for us," Jun mumbles.

I feel Tatiana's hand slip into mine. "I was looking around as much as I could while the others were coming down," she said, "I've tried to stay oriented to the back left corner, I saw some boxes stacked there."

"You're a genius!" I praise her, kissing in the direction of her mouth. My lips land on her chin, but it's close. "Did you all hear that? Let's link hands and move over there."

After some scuffling around, Tatiana leads us to the corner, where we find the cases of water and food and a pile of scratchy wool blankets.

"I have to admit," Meiying says after a while, "I'd rather starve for a week than sit in the dark. My father used to lock Jun and me in a closet as punishment, sometimes for days."

There's a shuffling sound, and I know Jun's moved closer to her. "Remember all the dirty songs we used to sing? We knew they could hear us and they were waiting for us to scream or cry, so we sang. It used to drive the guards insane," he chuckled.

"We never cried after the first time," Meiying said.

"How old were you, the first time?" Tatiana asks.

"Four years old," Meiying replied. "Right, Jun? We were four?"

"That sounds right," he agrees casually.

Tatiana doesn't say anything, but she squeezes my hand.

I've always had a pretty good internal clock, so I'm guessing it's been about a day and a half when Kon and Mariya start bickering again.

"You could stop being such an aggressive asshole, for starters," she snaps.

"We both know that's not going to happen," he chuckles, "you should probably get used to it."

Jun and Meiying start singing in Mandarin, something that I'm sure is utterly filthy.

Kissing Tatiana and bumping noses, I tell her, "I'm going to take another circuit around the pit. Maybe I'll find something."

"Be careful not to fall through the grate," she reminds me.

We were all relieved to find a small opening covered by an iron grate in the opposite corner of the pit that we use as our toilet. It's gross as fuck, especially for the women, but it cuts down on the smell.

Being deprived of one sense does make the others work harder. My fingers feel especially sensitive. I've circled this room enough that I think I know every bump, every depression but I can't help feeling like I'm missing something. Counting each seam of the concrete slabs, I move past the first corner.

On the next wall, opposite from where the rest of the group are sitting I slide my hands higher, looking for a ledge or... I'm not sure. When my hand brushes over a circle of cold metal, I stop. I don't remember feeling this before. Have I just never reached this high? Pulling on the ring, it pops out of the depression in the wall and I feel a slight give.

"Hey Kon, come over here. Follow the wall to your left. I'm right across from you."

It doesn't take him long to join me. "What have you found?" he asks quietly. I guide his wrist up to where I'm gripping the metal ring.

I can feel the edges of a door or something," I said, "I can't pull it out by myself."

"What if it's some hatch that lets the seawater pour in and drown us?" he asks.

"Optimistic," I said.

"Pragmatic," he shoots back. "You know our Dean."

"There's something more here," I insist, "I know it."

"Let's do it," he sighs. "One, two, three!"

We both pull, grunting with the effort, and the concrete slab slowly swings outward. A light clicks on at the opening and there's a collective yelp as we all shield our eyes.

"Well, damn it! This has been here the whole time?" Meiying snaps.

It's a bunker, still concrete walls, but there are bunk-beds, shelves for food and books, a small stove, and even a separate bathroom.

"Pillows..." sighs Tatiana like she's petting a kitten. "Oh! And changes of clothes!"

"Fuck that, there's a toilet!" Jun says, "And toilet paper!"

"Most importantly, lights," I said, finding a switch that turns on several more lightbulbs, illuminating the bunker.

"If this was a Leader's challenge," Tatiana said, kissing me, "you would win hands-down."

"Who's to say it isn't?" Jun said.

Mariya pulls down a piece of paper tacked to the wall.

Dear students, she reads.

If you are reading this, clearly, you have found the bunker. There is a digital device with a countdown for the remainder of your stay on the shelf by the stove. Hopefully, you have found this sooner than later.

On the final day when we open the hatch at noon, I expect you to all be back in the pit, looking and smelling quite unpleasant, as if all your time had been spent there. You will never speak of this to another soul. If anyone else on campus ever finds out about this, there will be another collective punishment. It might involve my power tools. Govern yourselves accordingly.

Dean Christie

"Is it sick that I like her?" Tatiana asks.

"Well, we are at a college for criminals, sociopaths, and the occasional madman," I said.

"I'll be christening that bathroom now," Jun said gleefully, slamming the door.

When the steel hatch opens, we're all blinking up pathetically, dirt smeared on our faces, back in our smelly sweats, and racing up the metal rungs to leave the pit.

Nearly the entire student body is there, eager to enjoy our humiliation. Dean Christie has her arms folded, wearing one of her comfort over fashion pantsuits in black.

"Do you feel that you can stay in compliance with school policy for the remainder of your stay here?" she asks sternly.

"Yes, ma'am," we all chorus.

"Very well," she says. "You may return to student housing and take…" she gives a pointed sniff, "very long showers."

CHAPTER THIRTY-SIX

In which there is so much sex.

Lany - XXL

Tatiana...

"Very long shower, accomplished," Lucca says with great satisfaction, lifting me and racing into the bedroom, where I am thrown, flying onto his mattress.

Back again on my... uh... back, but this time naked and helping Lucca pull off his towel. My hand strokes the impressive swell of his cock as my other one clutches a handful of his hair, moaning as his lips moved over mine.

Sliding just the tip of his tongue between the seam of my lips, he traces my teeth, sliding slickly in and out, in and out, and god, do I hope his dick will be doing just the same thing soon. My greedy boyfriend has other plans, and with a wink, he throws my legs over his broad shoulders and dives for my center.

"*Bozhe moy*, what areyoudoingthat's-" I can feel his laughter, muffled against my center as he licks and sucks along me, driving his tongue up my channel, and then latching on to my clitoris, sucking with an enthusiasm that sends me into my first orgasm, legs straight and toes pointed as I gasp.

One thick finger, then another slide inside me with care, gently stroking and scissoring up my passage as Lucca praises me in a flatteringly hoarse voice, "Good girl. Now you're going to give me another one."

"Oh, I..." I moan, back arching as he finds that soft spot inside that he scratches very gently, with just the tip of his fingernail and it sends me into a spasm. My fingers spread out over the skin of his back, absently marking the scar tissue and beautiful musculature of his shoulder, and my palms smooth down the bulk of his biceps and warm flesh. "Come here, *velikolepnyy*," I pant, "I want to kiss you some more, okay?"

But as he slides up, I slide down, winking on my way before my mouth latches on to the thick head of his cock. "Oh, you bad girl!" he groans, and then louder as I smoothly slide him to the back of my throat, and then down it, not stopping until my nose touches the crisp curls at the base of him.

Pulling air in through my nose, I sigh happily. Lucca is thick. Impressively, perfectly, wonderfully, porn-star worthy, well, way past porn-star worthy thick. And throbbing in my mouth and I am going to make sure the first time he comes tonight is as strong as the ones he's given me.

Cupping his heavy balls, I gently roll them between my fingers as I feel the thick muscles of his thighs tighten around my shoulders. "Mmmm-hmmm," I hum helpfully, pulling off his cock, suckling the tip, and diving back down again. I can feel his sculpted abdominals heaving against my cheek.

I want to make Lucca feel as overwhelmed as I do, knowing that I can make him feel better than any woman ever could. Any man, either. Anyone. And as he comes, I gleefully swallow him down, hearing his gasp as his beautiful body shudders. "You're going to..." he pants, "you're going to pay for that, *piccolo bacio*."

Rolling me over, he cages my head between his forearms, stroking the hair out of my eyes.

"I love you." He says it so sweetly, this man who I know can decimate a dozen enemies in minutes, and I know this because I've seen him do it, but his fingers are so delicate that I can barely feel them. "I want to be inside you, but..." Lucca swallows, staring down at me.

"But what?" I ask, stroking his shoulders, and running a finger over his lips. This beautiful, perfect, kind man.

"Only if you'll marry me. Not today. But soon. Because you are mine and no one else's, not someone your brothers can promise to someone for an *alliance*," he spat. "Mine forever."

I put a hand on the side of his face, thumb tracing his cheekbone. "I only want you. I want to be your… I'll be whatever you want. Your wife, your intended. I just want you." The relief in his eyes makes me tear up a little, but I spread my thighs invitingly as he moves between them. The thought of looking a lover in the eyes has always seemed too… personal. Too intrusive. But Lucca and I stare at each other, mapping each expression and savoring each moan as he slides inside me, painfully slowly, one taunting inch at a time. "Um…" I wheeze when he stops at the top of me, groaning and dropping his head onto my chest. "You're… give me a minute, *dorogoy*, sweetheart…"

"*Dio, tesoro.* God, baby… you're so good," he whispers in a newly dark tone that makes me shiver. "I'm going to fuck you senseless."

"Oh- okay," I whimper as this gorgeous, gigantic man begins moving inside me, agile hips sliding in, then scooping up and back to do it again. It stings. In the best, possible fucking way it stings and that is perfectly fine because the piercing on his cock is sliding along inside me, striking nerve endings like match tips and I am on fire.

He waits until I come the first time, groaning as I tighten hard enough to hold his cock at a standstill until I can relax my convulsing muscles enough. It's hard; I want to keep him inside me, feel the ring on his cock rub me into madness and he feels so perfect where he is. With a mischievous wink, he pulls me up, sliding his hands under my butt and standing, thick legs planted, and begins bouncing me up and down on his slick cock, making my thighs and his wet from my finish.

"Go ahead and wrap your arms and legs around me like a howler monkey on a palm tree," he laughs, "I love it."

I gasp and moan my way through another orgasm before his fingers tightened painfully on my ass and he joins me.

Barely conscious, I feel my beautiful, wonderful Lucca put me on the bed and wipe me clean with a warm cloth. "I love you," he whispers, "I'll love you forever."

"I love you, sweetheart," I mumble sleepily, "thank you for not giving up on me."

"You never told me," he says, rolling me on top of him and tracing shapes on my back. "What did your brothers ask about us?"

I look up, lacing my fingers together on his chest. "It's not like we have had a moment alone since we got you out of the hospital. I told them the truth. That we had been together since before they promised me in marriage. That we both tried to honor it until you saved my life again. That I was staying at the Academy, and I was staying with you."

He put an arm behind his head, looking up at the ceiling. "That explains my visit from Roman."

"What?" I bolt upright. "You never told me about this!"

"No time, remember?" he said with a sweet smile, stroking my arm. "I told him that my intentions were honorable-"

I can't hold back my laughter.

"My intentions toward you *long-term* were honorable," he corrects. "I said that I would ask for your hand in marriage when we had graduated. There might have been some mention of how productive recent marriages between the Russian and Italian syndicates had been."

"That's so smooth!" I said, "I'm very impressed."

"Then, I told him that I would marry you with or without his approval, but that I hope to earn it."

"Oh, you love pushing your luck, don't you?" I said.

Lucca shrugs. "It went well. His hand only drifted toward his gun twice."

Howling, we rolled around over the crumpled sheets. I never knew how good it could feel, to laugh with the man I love, sweaty and naked.

"Very well, what about Dario? How did that go?" I know I'm frowning and not looking at all receptive. But I'm still so angry at his family.

"We spoke for a while, he said he had some reading to do and that he'd check in with me later," Lucca said, brows drawn together. "The next day, Giovanni and Dario called me. They apologized. I don't think those words have ever left their lips before. They looked like they were in pain."

"Good!" I mumbled spitefully.

"Giovanni said something interesting," he said, eyeing me. "He said that even without the bank records, my 'performance' showed courage and honor, and they were proud to call me their brother again."

"That's wonderful!" I said, kissing him.

"You wouldn't happen to know anything about some bank records, would you?" Lucca said, flipping me over and pinning me down.

"Are you angry at me?" I said, searching his face. "You have every right to be, I know that."

"I was being proud and angry," he said, punctuating his words with kisses down my neck. "But the one-two punch of the truth and my - as Dario said - *performance,* was a good humbling moment for them. They don't get many of those. Giovanni asked if I would come home this summer, and bring you. He wants us to get to know his son and his wife."

"What did you say?" I ask, circling his dusky nipple with my fingertip.

"That I would let him know," he says with a dark smile. He grins at my look of disapproval. "They deserve to suffer for a while, and we have the rest of this school year to handle."

"It can't be as rough as the first half, so that's something," I said hopefully.

"You know you're begging for bad luck with a statement like that, don't you?" My dark and terrifying man looms over me.

Wrapping my arms around his neck, I whisper, "Bring it on."

What happens next for Lucca and Tatiana? Will they ever get a moment alone without someone trying to murder or abduct them? Read on for a look into their lives, eight months later in the extended epilogue.

A FAVOR, PLEASE?

If you enjoyed the adventures of Lucca and Tatiana, can I trouble you to leave a review? Reviews are the lifeblood of independently published books and mean the difference between success or failure. Even a couple of sentences about something you enjoyed in the book means so much. Thank you for your time!
https://amzn.to/3QAmjg8

Also: don't forget to download the extended epilogue to Lethal, a look into Lucca and Tatiana's life about eight month's later. You can find it here.
dl.bookfunnel.com/zfr3jocl0i

Did you like the ever-bickering Konstantin and Mariya?

They will be back with their own story in Malice - A Dark College Bratva Romance, live on Amazon on December 26, 2023.

THE TOSCANO MAFIA SAGA

Beautiful, dangerous men and the women who (sometimes) redeem them.

Deceptive - An Arranged Marriage Mafia Romance

I may be Ekaterina Morozov, dutiful Bratva Princess, but I am not the sweet, well-behaved girl that everyone thinks I am.
I'm promised to Don Giovanni Toscano to create an alliance between his famiglia and the Morozov Bratva. I'm expected to step into my role as a Mafia bride and give up my dreams of a normal, happy life.

I'm having second thoughts.

Unfortunately, Giovanni is exactly the man everyone thinks he is: autocratic, lethal, and he never accepts less than what he thinks he's due.

Which in this case, is me.

Deconstructed - An Arranged Marriage Mafia Romance

When I went hunting a monster in the Black Forest of Germany, I discovered someone far more challenging than the lunatic who bought and sold women.
There was a girl, chained in his basement. When I tried to rescue her, she took matters into her own hands. She knocked out my best man and stole his wallet. And his gun. And disappeared. I'm

never letting him live that one down.

Letting her get away? That's on me.

She's the most cunning girl I've ever met. She likes to run. Well, I like to chase. Aren't we a match made in hell? Because when I catch her, I'm keeping her.

Deconstructed - An Arranged Marriage Mafia Romance can be read as a stand-alone with a HEA and no cheating. It contains dark themes and is for 18+ readers only.

Lethal - A Dark College Bratva Romance

There's no mercy at the Ares Academy. Not for me.
Named after the God of War, this college doesn't teach math or literature. Students here are the monstrous offspring from the most powerful families in the world of organized crime, they come here to learn how to terrorize, murder, extort, and find their seat of power.

My brother, the Pakhan of the Aslanov Bratva thinks I'll be safe here?

I have to survive this place. There's nowhere else for me to go.

Lucca Toscano is everything I'm not: strong, powerful, and courageous. He's beautiful, but so angry. He can teach me how to thrive in this school for villains, if I can be brave enough to give him what he wants in return.

Lethal - A Dark College Bratva Romance can be read as a stand-alone with a HEA and no cheating for 18+ readers only. Please read the trigger warnings in the preface. Lethal is the third book in the Toscano Mafia Saga and the first book in the Ares Academy Series.

THE MOROZOV BRATVA SAGA

The dark and dangerous men of the Morozov Bratva and the woman who (sometimes) redeem them.

Mistaken - An Arranged Marriage Bratva Romance

What happens after a mistaken identity, a kidnapping, and a terrifying chase through the woods?
Something much worse. Marriage.
Maksim Morozov is the billionaire Bratva King of New York City. He takes what he wants. Unfortunately, that includes me. That's what happens when you're in the wrong place at the right time.

He thinks he will keep me locked up in his penthouse like a princess in a tower. He thinks I'm a commodity to be used, like the other women raised in his world.

What's worse? Maksim Morozov wants to own me, body and soul.

So, in the weeks between a Christmas wedding and Valentine's Day, he's about to find out that owning me is not going to be that easy.

Mistaken - An Arranged Marriage Bratva Romance contains dark themes and is for 18+ readers only.

Bedazzled - An Arranged Marriage Bratva Romance

I wanted Tania. She was light. She was the lynchpin that kept me from flying into madness.

My father taught Maksim and me with fists and cruelty that we were not allowed to want anything more than the life we were born into.

Tania showed me there could be more for me. But when I was kidnapped and tortured by a rival mob, I came out of it a different man.

I was a fool. I'm covered in scars and now I truly see my place in the Morozov Bratva. There's no room there for happiness. There's no room there for her. But I can't let her go.

Hellion - An Arranged Marriage Bratva Romance

How could I marry the granddaughter of the monster who murdered my entire family?
After I took my revenge on the patriarch of the O'Connell mob, there was only one choice. Marry Aisling O'Connell and solidify my new empire. Even if I have to drag her kicking and screaming to the altar. And after seeing the rage and hate in her green eyes, I know that's exactly how this is going to turn out.

She has every reason to hate me. But she's still going to be mine.

THE CORPORATION - DARK TALES OF LOVE, LUST, AND MURDER

The dark and dangerous men of The Corporation and the women who (sometimes) redeem them.

The Reluctant Bride - An Arranged Marriage Mob Romance

Wait. What do you mean, my dad gave me to you?

I was ready for a fresh start in England, a career with the London Symphony Orchestra. But my father's "underperforming" company is bought out by The Corporation. Suddenly, I'm being told I'm marrying the tall and terrifying Thomas Williams, because dad would rather trade me to keep control of his company. Thomas tells me that it "looks better" to be a married man as his organized crime empire starts a partnership with the Russian Bratva Syndicate.

Really?

I'm a wife. I have a giant diamond ring to prove it... and a husband who can be kind in one moment and scary in the next. And there's car chases, and assassination attempts. There's a body in my cello case! Who has a marriage like this?

But by the time we're in St. Petersburg and surrounded by new friends and old enemies, my gorgeous, terrifying husband might just need me.

The Reluctant Bride is a Dark Mafia Romance and is 18+ only.

The Reluctant Spy - An Arranged Marriage Mob Romance

Maura MacLaren - mousey, dowdy, and very, very good with technology - is a perfect Corporation employee. Brilliant at her job, smart enough to know to keep her head down, and in debt to the criminal enterprise that gave her a chance when her past left her with nowhere to turn. But this puts her under the watchful eye of the Corporation's diabolical, gorgeous, and utterly unforgiving Second in Command, James Pine.

Pine has been sent by the head office in London to be sure nothing will go wrong with the Corporation's largest deal to date. The last thing a man in his dangerous position needs are feelings, or surprises. Especially feelings for a nerdy underling who is turning out to be full of surprises, including a sensually submissive nature that Pine finds too compelling to resist. But Pine is as cold-hearted as he is handsome and he never denies himself what he wants.

But when Maura's darkest secret puts her life and Pine's deal in danger, they both find themselves shocked at the sensual depths he will drag her to for revenge. And the lengths he will go to in order to save her life.

CAPTIVE BLOOD

Blood Brothers - Captive Blood One

"It'll be good for you," he said. "The stalker will never find you there." My agent sends me to stay on an Oregon mountaintop, cared for by a surly handyman named Steve, who looks like a supermodel ... lumberjack ... Greek God sort of guy.
I'm supposed to feel safe here? I keep having all these dreams ... dreams where Lumberjack Steve is biting me. Now, I'm losing time. Losing blood.
And I think it's possible my stalker is closer than I thought.

The Birdcage - Captive Blood Two

Black Heart keeps me in the Birdcage, high above the blasted remains of the earth after the Night Brethren plunged us into darkness. At the gate of his mansion, the Shadows wait to tear screaming humans into pieces of blood and bone. In the Birdcage, the vampire who keeps me is growing impatient. What does he want? My blood? My soul? I don't have long to decide whether to take my chances with the Shadows or find out what Black Heart intends to do.

To make it worse? He's not the only monster who wants me.

ABOUT THE AUTHOR

Arianna Fraser

Working as an entertainment reporter gives Arianna Fraser plenty of fuel for her imagination when writing romance-suspense stories. There will always be an infuriatingly stubborn heroine, an unfairly handsome and cunning hero - or anti-hero - romance, shameless smut, danger, and something will inevitably explode or catch on fire. She is a terrible firebug, and her husband has six fire extinguishers stashed throughout the house. She is also very fond of snakes.

When she's not interviewing superheroes and villains, Arianna lives in the western US with her twin boys, obstreperous little daughter, and sleep-deprived husband.

Join her email newsletter to keep up with new releases and she'll bribe you shamelessly with a free book! https://dl.bookfunnel.com/4cnao7l0mg

Have a thought? Wanna share? ariannafraser88@gmail.com

Find her on Tumblr: https://www.tumblr.com/blog/view/ariannafraserwrites
On Instagram: https://www.instagram.com/authorariannafraser/
On Facebook: https://www.facebook.com/profile.php?id=100061004614712
On Bookbub: https://www.bookbub.com/profile/arianna-fraser
On Pinterest: https://www.pinterest.com/AuthorAriannaFraser/author-arianna-fraser/
On Goodreads: http://bit.ly/ariannafrasergoodreads